WHEN HEROES FLEW

THE ROOF OF THE WORLD

H.W. "BUZZ" BERNARD

Severn River
PUBLISHING

Severn River Publishing
www.SevernRiverPublishing.com

ISBN: 978-1-64875-224-7 (Paperback)
ISBN: 978-1-64875-225-4 (Hardback)

ALSO BY H.W. "BUZZ" BERNARD

The When Heroes Flew Series

When Heroes Flew

The Shangri-La Raiders

The Roof of the World

Down a Dark Road

Standalone Books

Eyewall

Plague

Supercell

Blizzard

Cascadia

Never miss a new release! Sign up to receive exclusive updates from author Buzz Bernard.

SevernRiverBooks.com

To Barbara, my wife and Kennewick angel,
and to the memory of the men
who flew the Hump

"I would rather fly a fighter against the Japs
three times a day than fly a transport over the Hump once."

-Tom Harmon, Heisman Trophy winner and
decorated WWII US Air Forces fighter pilot

PART I

THE HUMP

1

Dum Dum Airport
Calcutta, India
Early August 1943

I couldn't wait to depart Calcutta. The crush of people. The poverty. The suicidal traffic. The stench of garbage rotting in open sewers. And the specter of death that hovered over the city like the clutching monsoon humidity.

Something that had become known as the Bengal Famine stalked the region. People lay dying in the streets. I'd heard stories of GIs trying to help the starving by offering them corned beef and hard tack—canned rations left over from the Great War. But their attempts to be humane were waved off. "No, no," the skeletal beings would mumble as they shook their heads and turned away. Their Hindu faith prevented them from eating beef.

Each morning the Indian military would sweep through the city, gather the corpses, and stack them on ox-drawn carts.

I wanted out of Calcutta. I wanted away from the madness. And I knew I soon would be. In my rumpled, sweat-stained Army khakis, I stood on the edge of a taxiway and gazed upward at the gray overcast draped across Calcutta like a tattered funeral shroud. It was from that shroud I expected my savior to emerge.

Except this would not be a metaphysical emancipator, it would be one of steel and aluminum—a C-47, a Gooney Bird, the military version of a DC-3 airliner. It would not carry me home, but at least it would deliver me from Calcutta. I hadn't been in the city that long— just a few days waiting for the plane that would bear me deeper into the Indian subcontinent —but I knew nothing could be worse than remaining in that teeming, fetid metropolis.

Boy, would I ultimately be proved wrong about that. And a few other things.

Right on time, the C-47 burrowed out of the low-hanging cloud deck and settled onto the runway. The dual-engine Army-green bird taxied toward me. As it drew closer, I could see a caricature of Donald Duck painted on its nose. And beneath Donald, the name *Betsy*.

Betsy came to a stop, the pilot cut the engines, and two Army Air Forces officers clambered down from the crew door onto the tarmac and strode toward me. The lead officer, gangly and youthful-appearing with thick black hair, smiled as he approached.

"Lieutenant Colonel Ellsworth," I sang out, "great to see you." I saluted as smartly as I could, hoping that might override my dumpy military appearance.

"Dick," he said, "call me Dick." He returned my salute and we shook hands.

He turned to his companion. "Tex, this is Major Rodger Shepherd," he said, introducing me. "He's going to be my director of operations. Rod, this is Major Harry Albaugh, my chief pilot. He goes by Tex."

I shook hands with Tex.

"Rod," Ellsworth said, "throw your stuff in *Betsy*, then join us. We'll probably be here about an hour to grab some grub, refuel, and pick up a nurse. Then we'll head north to Assam."

Assam, I knew, sat in the far northeast extension of India, essentially as a landlocked peninsula between the sawtooth Himalayas of Nepal and the steaming rainforests of Burma. This would be my first trip there. Even though I had pilot's wings, I also had a master's degree in meteorology from Cal Tech. That, I assumed, made me top candidate to be Lieutenant Colonel Ellsworth's director of operations, not for a flying unit but for the Tenth Weather Squadron. I really wanted to fly, of course, but figured that as a staff officer, I'd at least have a relatively safe job. That would turn out to be one of the other things I would be terribly wrong about.

A third thing would be of an entirely different nature. It would be a lesson I would carry with me to my grave. I would discover that the difference between love and disdain for an individual does not spring solely from that individual's own actions. It can sometimes be born of your own.

I stowed my duffel in *Betsy*. I didn't have much. I didn't need much. I'd spent most of 1942 in the South Pacific flying a Gooney Bird, ferrying troops and supplies to and from Henderson Field on the war-ripped island of Guadalcanal. In early '43, I'd returned to the States to be with my wife, Trish, who was fighting a losing battle against leukemia. I held her hand as she took her final breath in Letterman Army Hospital in San Francisco. We hadn't been married long, only three years. We'd taken our vows right after I'd earned my master's. Three years. I often wondered, wrapped in my miasma of grief, if God had taken a particular dislike to me.

For a few weeks after Trish's passing, I didn't feel like carrying on with my own life. But with my country at war and

me with flying skills, I knew that burying my head in the sand
—or drowning myself in shots of whiskey—would be the most
selfish act I could imagine.

I sucked it up and went back to work. I thought the Army
would return me to the South Pacific, but as it often goes, the
Army marches to its own drummer. They ordered me to Reno
Army Air Base in Nevada. They wanted me to learn how to fly
the biggest, fattest, most costly transport in the world, the
Curtiss-Wright C-46 Commando. The name Commando
never really caught on. Pilots developed different nicknames
for the beast—Ol' Dumbo, the Flying Whale, and the Curtiss
Calamity.

After I completed my training, I guessed I'd be assigned a
flying job. Wrong again. My orders dispatched me to the Tenth
Weather Squadron in the China-Burma-India, or CBI,
Theater. As I said, I didn't have much in the way of posses-
sions. Three sets of khakis, my flight jacket—not needed in
the sweltering Indian heat—a few books, toiletries, and some
photographs of Trish.

After I stowed my stuff in the Gooney, I joined Ellsworth
and Tex at a rusted metal table in an outdoor canteen covered
by a tin roof. The mumble of distant thunder rode a soft
breeze.

"More rain coming," Ellsworth said. He shoved a small bag
fashioned from newspaper across the table toward me. The
bag contained *jhal muri,* spicy puffed rice, an Indian specialty
I'd come to enjoy. We slapped the rice into our mouths using
the palms of our hands. The rice bore hints of mustard, lemon
juice, onions, and green chilis. We washed it down with warm
beer . . . safer to drink than the water.

The rain arrived shortly, hammering down on the tin roof
with the intensity of machine gun fire.

"Does it rain every day?" I asked. It had so far during my short stay in Calcutta.

Ellsworth wiped his mouth with the back of his hand. "Not every day, but at this time of year here in Calcutta, with the southwest monsoon in full cry, probably two out of every three days."

"You think this is bad," Tex interjected, "there's a place northeast of here, in the Khasi Hills—we'll fly over them on our way to Assam—called Cherrapunji that gets drenched by over four hundred inches of rain per year."

"Say again," I said.

Tex smiled, then took a swig out of his beer glass. "Over thirty-five feet every year. Sometimes more."

"Jesus, Joseph, and Mary," I said.

"So now you begin to get a hint, just a hint, of the challenges facing the Tenth Weather Squadron," Ellsworth said. "We're responsible for weather support covering an area of more than twelve million square miles."

"Twelve million?" I said, almost choking on a mouthful of *muri*.

Thunder reverberated over Dum Dum as Ellsworth nodded. "The region that falls under the Tenth's purview extends from Cocos Island southwest of Sumatra—that's in the Southern Hemisphere, by the way—to Urumchi in far northern China, just west of Mongolia.

"We're tasked with supporting three different air commands, the Tenth, the Fourteenth—the former Flying Tigers—and the Air Transport Command's CBI Wing. The ATC guys are the ones who fly over the 'Hump.' Forecasting for that mission is an almost impossible challenge."

I cocked my head. "The Hump?" I'd never heard of it.

"That's what the guys call the air route from India to China over the Himalayas. We're scheduled to get briefed on it after we get to Assam."

Ellsworth checked his watch and stood. "Well, we'd better hit the trail. Let's find our nurse and get going."

The rain shower passed. A small hole, the size of a camera aperture, opened in the clouds and allowed a brief burst of sunshine to strike Dum Dum with the intensity of a mortar shell. Steam rose in a quivering dance from the roads and runways. An enervating steam bath settled over the airport as I followed Ellsworth and Tex back to *Betsy*. Tiny freshets of perspiration drained down my body. Oh what I would have given to be back where I grew up, in the semiarid summers of the Idaho Panhandle.

Outside the C-47, an Army nurse, a captain, waited for us. She saluted as we approached. "I'm your passenger for Chabua," she said.

I looked at Tex. "Chabua?"

"That's the base in Assam we're headed for."

I nodded.

"Rod," Ellsworth said, "could you help the captain onboard while Tex and I run through the preflight?"

"Yes, sir," I said. I stepped toward the nurse. I couldn't help but note her attractiveness. Trim, endowed like, well, Mae West—apparent even in loose-fitting khakis—short blond hair, and piercing blue eyes. Her face, with high cheekbones, bore a soft, angular cant. She didn't smile as I stepped in front of her.

"I'm Major Rodger Shepherd," I said. "You can call me Rod. What do you prefer to go by?"

"Captain Johannsen," she said in a firm tone.

"I mean, you know, just casually."

"Captain Johannsen is fine, Major."

Her curt reply brought me up short. But perhaps it had been a long day for her already.

"Let me get those bags onboard for you," I said. I reached for two small duffels that sat on the ground on either side of her.

"I'm not helpless, Major, I got 'em." She snatched them off the wet ramp and strode toward the crew entry door.

I shrugged and followed her.

She stowed her duffels in the rear of the plane, then sat in one of the fold-down wooden seats—normally used for carrying paratroopers—that lined the sides of the aircraft and faced inward. She belted herself in. I took a seat across from her.

I noticed she wore the wings of a flight nurse on her uniform.

"Do much flying?" I asked.

"Some."

"Where are you headed?"

"Chabua."

"As a flight nurse?" I nodded at her wings.

"No."

She didn't seem much of a conversationalist. But I persisted . . . just because there was no one else to talk to.

"There's a hospital at Chabua?"

"The Ninety-fifth Station Hospital."

"Permanent change of station?"

"TDY. My normal duty station is the Army Hospital here in Calcutta."

"Where before that?"

"Around."

Lieutenant Colonel Ellsworth shut the crew door. "We're ready to go. Should be landing at Chabua in about three and a half hours." He stepped back into the cockpit.

He and Tex cranked the engines. A soft, resonant vibration rippled through *Betsy* as the twin Pratt & Whitneys coughed and sputtered, then roared to life, first the right one, then the left. An amalgam of exhaust fumes and the stench of Calcutta —the last I would ever sample, I hoped—sifted through the cabin.

"That aroma won't last," I shouted to the nurse.

"I've flown before," she responded. It sounded like a reprimand.

The taxi and takeoff proved smooth, but once we punched into the clouds a jouncy ride took over. The Gooney Bird thumped up and down in thermals and air pockets. Nothing severe, mind you, but continuous.

"You okay, Captain?" I raised my voice to be heard.

She flashed a quick glower at me, a reminder that she'd already told me *I've flown before.* At that point I realized any further attempt at chitchat would be pointless. I didn't know what Captain Johannsen's problem might be and didn't care to find out.

The plane continued to climb, to around ten thousand feet I guessed, and the flight smoothed out except for occasional jiggles. My thoughts and memories drifted to Trish and her easy-going, bubbly disposition—at least before she was hospitalized—and to what a stark contrast it provided to the icy personality of the woman who sat across from me. God, how I missed my wife.

I eventually nodded off and woke only when I felt the transport begin to descend. If I had known then what I would soon come to learn about the Assam region of India and flying the Hump, I would have been a hell of a lot more apprehensive.

2

Chabua, Assam, northeast India
US Army Air Forces base
Early August 1943

Betsy rolled to a stop in front of the base operations building at Chabua. The airport sat in the broad, flat floodplain of the headwaters of the Brahmaputra River. From Chabua, the river flowed westward for several hundred miles, then turned southward, joined other streams, and eventually emptied into the Bay of Bengal east of Calcutta.

Ellsworth and Tex cut the engines. I allowed "Captain Nurse" to retrieve her duffel bags, then grabbed my own. I didn't offer to help her this time. She threw her baggage down onto the tarmac, scrambled out the crew door, grabbed her stuff, then disappeared into a misting rain toward base ops. She didn't say a word to me. As physically attractive as she appeared, I hoped I wouldn't run into her again.

Base ops proved primitive—a wooden and stucco structure with a thatched roof. The control tower, of similar construction, sat adjacent to it. But after flying out of Henderson Field on Guadalcanal, I'd become used to primitive. At least Chabua sported a concrete runway. Not the Marston Mats—pierced steel planking—of Guadalcanal. There, the mats sat on a mixture of gravel, coral, and clay.

I joined Ellsworth and Tex on the rain-puddled tarmac and, chatting about the flight to Chabua, we headed toward base ops. I noticed a number of additional aircraft perched along the edge of the taxiway—other C-47s, a few C-46s, and one or two hulking C-87s, the transport version of the B-24 heavy bomber.

Upon entering base ops we found an uproar. Ellsworth cornered a major, who seemed to be in charge, in an attempt to find out what was going on. They held about a five-minute conversation. Then Ellsworth motioned me over.

"Rod," he said, "I hate to do this to you, but you've got a chance for a short-notice orientation trip, an opportunity to get familiar real quick with the topography and jungles around here."

"Yes, sir. What's going on?" I didn't exactly get a warm, fuzzy feeling about things.

"There's a rescue mission scheduled to depart Dinjan, one of the auxiliary airfields near here, in about an hour. You're welcome to go along and gather some firsthand knowledge about operations here. I'd go myself, but I've got a briefing to get me up to speed on missions over the Hump scheduled, then I've got to scoot back to headquarters in New Delhi tomorrow afternoon. I'd like you to remain here, in Chabua, fly some resupply sorties to China, and get into the thick of operations so you'll understand what's really needed, and where the shortcomings are, in terms of weather support."

"Okay. I didn't come to India to sit on my butt."

"Great, Rod. The major here says a jeep can run you over to Dinjan. It's just a few minutes from here."

"What's with the rescue mission?" I asked, wondering what I had "volunteered" for.

The major with whom Colonel Ellsworth had been talking spoke up. "It's kind of a big deal. A C-46 lost an engine near the India-Burma border a few hours ago and crashed behind enemy lines. The crew and passengers bailed out."

"Passengers?"

"Yeah. The kind of folks we don't want the Japs getting their hands on—"

Outside, a plane cranked its engines with the roar reverberating through the ops building. After the bellow subsided, the major continued.

"The manifest included John Davies, Jr., a political advisor to General Stilwell—commander of US forces in the CBI Theater—a group of high-ranking Chinese Army officers, and a pretty well-known war correspondent, Eric Sevareid of CBS."

I issued a low whistle. I'd heard Sevareid on the radio back in the States.

"Well, let's get going then," I said.

"I'll take care of your baggage and get your quarters lined up here," Ellsworth said. "See you tomorrow."

I certainly hoped so.

A few minutes later I found myself rattling over a muddy, rutted road in a beat-up jeep. A young private, who probably should have been in high school back in the States, sat at the wheel. Gently terraced green fields—tea plantations, I later discovered—and stands of tall grass and tropical trees sprawled out all around us. At least the rain had tapered off, but ragged, ashen clouds paraded overhead, and the humidity remained oppressive. My uniform began to feel like something you mopped with, not wore.

"How far to Dinjan?" I asked the driver.

"It's only a whoop and a holler away, sir."

So, not far, I guessed.

"I gather there's a rescue unit at Dinjan?" I said.

"No, sir. I don't think so. Nothin' formal anyhow. From what I done heard, it's an outfit called Blackie's Gang." The private's voice carried an Appalachian twang.

"Blackie's Gang?"

The jeep hammered into a deep pothole and we both managed to jounce about a foot into the air.

"Sorry, sir."

The private kept control of the tormented vehicle and we continued to slip and slide toward Dinjan.

"Ya asked about Blackie's Gang," he said. "I think it's kinda like a seat-a-the-pants operation run by a Captain Porter—Blackie, he's called. He and his men go out searching for downed fliers. When—well, if—they spot 'em, they drop food and other supplies and stuff. After that, a plane goes out every day, circles around, drops more supplies, and tries to direct the guys outta the jungle."

"No way to pick them up?"

"No, sir. The Japs done took over the only airfield in northern Burma. And the jungle's thicker 'n' darker than my Aunt Bessie's shoo-fly pie, so there ain't no other places to land. The guys have to walk out."

"What if they go down in the mountains?"

The private shook his head. "They ain't gonna walk outta there. Usually in the mountains they just crash. Most of the time, we don't even know where." He paused. "The pilots, they call that route the Aluminum Trail. So many wrecks."

"Jesus," I muttered.

Dinjan, Assam
US Army Air Forces base

Dinjan appeared pretty much the same as Chabua—a thatched-roofed control tower and base ops building, muddy roads and puddled runways, cargo planes dotting the tarmac. A lot of activity seemed centered on a C-47 being loaded with rescue gear and emergency food supplies.

"Blackie's Gang," the private said, nodding in the direction of the plane. He brought the jeep to a stop next to a captain who seemed to be directing things.

"Thanks for the lift, Private," I said, and jumped out.

I approached the captain. "Sorry to intrude," I said, "I'm Major Rod Shepherd, Tenth Weather Squadron. Heard I might be able to catch an orientation ride with you . . . if you're the guy they call Blackie."

"Yes, sir. That's me. Captain John Porter." He ran his gaze over me, making a quick appraisal, then shouted at a sergeant to pick up the loading pace.

"Sorry," Porter said, "kinda busy at the moment. But, yeah, you're welcome to join us. Probably put you to work, though."

"I didn't come to sightsee."

"Okay, you got a weapon, Major?"

I laughed. "I landed in Assam less than an hour ago."

Porter turned away from me. "Sergeant Cavanaugh," he yelled, "get this man a .45 and a Bren. He's coming with us."

A lean sergeant with close-set eyes motioned for me to follow him. We entered a warehouse—thatched roof, as usual —stocked with all manner of rescue gear, food rations, and a variety of weapons.

"Wait here, sir," Cavanaugh said. "I'll be right back." He scurried into the depths of the supply depot.

I scanned the stash of rescue provisions—medicines,

bandages, boots, clothing, compasses, maps, radio receivers and transmitters, signal panels, playing cards, books, Bibles, and various cheap-looking but shiny trinkets. I wondered about the trinkets.

Cavanaugh returned in short order and handed me a Colt .45 with a couple of ammo clips and a shoulder holster. I strapped on the Colt, then the sergeant handed me another weapon. It appeared to be about four feet long with a wooden stock, a pistol grip behind the trigger, and a carrying handle on top of the gun's barrel.

"What's this?" I asked.

"British Bren. Best light machine gun in the world."

"Well, Sergeant, I'm qualified with a .45 but not with a machine gun."

"Easy to use as a Colt," he chirped. "This curved magazine"—he handed me one—"holds thirty rounds and fits into the top of the gun. You cock the Bren by pulling back this handle." He pointed it out to me. "When you're ready, just squeeze the trigger. Blam, blam, blam."

"Right." I'm certain I sounded dubious, because I was.

The sergeant gave me a satchel with additional magazines. "Blackie always has his copilot carry a Bren in his lap, and he likes to keep another one ready for action in the cargo area— that'll probably be your assignment today. I doubt that you'll need to use it. But you never know. Gotta be ready, just in case."

"In case of what?"

"Well, if you get jumped by Jap fighters or something."

I shook my head. Not only had I never fired a machine gun, I certainly had no idea how I'd be able to hit a target moving at three hundred miles per hour from a platform moving at two hundred.

We headed out of the warehouse. I toted the machine gun in my left hand and carried the satchel in my right.

"Oh, I wanted to ask, Sergeant, about the trinkets you got stowed in the depot. What are they for?"

"Friendly natives will sometimes help downed crews. So we like to drop items the guys can reward any friendlies with, or maybe use to barter for special services."

"Any unfriendly natives?" I asked. I meant it as a joke.

"Well, maybe. We've heard there are headhunters in parts of northern Burma."

I expelled a long breath. "So we've got Japs, headhunters, and plane-eating mountains lying in wait for us? Anything else I need to know about?"

He shrugged. "In the jungle? Sure, tigers, pythons, leeches, cobras, dysentery—"

"Okay. That's enough. Thanks, Sergeant. How do I get out of this chicken shit outfit?"

He let loose a hearty guffaw.

We reached the plane, the sergeant wished me well, and a stocky crew chief helped me aboard through the freight door near the tail of the aircraft.

Blackie—Captain Porter—had the engines cranked and the bird taxiing before I could even get strapped in.

We took off and punched quickly into the clouds. I felt the Gooney Bird climb steeply as it banked toward the east and the jungles of Burma.

Once the plane leveled out, the crew chief came over and introduced himself—First Sergeant Alan Wardlaw—and explained that we'd just climbed over the "First Ridge," the first range of mountains to the east of the Brahmaputra floodplain.

"We'll drop down to about a thousand feet above the

jungle now and start looking for signs of survivors. If we spot 'em, we'll drop some goodies to them."

"Do we know where to start looking?" I asked. I had to shout to be heard over the reverberating roar of the twin engines.

"We've got a pretty good idea. The radio operator of the C-46 got a message to us just before he bailed out. He apparently tied down the transmitter key, so we got an excellent fix on where the plane crashed."

"How many onboard?"

"Twenty-one including the crew."

"Wow." I unbelted and stood, then nodded at the Bren gun I'd placed on the seat next to me. "Think I'll need that?"

"Doubt it, sir. At least we haven't on any of our rescue trips yet."

"Good. Because the only thing I might be able to hit with it is a battleship. At anchor."

"Not many of those in the jungle, sir." The sergeant flashed me a quick grin from a ruddy face that suggested he'd flown more than his share of missions . . . and probably downed more than his share of booze.

We hit a thermal. The C-47 leapt skyward, then dropped sharply. A quick, brief rollercoaster ride. I grabbed at the fuselage frame to maintain my balance.

"Tell you what, sir," Wardlaw said, "let's get you tethered in. I'm gonna pull the panel on the passenger door. You can help me throw stuff out when we spot the survivors."

He got me secured to the interior of the aircraft, yanked the panel from the door, then handed me an interphone headset. "So you can hear what's going on," he said. "Don't forget to unhook it before we start pitchin' things out."

Below us, a vast green carpet—the canopy of the Burmese rainforest—unfolded as the Gooney Bird growled eastward in search of the downed aircraft and survivors. The thick growth appeared dark, impenetrable, and inhospitable. I didn't see how anything not native to it could survive in it for long. I hoped I'd never have to find out.

Blackie's voice came over the interphone. "I've got a billow of smoke at our two o'clock. May be our bird. Let's take a look."

Blackie banked the C-47 slightly to the right. In short order we roared over the crumbled and smoking wreckage of a C-46. It sat at the end of a short swath of jungle that had been ripped open as the plane ended its life.

"We'll continue toward the east," Blackie said. "Hopefully we'll find some survivors."

"I'll keep watch out the port door," Wardlaw said to me. "You've got a window there you can look out and scan to the starboard."

I nodded. The aircraft lifted a bit to climb over a shallow ridge, then held at that altitude to provide us wider angles over which to search.

The bird jiggled and bounced as it plunged into a rain squall. The visibility dropped to nil, temporarily negating our search. The burst of rain swept away and we circled back over the area to make another pass.

I felt the plane slow as we began our second run away from the gouge the downed plane had carved through the rainforest.

"Got something," Wardlaw yelled.

The plane dipped its left wing toward the rainforest. I unhooked my interphone and went to stand behind Wardlaw to look out. In a small clearing adjacent to a stream, a group of men gave us vigorous waves. Blackie acknowledged their signal with a wing waggle. He circled the area, climbed a bit, then made an approach from the southwest.

Wardlaw pointed at a trio of survival packets with attached parachutes. "When the bell sounds, push those out." He raised his voice to be heard over the bellow of the Pratt & Whitneys and the rush of wind, bearing raindrops and exhaust fumes, filling the cabin.

"Roger that," I yelled.

"There's some C-rations, a couple of Springfield rifles, and a signal panel in that first one," he screamed. "Then we got a radio receiver and a Gibson Girl transmitter."

The Gooney Bird quivered, the bell rang, and I pushed. One, two, three. The first two packages exited nicely, the 'chutes opening quickly. But the parachute tied to the Gibson Girl—the hourglass-shaped transmitter—became a streamer and the hand-cranked radio smashed hard into the ground, shattering.

"Damn it to hell," Wardlaw screamed. "Shit. Well, we'll get another one to them tomorrow." He slammed the panel back into place on the passenger door.

"Did you get a count on survivors?" I asked.

"Looked to me like about a dozen and a half or so," he said.

"So most of them made it?"

"Appeared that way."

Blackie shouted something from the cockpit. Wardlaw jammed his headset on. I did the same.

"Got some natives about a hundred yards upstream from the flyboys," Blackie said. "Can't tell if they're friendlies or not. We're gonna go around and take a look. Major, get ready with the Bren."

"Headhunters?" I asked.

"If they are, you'd better be a damned good shot."

Great. My first try with a British light machine gun and I won't have a battleship to aim at. I hoped I wouldn't blow a hole in the side of the Gooney.

Wardlaw pulled the panel back off the door. Blackie brought us around, dropped low, and we checked out the natives.

"Look harmless enough," Blackie said from the cockpit.

I glanced down as we zoomed over them—four brown-skinned, black-haired men wearing, well, not much. They carried spears but had jammed them into the ground and waved at us as we flew overhead.

"Not trying to hide from anybody," I said.

"I think they're okay," Wardlaw responded.

I exhaled a long, slow breath and placed the Bren back on the seat. I wouldn't have to make a fool out of myself after all.

We made one last pass over the survivors, I assume to confirm their position and radio them that there'd be a plane back tomorrow—with a new transmitter—and that a native greeting committee was on their way to welcome them.

3

Chabua, Assam, India
US Army Air Forces base

I arrived back at Chabua after sunset. I found that Lieutenant Colonel Ellsworth, as promised, had arranged for my quarters. Called a *basha,* it looked like something built by one of the Three Little Pigs. It sported a thatched roof, bamboo frame, woven bamboo walls, and glassless windows—really just small, square openings. At least it had a cement floor. At one end of the hut, a faucet and an overhead pipe—for showers— offered cold water. I was later informed the *basha* had once housed Indian tea plantation workers. Now it served as a barracks for about fifteen American aviators.

The beds, canvas, were draped with mosquito netting. Bone-tired, I plopped down on my cot. My duffel bag sat on the floor.

An officer who claimed a bed adjacent to mine walked over and introduced himself. "Captain Olney Farraday, Kenosha, Wisconsin." We shook hands.

"I know you're exhausted," he said, "so I'll be quick. Don't plan on storing any clothes in here. They'll mildew within days. Best to wear everything you own . . . on a rotating basis, naturally."

"Naturally," I said as I removed my boots.

He nodded at my footwear. "When you get up in the morning, check your boots before you put them on. Scorpions like to nest in them. Guys have said they've seen scorpions as big as crayfish running across the floor. If you ever get stung by one, you'll wish you'd been shot by a Jap instead."

I rolled my eyes. I wondered if I wouldn't have been better off getting reassigned to Guadalcanal.

"Also," Farraday continued, "you might wanna peek under your bed any time before you put your feet down. Just to make sure there isn't a python or cobra snoozing there. The cobras around here aren't defanged like the ones used by the snake charmers in Calcutta."

"Jesus," I muttered, falling back onto my cot and pulling the mosquito netting over it. "Anything else?"

"I guess not. Any tigers are usually long gone by sunrise."

I sat up so quickly I almost tweaked my back. "Tigers?"

"Rare," Farraday said, "and they usually hunt only in the dark."

I didn't know if he was kidding or not. "What if I have to take a piss in the middle of the night?" The latrine sat about fifty yards from the *basha.*

"Don't." Farraday chuckled.

I didn't try to analyze his warning. Sleep overwhelmed me like a tsunami.

The next morning I went for my medical checkup—which proved to be something short of cursory.

The flight surgeon asked me if I had a cold or an upset stomach.

"No," I answered.

"Qualified for flight," he barked. He stamped my orders and handed them back to me. "Go see the dental technician. He's next door."

The technician took a quick look inside my mouth. "Ah, good teeth. You'll be a cinch to identify."

Exactly the words a pilot wants to hear. What in the hell kind of mission had I been pitched into?

Next, I got issued my equipment. I had turned in the .45 I'd been given at Dinjan. Here at Chabua I was provided another along with three clips of ammo. One clip contained birdshot —much to my surprise—for killing small game for food. The others held heavy slugs for bigger game, including Japs.

The supply sergeant handed me a trench knife. "Good for opening cans of Spam. Also for cutting yourself loose from your parachute harness when you bail out and maybe end up hanging upside down in a tree."

I noticed he didn't say *if* I had to bail out. I examined the knife.

"Carry it in your holster," the sergeant said. "That way you won't forget it and it'll be within easy reach."

I looked askance at him.

"There's a tale going around," he said, "of a radio operator who jumped and landed in the top of a tree deep in the Burmese jungle. He ended up suspended ass over teakettle in his harness. He'd forgotten his knife. He used five shots from his pistol trying to slice through the straps. It didn't work. Army ants, leeches, and the heat got to him. He put the sixth round in his head. Two rescuers found him, or at least what was left of him, days later."

I fell silent. The story seemed too graphic not to be true.

"Okay," the sergeant said, "here's your first aid kit." He handed me a small canvas packet with four straps. "Fasten it to your parachute harness on the right lift-web, label facing out."

Next he gave me a leather flight jacket with a large American flag sewn on the inside back.

"The flags used to be on the outside," he said, "but we discovered that only provided swell targets for the Japs."

I knew I wouldn't need the jacket while on the ground in a tropical rainforest, but airborne at ten or fifteen thousand feet —assuming I got the chance to fly again—it would be welcomed.

"There're also some 'blood chits' on the inside of the jacket," the sergeant noted.

I took a look. A couple of colorful silk patches, about eight by ten inches, had been stitched into the leather.

"They promise rewards to villagers or tribesmen who help downed flyboys get to the nearest allied base," the sergeant explained.

"Do they work with headhunters?"

The sergeant shrugged. "I'm not sure we know."

The news just kept getting better and better.

Lastly, I stopped at the parachute loft and received my 'chute. Normally, in transports, we sat on the 'chutes without fastening on the shoulder and leg straps. We buckled up only if we knew we were in trouble—fire, engine loss, severe icing, those sorts of things.

I had a briefing set up with Ellsworth at base ops at eleven hundred hours. I plodded off through a drenching rain along a muddy street. It flowed with water that came halfway to the top of my flight boots.

I found Ellsworth, along with a beefy major built like a beer keg, in a small corner office. Ellsworth introduced the major as Vinnie Hatcher.

"Major Hatcher is in charge of operations here," Ellsworth said.

Hatcher, who I'll bet could have lifted a fifty-five-gallon drum of avgas on his own, sported a face that looked as though it could have been featured in a magazine ad for headache medicine. I gathered he'd been through a lot here at Chabua.

He stepped forward and we shook hands. "Have a seat," he said. His voice carried the rasp of a heavy smoker.

I sat, along with Ellsworth, at a battered wooden table. Hatcher, a cigar clamped in his mouth, moved to a large map pinned to one of the walls. Along another wall sat a couple of metal bookcases caked with green-black mold.

Hatcher's cigar issued a poisonous smog I thought should have killed any mold. The smoke bore the essence of burning diesel fuel and stale vomit. Fortunately, the window on the exterior wall of his office sat wide open. I shifted my chair closer to it as he placed his cigar in an ashtray, stepped to the map, and began to speak. His words mingled with the hammering rain pounding down outside.

"Lieutenant Colonel Ellsworth, Major Shepherd," he said, "welcome to the western terminus of the Highway to Hell. You're probably wondering why we're here. What the hell this 'flying the Hump' business is all about."

We both nodded our assent.

"Once upon a time, in early 1941, we funneled war materiel and munitions to our friends, the Chinks, via the Burma Road. Supplies entered Burma through the port at Rangoon, held by the Brits, then moved north via railroad through Mandalay to Lashio in east-central Burma near the Chinese border." He used his finger to point at the map.

"Lashio is where the Burma Road began. Seven hundred miles of twisting, perilous travel to Kunming, China, over the southern reaches of the Himalaya Mountains. Kunming is where General Claire Chennault and his renowned Flying Tigers were headquartered . . . still are, although now they're part of the Fourteenth Air Force. They were charged with protecting the Burma Road."

Hatcher picked up his cigar and I snatched a deep breath of fresh but humid air before he could pollute it with a puff on his stogie. He exhaled and the room fogged up. He put down the cigar and continued his briefing.

"In early '42, the Japs invaded Burma and drove the Brits back into India. That put an end to using the Burma Road. The Nips took control of the southern two-thirds of Burma and also captured the only usable airfield in the northern part of the country at Myitkyina. Enter the ATC—the US Army Air Forces' Air Transport Command."

"If I may ask a question," Ellsworth interrupted, "aren't there any other ways of getting supplies to China?"

"In short, no, sir. From 1937 to '41, stuff came in over the ancient Silk Road from Russian Turkestan through Sinkiang. But the Russkies signed a nonaggression pact with the Japs in April '41, so that shut down that route. And the Japs hold all the east coast ports and railheads in China, so nothing gets in from that direction. That leaves resupply via air the only viable way."

I decided to enter the dialogue. "Pardon my ignorance, but why is it so damned important to get supplies to the Chinese in the first place? We've got our own war to fight now."

"A lot of people have been asking that question, Major. And the answer is pretty simple. Three million Chink soldiers are keeping over a million and a quarter Japs tied up in China. That's over a million of the little buck-toothed bastards who can't shoot at us in the South Pacific as we slog through island after island down there. So the Chinks, while fighting their own war, are helping us win ours."

Hatcher reached for his cigar again.

Ellsworth raised his hand like a traffic cop signaling stop. "Please," he said.

Hatcher frowned, but said, "Yes, sir."

"Thank you," Ellsworth responded. "I don't think I received a vaccination for that." He nodded at the half-smoked stogie. Hatcher laughed.

"No problem, sir. You pick up a lot of bad habits around here after a while."

"Okay," Ellsworth said, "tell us about this Hump business."

Hatcher turned back to the map. "There are two main air routes from Assam to Kunming where most of the supplies are taken. There's a northern track, and a southern. Either way, five hundred miles of hell."

He traced a course on the map with his finger. "The northern route goes over far northern Burma, then crosses the main Hump, as we call it, the fifteen-thousand-foot-high Santsung mountain range. The range, an extension of the Himalayas—the roof of the world—from Tibet, runs between the cavernous river gorges of the Salween and Mekong. Believe me, gentlemen, the entire route is a gauntlet of towering rock piles waiting to snatch planes from the air, but the Santsungs are the most dangerous ramparts. Cumulo-granite, to use a weather-related term." Hatcher issued a rueful smile.

"The southern route," I asked, "what's that like?"

"Infested with Japs," Hatcher answered. "It's an easier path, because the mountains are lower, but ever since the Brits lost the airfield at Myitkyina to the Nips, the skies are filled with Jap fighter patrols. Our transports are unarmed and don't have fighter escorts. Bottom line: on the southern track, our birds are aluminum ducks in a shooting gallery."

"So it's the northern way or nothing?" Ellsworth said.

"Yeah, and that cuts way down on the tonnage we can carry, because we have to load the birds a lot lighter so they can squeeze over the Santsungs. We've got some of the new fat boys now, the C-46s, and they can carry a hell of a lot more crap than the Gooneys, and that helps. But we still can't fill 'em up."

My attention was yanked away from the briefing as a grumpy-looking monkey—an Assam macaque, I later learned —suddenly appeared on the window sill. Its long fangs looked as big as a tiger's.

Major Hatcher spotted it, too. "Hey, you little bastard, get the hell out of here," he bellowed. He charged at it, waving his arms. The monkey screeched and bolted off into the downpour.

"Don't ever let 'em inside," Hatcher warned. "They'll rip things apart looking for food. And don't try to make friends with them. With those teeth they'd just as soon tear into your arm as a banana."

He muttered to himself as he stepped back to the wall map.

"So what kind of tonnage are you boys actually delivering?" Ellsworth asked.

"Not nearly what's been promised," Hatcher answered. "The White House and War Department, which don't have any notion of what the hell it's like over here, set next month's goal at ten thousand tons. We'll be lucky to haul four thousand.

"Plus, we've got *three* different kingpins screaming for more and more supplies. Number one is that little 'peanut'— as General Stilwell calls him—Generalissimo Chiang Kai-shek, head of the Chinese government in Chungking. He keeps begging Washington for increased amounts of weaponry, ammo, and food so he can fight the Japs."

Hatcher gave us a squinty-eyed glare. "But, shit, just between us girls, much of what Chiang gets is going to his civil war against Mao Tse-tung's communists. Damn Chinks are fighting each other for control of China after the Japs get booted.

"Then there's General Claire Chennault of Flying Tigers fame. He needs hundreds of tons of fuel in Kunming to keep his fighters in the air. We can't deliver enough. Finally, you've got crusty ol' General Stilwell himself. He wants his cut to help re-equip and retrain Chink ground forces. He'd like them to help us retake Burma ASAP."

Ellsworth expelled a long breath. "Talk about an impossible task."

"As Stilwell so eloquently once put it," Hatcher responded, "'It's like trying to manure a ten-acre field with sparrow shit.'"

Ellsworth laughed. A sharp knock sounded on his office door.

"In," Hatcher growled.

A string-bean corporal entered and handed Hatcher a sheet of yellow teletype paper. A message.

4

Hatcher read the message, then looked at me.

"I understand you went out with Blackie and his crew on a search mission yesterday," he said, more of a statement than a question.

"I did."

"Well, just to let you know, they dropped another radio transmitter to the survivors this morning. I guess the first one busted apart. Bad 'chute."

I nodded.

"So we got a message back from the guys on the ground," Hatcher said. "Everyone, except for the copilot, made it out before the C-46 crashed and exploded. The copilot's 'chute got fouled in the plane's tail when he tried to jump and he went down with the bird." Hatcher fell silent for a moment, staring out the window at the downpour before continuing.

"The radio operator broke his ankle when he landed, and there's a corporal that hasn't been located yet. They think he may have landed quite some distance from where the rest of them did. It turned out that the location where most of the guys came down is fairly well populated with natives. Some provincials found them and led them to a village."

"That war correspondent, Sevareid, is he okay?" I asked.

"Must be," Hatcher said. "Nothing in the message says he isn't."

"So what happens next?" Ellsworth asked.

Hatcher studied the message again, then said, "We're going to drop three medics in on them this afternoon. A Lieutenant Colonel Flickinger—I know him, good guy, an Army flight surgeon—will head the team. He'll make sure the survivors are in good enough shape to walk out of there."

"They have to walk?" I said.

Hatcher snorted a soft laugh. "There's absolutely no place near them where we could land a rescue plane. And the nearest British base is a twelve-day thrash through the jungle."

I shook my head in dismay. "So how do they get back here?"

"Like I said," Hatcher responded, "they walk. We'll send a rescue team in on the ground to lead them out. And we'll keep everyone supplied and informed by air until they reach safety. That means there will be a plane over them every day, sometimes more often. But the whole process could take a month or more."

"Good grief," Ellsworth muttered.

"Colonel," Hatcher rasped, "they aren't in Kansas out there. They're in the goddamned jungle with wild animals, headhunters, leeches, snakes, and Japs. No roads or marked trails. No roadside diners. I'll tell you what, though, they're lucky."

"Yes?"

"Yes." Hatcher once again pointed at the map on the wall. "See these pins stuck in the map?"

Ellsworth and I both nodded. Colored pins, dozens, formed an uneven line stretching between India and China.

"Headstones," Hatcher said, his voice just above a whisper and choked with emotion. "Grave markers for kids who will never go home, whose bodies will never be found, whose families will never receive their remains. American boys who died on a rock pile in this Godforsaken, backwater land ten thousand miles from home."

"How many?" Ellsworth said softly.

Hatcher shook his head. "We may never know for sure. Record-keeping is a train wreck. But last month alone there were over two dozen crashes and maybe thirty fatalities." He jabbed at the parade of pins with his finger. "That, gentlemen, marks the Aluminum Trail. On a clear day—which isn't very damn often—you can navigate your way to Kunming using the wreckage."

He sat heavily in his chair across from us and didn't speak for a bit. The only sound came from the rain beating down on the thatched roof.

After a short while he spoke again. "You know, what really pisses me off is that the guys who fly the Hump aren't even recognized as being in combat. ATC is derided by combat crews as standing for Allergic to Combat, or Army of Terrified Copilots. Well, shit, we may not be fighting Japs every day, but they're sure out there hunting for us. And if a Jap fighter doesn't knock us out of the sky, the weather or the terrain will make every attempt to make up for that.

"Begging your pardon, sir, but the weather forecasts we get are next to worthless, and the aeronautical navigation charts we have are unreliable. Some of them were copied from maps the French originally drew. And they used meters to designate the topography, and sometimes the meters were never converted to feet. That can get you into trouble real fast. You know, there are stories floating around of pilots who've strayed into Tibet and reported seeing mountain peaks higher than Everest."

Hatcher, with a wistful expression, eyed his smoldering cigar stub, then leaned back in his chair and placed his hands behind his head.

"And it's not just the weather and the mountains that are killing us," he went on. "It's the quality of pilots we're getting. We're low man on the totem pole, bottom feeders in the lake, when it comes to getting new flyboys. The Army's shipping us so-called pilots, kids, who've never flown a twin-engine aircraft, who have only a few hours on instruments, and who wouldn't even qualify for a copilot's seat on a commercial airplane back home.

"And, Jesus, look at the planes we're flying. The C-47, the Gooney Bird. It was never designed to fly over mountain ranges like the Himalayas. Yet we had one bird that hauled a full load over the Hump at twenty-four thousand feet. Twenty-four thousand! And then there's the new C-46. I'll emphasize the word 'new.' It was rushed into service before the bugs were fully worked out. So the guys flying the C-46 are not only challenging the weather and the terrain, they're goddamned test pilots, too."

Hatcher focused his gaze on me. "Major, I understand you're a C-46 jockey."

"Yes, sir."

"Well, believe me, even though you may be staff officer for Colonel Ellsworth here, you'll get your chance to fly all you wish. A pilot with experience at the controls of a Commando will be like a minor god at Chabua."

I wanted to fly, of course, but wasn't sure about tackling the

Hump. On the other hand, I knew that getting airborne and flying the Assam to China route would be the best way to learn firsthand what the weather support shortcomings were. I looked at Ellsworth.

"Perfect," he said, and patted me on the back. He turned to Hatcher. "Major, I can't do anything about your aircraft, pilots, or nav charts, but I can address your weather needs. It would help if you gave both Major Shepherd and me a primer on the kind of conditions you folks face tackling the Hump."

Hatcher burbled a sardonic chuckle. "Sure. There are sometimes winds howling over the crests of the ranges at more than a hundred miles per hour—hurricane-force blasts that can slam you into a mountain before you can even say, 'Oh shit,' which are too often a pilot's final words around here.

"There are updrafts that hurl you heavenward so hard you'll be glued to your seat like a damn butterfly pinned in a display case. The downdrafts are equally as violent. Easy to whack your head on the cockpit ceiling unless you've belted yourself in like Harry Houdini before an escape attempt. Believe me, the turbulence can be so extreme it's caused more than one bird to turn turtle, flipping completely upside down.

"Then there's the icing. Ice buildup can change your aerodynamics from that of a flying machine to a cannonball in a matter of minutes. Wings have been bent and warped from ice accretion. And more often than not, the only thing you can really see up there is your instruments. Most of the time, especially during monsoon season, you're in clouds so thick you might as well be flying through gray gumbo. If you don't trust your instruments or don't know how to use them . . . well, I hope you've made peace with your Maker."

Pilots, I knew, tend to exaggerate, so I thought perhaps Hatcher was merely following unwritten protocol. I was to learn later, maybe he'd been downplaying things a bit.

"What about weather support?" Ellsworth asked. "Any at all?"

"Nothing that really helps," Hatcher responded. "I mean, there's a couple of weather guys here at Chabua and at the other airfields in Assam, and there's an officer and six enlisted folks in Kunming. But let's be realistic, in between Assam and Kunming, over five hundred miles—New York City to Detroit —we got nothing, Nobody on the ground and no observations. The only way we know what's going on over the Hump is by talking to the last crew that flew it . . . if they made it. And half the time if they did make it, they don't bother to leave a report."

Ellsworth sighed. "Well, I've got my work cut out for me, then."

After the briefing, Ellsworth and I stepped outside. The rain had ceased, the clouds had parted, and the soaked landscape steamed in shallow mist as shafts of sunlight warmed the earth. Soldiers and Indian workers loomed in and out of the drifting fog like evanescent ghosts.

"I'm heading back to New Delhi this afternoon," Ellsworth said. "It's pretty obvious I'm going to have to find a way to get a heck of a lot more manpower in here. We need observation teams in northern Burma, maybe even Tibet. We need more men in China to debrief pilots. And we need upper-air crews with their pilot balloons and radiosonde equipment throughout the theater. I don't know how in the hell we're expected to generate weather forecasts for an area that covers over a tenth of the northern hemisphere with a little over a hundred guys. Yeah, the Indian met office is helping us, but we still need observations. We don't have any idea whatsoever about what's happening in the Bay of Bengal, the Arabian Sea, Pakistan, Afghanistan, or Iran. And yet we're expected to churn out forecasts for the most dangerous flying conditions in the world."

"Looks like I'll get to find out firsthand just how dangerous," I offered.

Ellsworth rested his hand on my shoulder. "You'll do fine, Rod. You're an experienced pilot. You've got weather savvy. I think you know how to stay out of trouble."

Did I? "Thanks for your vote of confidence." But I wondered if I had my own vote.

"It's not just a pro forma pat on the back. I've studied your record. I'm aware of the personal tragedy you've been through. I have an inkling how hard it must be to carry on. And yet here you are, doing your job, serving our country, and carrying out your duties as a United States Army officer. I applaud that. I salute your integrity."

His words sounded genuine, heartfelt. "Thank you, sir."

He looked around, as if to make certain no one was overhearing our conversation, then motioned for me to step behind a corner of the ops building with him.

"I haven't been here long," he said, "but long enough to notice a few things." He took another quick glance around us, then lowered his voice. "I know conditions are intolerable—stifling heat, suffocating humidity, seas of steaming mud, mosquitos, rats . . . well, you know. And I understand the guys don't have access to laundry services and barbers, but they look like a bunch of rag-tag, rail yard hobos. Unshaven, scraggly hair, dirty uniforms. Worse, flying operations are run like some sort of flying club. The pilots decide when they fly, what route, how much cargo. In other words, they're their own schedulers, dispatchers, and weather officers. No one's in charge."

I knew I was hearing the West Pointer in Colonel Ellsworth coming out. I believe he'd been commissioned at the Academy in '35 or '36. So I understood his remarks went deeper than off-the-cuff chitchat.

"Just a heads-up," he went on. "The jungle drums at head-quarters in New Delhi say there's a new commander of Hump operations inbound. You're gonna see some big changes here, real quick. And there's gonna be guys looking for new jobs."

"Major Hatcher, maybe?"

Ellsworth smiled but didn't say anything.

"So who's the new bossman?" I asked.

"Rumor has it it's a Colonel Thomas Hardin, a veteran pilot and reserve officer who was a vice president at TWA. He got called to active duty in '42 as a light colonel. Less than two weeks later he was promoted to full bird and ordered to North Africa as chief of operations for the Africa-Middle East air transport wing. He had his men there flying in *harmattans*—Saharan dust storms—when the Brits wouldn't do it. That tells me you'd better expect some big changes for Hump operations."

"Hard ass?"

"Keep your uniform pressed and your boots clean."

"How in the hell can I do that when—"

"From what I've heard, Hardin won't care."

We said our goodbyes. Ellsworth departed for New Delhi, and I slogged through shoe-top-deep mud to the chow hall for a late lunch. The place was mostly deserted, but I was able to scrounge a plateful of powdered eggs, beans, cabbage, and some French-fried Spam that tasted halfway—well, maybe a quarter of the way—decent. The beans and cabbage could be gas-makers at altitude, but as far as I knew I wasn't scheduled to fly today.

As I jammed the last forkful of beans into my mouth, I noticed a figure hunched at a table in the far corner of the facility. Captain Nurse. Like me, she sat alone. She gnawed on a thin sandwich and sipped coffee. She flashed a glance in my direction but didn't acknowledge my presence. Well, screw her. I'm sure every GI in Assam had problems of one sort or another, or lugged around personal baggage, but that didn't preclude you from being civil. Fine, if she wanted to be an Ice Queen, I'd let her rule to her dark little heart's content.

Finished with my meal, I sat back in my chair and lit a Lucky Strike. I didn't enjoy smoking that much, but sometimes it gave me an excuse to just relax for a few moments. I tipped my head back and slowly blew a spiraling, translucent cloud of smoke toward the ceiling. As I did, I spotted a well-fed rat scuttling across a rafter like an overweight tightrope walker. In the overseas Army, I'd come to regard the vermin as chow hall mascots. As long as they stayed out of my "bedroom," I gave them their space.

Finished with my cigarette, I stubbed it out in an ashtray. That's when I noticed a bowl containing some sort of tablets sitting on the table. I bent forward to examine them, twisting the bowl in place to get a better look at them. I tried to figure out what they were.

"One with each meal," a voice behind me said. "They're atabrine tablets. They help suppress malaria."

I turned, but Captain Nurse had continued past me without stopping. I thought about saying thanks, but decided it didn't matter one way or the other. She stepped out the door and I guess headed back to the hospital. As she exited, Major Hatcher entered and strode to where I sat.

"Wow, who was that babe?" he said.

"The Ice Queen?"

"Oh? You've been rebuffed already?" He shot me a crooked grin.

"Never got the chance. I know her only as Captain Nurse. She's surrounded herself with tank traps and barbed wire, and apparently won't enter into a conversation unless threatened with bodily harm."

"Too bad. I'll bet she could offer a lot of bodily *comfort* to somebody."

"That I doubt," I mumbled.

Hatcher shrugged. "Anyhow, I thought I might find you here. Just wanted to let you know I've set up your orientation flight over the Hump tomorrow. You'll be hauling some fuel to Kunming in a C-46 with Captain Zimmerman."

"Experienced?"

"As much as anybody. He's got a couple of hundred Hump hours in."

"What time is takeoff?"

"Oh-six-hundred."

"Weather?"

Hatcher laughed. "Fifty-fifty."

"What's that mean?"

"You either make it, or you don't."

5

Chabua, Assam, India
US Army Air Forces base

A private rousted me out of my slumber at oh-four-hundred the next morning. But before I set foot on the concrete, I grabbed my flashlight and leaned over to peer beneath my cot. Nothing without feet appeared. Next, I shook out my boots. No crayfish-sized arachnids tumbled out. The day seemed off to a good start.

Outside, the private sat waiting for me in a jeep. The humid darkness, filled with the squeals, chirps, and squeaks of small animals and birds I couldn't identify, smothered me with the tenacity of an unwelcome steam bath. I sniffed the air. Something else, too.

"Jesus," I said, "what's that smell?"

"You'll get used to it, sir."

"Unless I die first. I thought the use of poison gas had been outlawed."

The private laughed. "It'll disappear when the sun comes up."

"Good grief. The stink's so thick you could slice it and use it for wheel chocks."

"It's the natives. They burn cow shit for their cooking fires."

"Must do wonders for flavoring the food."

I realized now, as a meteorologist, that the smoke from the fires must get trapped—right at nose-level, apparently—by a shallow, early morning inversion that would break when the first warming rays of the sun hit it.

We drove along a taxiway. I noticed a lot of maintenance crews at work on the aircraft beneath a blaze of floodlights.

"They must have a heavy repair and fix-it-up load," I said. "Looks like a lot of overtime being logged."

"Not really, sir. During most days, with even a little sunshine, the skin of an airplane gets so hot you can't touch it without getting blistered. So the guys work on the birds late at night and in the early morning. Usually isn't raining then, either."

We arrived at a large warehouse-like structure adjacent to the taxiway. "This is it, sir," the private said. "You should find Captain Zimmerman inside." I thanked the private and headed out of the darkness, humidity, and stench into the interior of the building. The only thing that turned out to be different inside was that it was bright.

A tall captain with curly red hair stood at the far end of the warehouse supervising the placement of fifty-five-gallon drums within some sort of outline on the floor. I approached him. He gave me a quick salute and introduced himself as Pete Zimmerman.

"Call me Zim," he said.

"What's going on here?" I asked.

"We've got the interior dimensions of a C-46 painted on the floor," he said. "We stack the cargo in here first. That way we can load the plane fast and efficiently, and make certain we've got nothing blocking the cargo door in case we have to jettison a fuel drum or two."

"Why would you have to jettison one?"

"If a drum leaks enough to get the cargo floor wet with avgas, you've got a flying bomb. A spark from a heater or static discharge, and boom, you're a memorial on the Aluminum Trail."

"This happens a lot?"

"Not a lot, but it happens. And between you and me, for some unknown reason, Dumbos, whether they're lugging fuel or not, tend to explode in flight. It occurs a lot more frequently with the 46s than with other birds. We don't know why yet, so we try to minimize any threats. You gotta remember, they rushed this plane into service. It didn't undergo the extensive testing that most birds get before they're pressed into combat operations."

So much for the day seeming to be off to a good start. I drew a deep breath. A mistake, of course, because the malodorous fumes of the Indian cooking fires launched an immediate assault. After my coughing fit subsided, I asked Captain Zimmerman for details on the manifest for our flight.

"We've got twenty fifty-five-gallon drums of aviation gas—avgas—ten pounds of nitroglycerin, and a couple of crates of med supplies."

"Nitro?"

"Yeah. At least if we blow up, we'll never know it." He flashed me a sad what-the-hell grin.

I needed to change the topic. "Did you check the weather yet?" I asked.

Zim shrugged. "What's the point? It's not like anyone really knows."

"Part of the reason I'm here is to take a look at weather

support," I answered. "I'm going to head over to base ops and see if I can dig up some info. I'll meet you at the aircraft. Tail number?"

"Five-oh-nine. It's parked not far from the ops building."

Behind the weather counter at base ops I found a bleary-eyed sergeant who greeted me with a tired smile. "Good morning, sir," he said with false brightness.

I returned his smile and nodded. "What time does the inversion break?"

He laughed. "Your first whiff of Punjab perfume?"

"We're a long way from Punjab."

"It's just what the guys call it. At this time of year, the inversion disappears about an hour after sunrise and so does the stink."

I introduced myself as the Tenth Weather Squadron ops officer, and the sergeant, Jim Howard from Kansas, quickly told me about the problems he faced as a forecaster.

"One thing they taught us back in the States at Chanute Field was single-station analysis. I gotta tell ya, sir, I never saw any use for that then. But here, wow. We get a few observations each day out of northern India. But nothing west of there from Afghanistan or Persia. And absolute zero out of Nepal and Bhutan, the Bay of Bengal, and the Arabian Sea. But at least by knowing the surface wind direction, pressure tendency, and cloud types here, we can make an educated guess at the overall weather pattern."

"I'm glad you paid attention in class, Sergeant."

"Me, too. But I gotta tell ya, sir, we're totally blind over northern Burma and the Hump itself . . . unless we get a pilot report, but most of the time the plane jockeys don't bother to give us one. So all I can do is toss speculations and assumptions at our flyboys, which means, quite frankly, a lot of them don't even bother getting weather briefings anymore."

"I understand the challenges and we're going to try to fix them, at least to the extent we can, and see if we can't make life a little easier for you guys. In the meantime, it looks like I'm going to find out firsthand what flying the Hump is like with little or no weather support. Wanna give me your 'speculations' on conditions en route to Kunming?"

"Your first trip, sir?"

"Over the Hump, yes. But I've logged more than a few hours at the controls of a C-46."

"The ol' Curtiss Calamity, huh?"

I sighed.

"Sorry, sir." He held up his hands in an apologetic gesture. "But I do have good news . . . I think."

"Try me."

"From the handful of obs we got out of India yesterday, there appeared to be a minimum of convective activity."

"No thunderstorms?"

"Yes, sir, as far as we could determine. There might have been a little patch of drier air over the area. So, projecting that downstream, I think that augurs well for your flight today."

"I'll let you know if it did when I get back, Sergeant." I assiduously avoided saying *if* I got back.

He wished me good luck and I went in search of tail number five-oh-nine. I found it quickly. Big, fat, and ugly, it appeared to be in the final stages of loading. Captain Zimmerman was doing the walk-around. I joined him.

"Everything looking okay?" I asked.

"Yeah, I think she's in good shape. So if you're ready, Major, we'll crank 'er up and set sail for China."

"We got a navigator or crew chief?"

"Nah. Usually the weather's so shitty a nav can't take star- or sun-shots, so we just fly compass headings and use time and distance. There are a few homing beacons en route, but we can handle those on our own. And we need a crew chief only if we've got passengers, which we don't on this trip."

"Just the two of us, then?"

"Yes, sir. An experienced pilot could even fly an Ol' Dumbo solo if he had to. All the controls can be reached from the lefthand seat."

"I'll wait awhile before I try that." Actually, I hoped I'd never have to try it.

A shallow mist hung over the field, but to the east, the sky had begun brightening as the sun lifted into a cloud-matted sky.

Zim paused before entering the aircraft. "Will you look at that," he said, "just look at that." He pointed at the sunrise.

A sudden sunlit eruption of brilliant colors had tinted the clouds in a kaleidoscope of reds, oranges, and shimmering pinks—as if God had taken a giant paintbrush and brushed the horizon with a glimpse of heaven.

"An' the dawn comes up like thunder, outer China 'crost the bay," Zim said softly.

I stared at him.

"Kipling," he said. "Sorry. I was studying English lit and poetry in college before I joined up."

"Poetry," I said, more a statement than a question.

The captain offered a sheepish grin. "Kipling wrote 'Mandalay' in 1890, sort of a romanticized memory of Burma, even though his geography was off. But that's poetic license, I suppose."

"What do you mean?" I asked, semi-curious. I checked my watch. Almost takeoff time.

"The opening verse of the poem goes:

By the old Moulmein Pagoda, lookin' lazy at the sea,

There's a Burma girl a-settin', and I know she thinks o' me;
For the wind is in the palm-trees, and the temple-bells they say:
'Come you back, you British soldier; come you back to
Mandalay!'
Come you back to Mandalay,
Where the old Flotilla lay:
Can't you 'ear their paddles chunkin' from Rangoon to
Mandalay?
On the road to Mandalay,
Where the flyin'-fishes play,
An' the dawn comes up like thunder outer China 'crost
the Bay!

"But Mandalay is inland," Zim continued, "so there are no flying fishes and no bay, and the sun rises out of French Indochina, not China proper. Technically."

I sensed I was being given a quick lecture, so decided to let the captain finish.

"So here we are in Assam," he went on, "about to fly over Burma on our way to China. And there's the dawn exploding over our flight path . . . like thunder . . . outer China 'crost the way."

But the resplendent hues had already faded, and the clouds had reverted to their more typical dichromatic grays and whites.

"I see," I said. "Well, let's fly off into the thunder, then." Bad choice of words, I realized too late. I hoped my uttering them didn't turn out to be literally prophetic.

We clambered into the C-46, Zim in the left seat, me in the right.

"I suggest you just sit on your 'chute for now," Zim said. "We'll have time to strap them on if we lose an engine. If we ram into something, it won't make any difference whether you got a 'chute on or not."

Another comforting thought.

The captain checked me out. "Good. You've got your jacket and heavy socks on. You got a blanket?"

I shook my head.

He flipped open the cockpit window and called to someone standing below, then turned to me. "We'll get you a blanket to wrap around your feet. It'll get damn cold at altitude and I don't like using the heaters. They're gasoline driven. If one of our avgas drums springs a leak, I don't wanna be mixing gasoline fumes with an open-flame heater."

"No point in making the dawn come up like literal thunder," I offered.

"Safety first, Kipling second. Let's do the checklist."

The bird, now buttoned up, stank of fuel, sweat, and—from the air that had snuck in from the outside—burning cow turds. We made a quick but meticulous run through the checklist, then cranked the engines, eager to be on our way.

The big Pratt & Whitneys, each endowed with twenty-one-hundred horsepower, spun the props lazily at first, then snorted to life in puffs of white smoke. Ol' Dumbo shook, creaked, and roared like a giant awakened from a deep slumber but ready to go to work.

We taxied out of the revetment, the C-46 lumbering like a drunken elephant. Ahead of us, a jeep, headlights flashing and horn blatting, charged down the runway.

"What's he doing?" I asked through the interphone.

"Making sure the runway is clear of cows and locals."

"Great. And we used to worry about birdstrikes."

Zim laughed. "Wait until you see the runway shenanigans at Kunming."

"What—"

"Not now. That would take all of the fun out of it. Let's do our engine run-up and make sure we got enough oomph to get us up. If we get anything more than a minimal mag drop of one hundred rpm at thirty inches of boost, then it's back to the roundhouse to get another plane. Most crashes happen on landings or takeoffs, and if we lose an engine on takeoff with a stuffed bird, we become part of the landscape. Don't want that to happen."

I agreed. We halted, held the brakes, and wound up the engines. They passed the test and we trundled into takeoff position.

The tower cleared us. Zim lined up on the center of the runway and locked the tail wheel. We started our run. We were on our way to China. I monitored the throttle and props. At eighty-five mph, Zim applied some back pressure to the control column and our bellowing Curtiss Calamity lifted off the concrete into a sky flecked with building cumulus. At least it wasn't pouring rain with a cloud ceiling hovering just above the deck. The last of the runway lights slid by beneath us.

Zim banked the plane and continued to climb.

"We're going to circle the aerodrome a couple of times to gain altitude," he said. "On this northern route, the first mountain range, the Mishmi Hills—'hills' is a joke, I think—comes up fast. We call it the 'First Ridge.' But they're just babies compared to what lies ahead."

Zim kept the engine superchargers on high blower as we climbed steadily, threading our way between billowing cumulus as we struggled to clear a rugged cordillera slathered with stands of heavy timber.

"Can't tell you what a beautiful day this is," Zim said. "Normally we're encased in clouds and can't see shit."

I had to admit, the scenery registered as spectacular. But I also understood that when it went into hiding, it waited to kill us. We wound through a pass at about twelve thousand feet. Nearby peaks loomed above us by another two or three thousand feet. Abruptly, we exited the mountains and flew out over a flat valley far below us with a river snaking through it.

"The Mali River," Zim said. "It flows south into the Irrawaddy. And directly beneath us, that's Fort Hertz down there, the last outpost the Brits hold in Burma. It usually has a radio beacon on if the Japs haven't grabbed it. Comes in handy where you're on instruments."

Ahead of us, more spiky mountains loomed on the horizon.

"Here comes the big boys," Zim said.

6

Airborne over The Hump
En route to Kunming, China

"Up ahead," Zim said, "those are the Kumon Mountains along the Burma-China border. Some of the passes there are over thirteen thousand feet in elevation. If you're flying on instruments, you want to be up around sixteen or seventeen thousand feet to make sure you don't bump into anything. Of course, you'll be on oxygen by that altitude, too."

Barren, rocky peaks jutted above the steep, green slopes like dragons' teeth, waiting to take a bite out of anything that ventured too close. Thermals, vertical spears of winds boiling up from the rugged terrain, began to lift Ol' Dumbo in sudden, sharp attacks. Then, just as abruptly, she'd lose the boost and tumble into invisible air pockets. At the same time, cross currents of wind, trying to find the easiest routes through the towering mountains, constantly pushed the plane this way and that onto different headings.

The C-46 shook and shimmied, though not violently, as it rode the vicissitudes of the bone-jarring turbulence.

Thank God, the twin Pratt & Whitneys thrummed away, oblivious to the brawling winds that assaulted the aluminum bird.

"Nice to be flying in quiet conditions for a change," Zim said. He appeared relaxed in his pilot's seat. "Wanna take the controls for a while?"

I guessed he wasn't kidding about the quiet conditions, so decided this was probably a good time to reacquaint myself with driving a Curtiss Calamity.

"Yes, sir. I got 'em."

Despite the portly appearance of the C-46, it moved through the air at a good clip. With a bit of a tailwind component, our ground speed registered two hundred fifty miles per hour. We swiftly crossed the crest of the Kumons, now smudged with building cumulus, and soared out over a deep gorge thousands of feet beneath us. The steep, sharp slopes of the mountains dove toward a river that wove through the narrow, green gorge like a thread of silver.

"That's the Salween River," Zim said. "Starts in the main Himalayas"—he inclined his head to the left, the north—"and ends in the Andaman Sea a thousand miles yonder." He tilted his head to the right, south.

As quickly as we'd swept over the deep gouge of the Salween, another wall of saber-toothed rocks loomed in front of us.

"Here comes the giants," Zim said, "the Santsung Range."

The others weren't giants?

"When you're in the soup," he went on, "you'll want to be at twenty thousand or higher going over these babies. If you encounter severe turbulence, maybe twenty-five. I haven't experienced it, but some of the guys said they've ridden a rollercoaster through here that hurls you up and down at five thousand feet per minute. And there's not a damn thing you can do about it except hang onto the controls and hope you survive the ride."

The plane continued to jump and bounce, a rubber ball in the sky, as we transited the range. Fluffy clouds hid many of the peaks; others, the tallest, wore caps of snow. The scene seemed surreal, coming, as we had just a couple of hours ago, from the steaming lowlands of subtropical India.

We quickly zoomed out over another cavernous river valley far below us. It sliced through the massive stacks of granite, the result, likely, of millions of years of gouging and carving, and snaked its way south.

"That's the Mekong," Zim said, "on its way to French Indochina and the South China Sea."

"Talk about an immense journey."

"Another fifteen hundred miles."

After an hour of me becoming reacquainted with the C-46, Zimmerman took the controls back from me. "You're a natural," he said.

"That's what I was afraid of."

We eased our way down from the mountains and sailed out over the Yunnan-Guizhou Plateau of southwest China, a flat, upland region of gently rolling hills, and home to our destination, Kunming. I'd spent a little time studying the city's climate. It received less than half the rainfall that soggy Assam did and, because of its elevation, over six thousand feet, boasted much cooler weather. July and August were its wettest months, but from November through April you could call it semiarid.

"Thar she blows," Zim said, and pointed dead ahead. I spotted several fighters, P-40s I assumed, lifting off from an aerodrome in the distance. South of the field, a broad lake, sitting in a basin guarded by accordioned slopes, sparkled in the late morning sun.

"Kunming coming up," Zim commented. "And to the south, that's Lake Tien Ch'ih. A great landmark."

Zim tried to raise the tower at Kunming for clearance to land, but to no avail. He looked at me and shrugged. "I know the landing pattern," he said, "and since it's VFR, we'll just go." As he turned to line up for his final approach, I glanced behind us to see if there were any ships following. There appeared to be three or four several miles out.

Kunming, China

As we neared the approach end of the runway, Zim had the flaps down and backed off on the power. We touched down at just over one hundred miles per hour.

"Doesn't seem too busy," I said. I thought there'd be a lot more activity on the field, but I spotted only a handful of GIs scurrying about.

"Yeah," Zim said, drawing the word out. Circumspection.

We taxied toward base ops, the wheels thrumming over the runway.

"Got that pierced-steel planking here, huh?" I asked.

"Not the concrete we have in Chabua, that's for sure. Usually there are dozens of coolies out here spreading gravel and flat rocks to place the PSP on—the runway needs constant maintenance—but I don't see any of the little buggers today."

I studied Zim's expression and saw puzzlement mixed with apprehension.

We pulled up in front of base ops, cut the engines, and clambered out of the aircraft—a bit more quickly than usual. We both sensed something was off.

We entered the ops building. Nobody behind the counter. No pilots filling out flight plans. No ops officers. I stuck my head into the weather office. Empty. Zim and I stared at each other. We both caught on at the same time.

"This way," he yelled, and we sprinted for the back door just as the first bomb hit. We dove into a slit trench as the second bomb rocked the base. Two more explosive eruptions followed, shaking the ground and rattling the ops building, but none seemed close to us.

"They're going after the main runway," someone else in the trench said.

"Guess we made it just in time," Zim responded.

"You guys from the aircraft that just landed?" another voice asked.

"Got a load of fuel from Chabua," Zim answered.

"Lord, I'm glad the Japs didn't hit that. Anyhow, welcome to Kunming. First trip?"

"Nope. Not hardly, but my copilot here, Major Shepherd, he's a virgin."

"I'm Major Leon Smith," the speaker said, "runnin' the shop today."

"I was so happy to be landing in VFR conditions," Zim said, "I forget the Japs attack in good weather."

The aircraft trailing us in the landing pattern apparently hadn't been ours.

No more bombs fell. "Guess Chennault's boys chased 'em off," Smith said. I assumed he meant the P-40s I'd seen taking off earlier. Zim, Smith, and I, along with several enlisted men who'd sheltered in the trench, stood, brushed the mud off our uniforms the best we could, and walked back into base ops.

Zim and Smith went off to arrange for getting our cargo offloaded, and I went to visit with the weather NCO, a Master Sergeant O'Malley. I explained to him that—in addition to being a Hump pilot—I was director of operations for Lieutenant Colonel Ellsworth's Tenth Weather Squadron.

"We're going to try to get things running a little better," I said. "Tell me what you need."

The floodgates opened. "Counting me," O'Malley said, "we've got six enlisted and one officer here. We run a twenty-four-hour shop and we're the only Army weather station in China. It's crazy, sir, we need weather teams in Chungking, Yunnanyi, Pao-Chan, Li-Shiang, and Kweilin at the very least. Criminy, we don't even have pilot balloon—pibal—capability here, so can't tell the aircrews what the winds aloft are directly over our own station. General Chennault, the crusty old bastard—pardon my French, Major—thinks we're a bunch of guys who flunked out of witchdoctor school and can't tell a cumulus from a cauliflower."

"That doesn't sound promising."

"I think he'd ship us all back to the States if he had his druthers."

Outside, the roar of aircraft engines, the growl of trucks, and the shouts of men filled the early afternoon air. The Kunming aerodrome sounded as if it was getting back to normal.

"Doesn't he understand weather is the most constraining factor in getting tonnage into China from India?" I asked.

"Of course he does, sir, but he believes we can't do anything about it."

"True, we can't. But with more manpower we could get more weather observations. At least then we'd know what's going on and what's likely to happen in the short range. If nothing else, we could make operations safer and more efficient."

"Well, good luck trying to explain that to Chennault. I hope you don't have to go up against him."

But I knew we would.

By late afternoon, our bird had been unloaded and taken

on a small amount of cargo—surplus military desks, chairs, and tables and a couple of Army officers—to be carted back to Assam. Too bad, I thought, I would have liked to have lingered a bit longer in Kunming and bask in its eternal springlike temperatures.

Captain Zimmerman let me take the left-hand seat and we taxied into takeoff position. The runway swarmed with hundreds of coolies in their wide-brimmed straw hats. They labored vigorously at repairing the damage the Jap bombs had done. Some shoveled stones and gravel while others pushed and pulled huge rollers to pack down the runway. They hadn't finished their tasks, but edged away from the center of the strip to permit our takeoff.

We received clearance from the tower and began our roll. It went smoothly. We hit sixty miles per hour and the tail-wheel lifted off the ground.

Then trouble. Without warning, a coolie separated himself from the throngs lining the right side of the runway and darted directly in front of Ol' Dumbo.

"Jesus," I screamed, and reached to slam the throttles shut.

"No," yelled Zim, and kept his hand on them, preventing me from cutting the plane's thrust.

I braced myself, expecting to feel a thump and see body parts flying through the air, spraying the windscreen with blood and gore.

But nothing. The coolie dodged death. We lifted into a cumulus-specked sky, my chest heaving in fright, my heart trying to jackhammer its way free of my body.

"What the fuck?" I bellowed. "What the fuck?" Not my usual language, but not my usual takeoff, either.

"You just killed a dragon," Zim said.

"I did what?"

Jouncing through afternoon thermals, we climbed steadily, heading toward the west-northwest.

"Chinese footbridges have sharp turns in them," Zim said. "Peasants think if they have a bad-luck dragon hot on their tail, they can dart around the turn in the bridge and the dragon will fall in the drink. Dumb dragon."

I stared at the captain.

"True," he said. "The homes around here all have alcoves just inside the front door. That's so bad-luck dragons can't sneak in."

I shook my head in disbelief. "So what's that have to do with a coolie trying to turn himself into mincemeat?"

"Not himself. The dragon chasing him. They figure if they can just barely dodge the props of an aircraft taking off, their personal dragon can't. End of bad luck."

"Or end of coolie."

"You know, sometimes I think these Chinks value life so little, they believe they'd be better off in their next reincarnation. Anyhow, we're under court-martial orders not to abort a takeoff if a coolie decides to lead his bad-luck dragon on a death chase."

Airborne over The Hump
En route to Chabua, Assam, India

We reached twenty thousand feet and I leveled out the C-46. The engines growled smoothly. Far to our south, cirrus outflows from billowing thunderstorms, smeared orange and pink in the setting sun, anvilled out over the jungles of southern Burma.

"Where the flyin' fishes play," I said.

Zim lifted his oxygen mask and smiled at me. He put the

mask back over his mouth and nose and spoke into the interphone. "Maybe I'll be able to make a poet out of you."

The sun slipped below the distant northwest horizon and darkness gathered us into its arms. I stayed on instruments as we flew in and out of cloud clusters. In the direction of Rangoon, a long way from us, lightning sheeted across the sky —back home I would have called it heat lightning—as the thunderstorms we'd spotted earlier let loose with a Fourth of July fireworks display.

I picked up the Ft. Hertz radio beacon over northern Burma, so knew we hadn't gotten lost. The tower at Chabua notified us that fog had formed over the field and appeared to be growing thicker.

"You feel comfortable taking her down?" Zim asked.

"As long as the Chabua ADF is working." Automatic Direction Finders broadcast radio signals pilots can home in on.

"I'll tune it in for you."

I got Ol' Dumbo lined up pretty well, but couldn't see the runway as we descended on final.

We crossed the middle marker at two hundred and fifty feet above the ground, right where we should be.

"Nothing," I said. My grip on the control wheel tightened. If it had been an orange or a lemon, it would have been squirting juice all over my lap.

"There's a red light on a breakaway pole about fifty yards short of the touchdown area," Zim said, his voice steady and calm. "Try not to hit it. The next guy in will be looking for it, too."

No sooner had he finished his words than the light flashed by beneath us. The first set of runway lights loomed out of the fog, like wolf's eyes at midnight. I hammered the aircraft down onto the runway and kept the nose pointed straight ahead.

Out of the windscreen on my side of the aircraft, I could

see only one successive runway light at a time. I coasted to a stop, but kept the props turning.

"Five-oh-nine," a voice from the tower said, "where are you?"

"On the runway."

"I hope so. Where? Give me a marker."

"Damned if I know. I can't see a thing."

"Okay, we'll send a jeep out to look for you."

A jeep with a FOLLOW ME sign on its rear found us after about a five-minute search. It led us to a revetment where we parked Ol' Dumbo and shut down the engines.

"Nice job," Zim said. "Couldn't have done better myself."

"Probably gonna need a new set of tires, though."

"Nobody will complain."

I filled out our post-flight paperwork while Zim helped our passengers deplane. By the time I'd finished and climbed out of the aircraft, I realized my personal overflow meter was registering yellow. I took a long pee behind the bird.

Following that, the jeep transported everyone to base ops where I turned in the forms I'd filled out.

"Okay," Zim said. "Now for the best part of the day. Follow me."

"Where are we going?"

"The dispensary."

"Why?"

"You'll see." He grinned and we slogged off through the humid darkness, the fog, and the muddy streets toward the hospital. A night chorus of insects, the occasional screech of a monkey, and the sporadic roar of a Pratt & Whitney being worked on accompanied us.

We reached the hospital and entered the dispensary where a bright-eyed corporal greeted us. "Yes, sirs?" he sang out.

"Whiskey, barkeep," Zim snapped, smirking.

I stared at him.

"Coming right up, Captain," the corporal responded. Zim turned to me. "Post-mission rations," he said. "Two shots of combat whiskey after each sortie. It's usually raw South African brandy. You'll sleep like a baby. Never hear the critters scurrying around in your *basha*."

Reason enough, I thought. I downed my first shot in one swallow.

The second one went down just as quickly.

"Okay, Major," Zim said, "I've got another trip scheduled for early tomorrow, so I'm off to beddy-bye."

I wanted some more time to unwind, so elected to sit in a chair in the dimly lit hallway outside the dispensary for a while. Farther down the hall, deeper in the interior of the hospital, I could see a couple of flight surgeons and several nurses making their rounds. The place didn't appear to be overly busy.

It reminded me of Letterman Hospital and Trish, a memory I didn't want. But it came, unbidden, anyhow. As I watched the nurses go about their business, I recalled a strange tale Trish had told me about a nurse at Letterman.

On the evening of the day Trish's doctor had given us the bad news—that there wasn't any more that could be done, that she had only a few weeks, maybe days, to live—I'd gone home. I'd needed to get some rest and pack some things with the notion of coming back the following day and bunking down in the hospital to spend as much time as I could with Trish . . . until the end.

When I walked into her room the following morning, she beckoned me over, and reached for my hand. After I kissed her, she told me, in a soft, broken voice, that a nurse had spent most of the night with her.

"She held my hand, read from the Bible, and talked a lot to

me about life . . . and life after death. She was very nice, extremely comforting. We even sang a few old hymns I remembered from my childhood."

I tried to respond, but my throat was so constricted with emotion I couldn't speak.

"She was a large woman and dark-haired," Trish continued. "She said she was from Pennsylvania."

I nodded.

"I didn't catch her name," Trish whispered. "Or maybe she didn't say it." She squeezed my hand more tightly. "Could you find out who she was and thank her for me? She was so kind."

"Yes," I choked out.

But first I went in search of a cup of coffee to give my emotions a chance to settle before I spoke to the nurses.

I approached the head nurse, described the woman who had sat through the night with my wife, and asked if I might have her name so I could personally thank her.

The head nurse, a matronly lady with sparkling eyes, stared at me as if I were a bum who'd just wandered in off the street. "First of all, sir, we don't have anyone on staff who fits that description. And besides, all of our nurses are from the western US. Second, no nurse would have had time to spend the entire night with one patient. We're too busy and stretched too thin."

"Maybe someone from another department?"

"Letterman has been my duty station for the past three years, sir. As chief nurse, I know virtually all the nurses in the hospital. I'm sorry."

So I never did find out who the nurse was. Maybe Trish had been hallucinating. I asked her if she thought that might have been the case.

"No. I know I get dopey from the medication at times, but

she was as real as you are sitting there now. I can still feel her grasping my hand. Feel her warmth."

Unbidden memories. Of Trish and her final days. Of a dark-haired nurse from Pennsylvania. If that's what she was . . .

Sitting there in the hallway of an Army hospital in India, the combat whiskey doing its job, my eyes misted over and my head dipped, partially in reverence, partially in fatigue.

A sharp kick to my flight boots snapped me upright.

"Doors are shut and bolted at twenty-two hundred hours," a voice said, somewhere between commanding and charming. Jesus, Captain Nurse.

I stared at her. She stared back. I swiped the back of my hand across my eyes, banishing the incipient tears and remembrances of my wife.

I thought I caught a flash of puzzlement, of softness, of empathy, in the captain's gaze, but it proved fleeting. She seemed to want to say or ask something. But she pinched her lips together and remained silent. As quickly as it had disappeared, the sternness in her countenance returned, and she spoke.

"You hear me?" she barked. "Sir."

I stood. "Were you ever a brunette?"

"What business of that is yours?"

"Were you ever in Pennsylvania?"

She didn't answer, just pinned me in a glacial glare.

"No. Of course not. Not the Ice Queen." The words came out before I could check them. Probably the South African brandy. But I only semi-regretted them.

"What?" The word cracked like a whip.

"You know, we hit it off so well, maybe we should grab a drink together sometime."

"Right after the war ends."

"You'll be last on my list."

"Fine. You keep your hands in your pockets and your pecker in your pants and we'll get along famously." She wheeled and stalked back down the hall toward the main hospital. I wondered what I'd ever done to alienate her. Never had I met a woman with such a Rita Hayworth body and a Lizzie Borden personality.

Inside the dispensary, the young corporal, having obviously overheard us, stood with his mouth agape.

"Wrong time of month for her," I said. "She's on the rag."

I returned to my *basha* and tumbled into a deep sleep. I did not dream of nurses.

7

Chabua, Assam, India
US Army Air Forces base
Early September 1943

August drifted into September in Assam. The monsoonal dumps of rain continued as did the unrelenting humidity. I swear to God, I could detect my straight, brown hair beginning to curl. Mildew readily colonized any articles of clothing that sat unattended for more than a day or two.

I flew a few more trips over the Hump, mostly on instruments, but made every effort to avoid the kind of conditions that might turn the Ol' Dumbos I piloted into markers on the Aluminum Trail. Unlike a lot of the guys, I spent time in the weather shop trying to figure out, with the help of the forecasters on duty, when the best flying days would occur. Given the acute data limitations we had, a lot of it turned out to be guesswork, but more often than not it turned out to be better than just winging it.

Mostly, I found myself bored to the point of stupefaction. If we flyboys weren't ensconced in the cockpit of a Gooney

Bird or a Commando, there wasn't a damn thing to do but sit around in the *bashas* and feel homesick and forgotten, or drink and play cards.

Mail arrived infrequently, but that made no difference to me. With no wife or kids, about all I had to look forward to was an occasional letter from Mom and Dad.

We didn't have a PX on base where we could buy razor blades or soap. They showed up sporadically in cargo shipments, or sometimes we could find the items in Kunming. Mostly, we didn't bother to shave, and bathed only infrequently . . . and got used to each other's BO.

It didn't make a lot of sense to send our uniforms to the "laundry service," either. Natives would wash our clothes, but would beat the crap out of them by pounding them with rocks or slinging them against wooden benches. So we generally wore our khakis muddy and wrinkled. That turned out to be fine, however, because they matched our muddied, weathered boots.

I mentioned that we drank. But not much. We had to be ready to fly. We did have an "officers club" at one end of a *basha* where we'd staked out an area with a few tables and chairs, and planted an ice box where we could keep our beer cold . . . unless we ran out of ice, which happened frequently. Once or twice I over imbibed, but made sure before I did I wasn't on the flight schedule for the following day.

We could get lost in our fears and doubts, too, although we rarely voiced them to one another. Fear clung to us like a dull headache—always there. Sure, combat pilots might refer to the ATC as Allergic to Combat, but don't tell that to a transport jockey who every time he lifts off for China knows there's a ten or twenty percent chance of not making it back. It's a risk we accepted. It's what happens when you sign up to go to war. Most of us tended to look through the other end of the telescope, however: that there's an eighty or ninety percent chance we'll make it home to enjoy our post-mission combat whiskey ration.

Yes, a few of the guys cracked. Got "Hump Happy," as we called it, and suffered a psychological breakdown akin to combat fatigue. Perhaps some got truly exhausted from too many trips over the Hump. Or not eating enough. Or not getting enough sleep. If a pilot really has logged too many hours, a furlough or trip home might help. As a last resort, a man can be removed from flight duty.

But sometimes, especially if the flyboy's a newbie who's lost his nerve after just two or three missions, he's told to suck it up and climb back into the pilot's seat. Or, perhaps to be on the safe side, the copilot's seat.

Whatever the view others might have of us, it takes a damn tough man to fly the Hump. Tough mentally. Tough physically. I know the ground pounders in the Army and Marines have it rougher than we do. But I'd challenge any of them to come sit at the controls of a transport in sub-freezing, zero-visibility weather, bouncing around at twenty thousand feet in an aluminum coffin, surrounded by piles of saber-toothed granite ready to eat you alive, and not lose control of their bowels.

One evening, as I sat in our shantytown officers club sipping a lukewarm beer, Zim entered.

"Got something for you," he said. "A couple of nickel nasties." He tossed a pair of well-worn paperback novels onto the table where I sat. Reading material—books, newspapers, magazines—was as difficult to come by at Chabua as were razor blades and soap.

The "nickel nasties," tawdry paperbacks featuring on their covers women wearing fewer articles of clothing than Fiji natives and boasting pontoons big enough to float battleships, had obviously made the rounds. They were wrinkled, crumpled, and barely readable.

"When you get tired of the porn," Zim went on, "you can try this." He placed a thin, nondescript hardcover book on the table.

"Looks like a textbook," I said.

"It is. Or it was. I used it at the University of Washington in one of my English lit classes, an introduction to modern poetry or some such thing. I thought you might like to browse it. At least you seemed to remember a few words from Kipling's verse."

"Thank you," I said, my gratitude genuine. "But to change the subject, did you say Washington?"

He nodded. "Class of '39."

I stood and grasped his hand. "Well, wonder of wonders. I graduated from there in '37, commissioned through ROTC, got my wings in '38. Pull up a chair. Sit. I haven't met a fellow Husky in a long, long time."

We chatted for several hours. I told him I'd been born in and grown up in Coeur d'Alene, Idaho. He'd been raised on a farm in Oregon's Willamette Valley near Newberg. It turned out we both loved fishing and had spent our winter and spring breaks plying the swift, twisting rivers in the rugged Coast Range of Oregon in quest of salmon and steelhead. Much of the timber there had been incinerated in a massive forest fire in 1933, but the fish still came.

"Favorite river?" he asked.

"I always did well on the Nehalem," I said. "You?"

"Caught a thirty-five-pound Chinook on the Columbia once. But mostly I fished the Trask and Wilson."

"Well, look," I said, "when this craziness is over, this stupid war, how about we spend some time together in the miserable cold, wet Oregon winters trying to deplete the number of fishies in the Nehalem, Wilson, and Trask?"

"Compared to what we have here, that would be heaven," Zim said, and took a big swallow of his beer, finishing it off.

It remained unspoken that we both expected to survive the war and get back to the States in one piece. Nobody ever talked about not making it, despite the fear that clung to us relentlessly, like jungle leeches.

Zim plunked his empty beer bottle back onto the table. "So let me ask you," he said, "there's this nurse—"

I laughed.

"What?" he said.

"I think I know what's coming . . . in a general sort of way."

"Well, some of the guys said you knew her. That you, well, had a run-in with her. That you might know why she's so . . . cranky."

"That's a kind description."

"Okay. Bitchy." Zim flashed a sad smile.

"She's had some harsh words for me," I said, "but I have no idea why. I've never said or done anything to her that would warrant the way she spoke to me. I really know nothing about her, except maybe she should be riding a broom instead of a C-46."

Zim chuckled. "She'd make a damn good-looking witch, though. You'll have to admit that."

I nodded. "I take it somebody else crossed swords with her?"

"I'd hate to see her with a sword. But she did happen to have a syringe in her hand when this particular event happened."

I leaned forward, eager to hear. The dark side of me, I suppose.

Zim continued. "So this lieutenant went in to get a tetanus booster and I guess made a pass at said nurse."

"Which wasn't well received, I'll bet."

"That would be an understatement." Zim swatted at a mosquito that had been making recon runs over us. "The nurse suggested he might want to keep his mouth shut or she might miss her target with the tetanus shot. She shifted the needle toward his, ahem, privates."

"So he didn't get a date?"

"After that, he couldn't get out of the hospital fast enough."

I shook my head, and again wondered what drove Captain Nurse. But I didn't allow the thought to linger. All I knew was, I wanted nothing to do with her. In a war zone, there's more than enough negativity and cynicism to go around without having to deal with an individual who is steeped in it. The Ice Queen may have a movie star's body, but she bore all the charm of a rotting corpse.

Major Hatcher, his rumpled uniform plastered to his body by rain and humidity, stomped into the little club. A soggy cigar sagged from his lips. "Guys said I might find you here," he said, his words directed at me.

"Beer?" I asked.

"Sure. Off duty now." Not that we were ever really "off duty."

Zim pulled a beer out of the icebox and set it in front of Hatcher.

"What's up, sir?" I said.

"Two things. First, I've got some news about that war correspondent, Sevareid, and the guys who bailed out over Burma a couple of weeks ago. And second, I've got a message for you from your boss in New Delhi." He slid a folded piece of teletype paper over to me.

"Tell me about the Sevareid guys," I said.

"They're fine. It took two or three weeks, but a ground search-and-rescue party finally reached them in the native village where they'd taken shelter, and walked them out. Apparently Lieutenant Colonel Flickinger—remember, he was the flight surgeon who parachuted in to help them—got everything organized in military fashion and kept the men in good shape. He gave everyone specific duties and they all pitched in."

"Even the civilians?"

"You bet. John Davies, Stilwell's political advisor and a professional diplomat, took over negotiations with the natives and made sure they understood they'd be handsomely rewarded for their help."

I thought back to the trinkets I'd seen in the warehouse in Dinjan.

"So, no heads were lost?" Zim asked.

Hatcher attempted to relight his waterlogged cigar but managed only to create a dense smoke screen.

"Let it smolder," I said, noticing the acrid emissions seemed to hold off strafing runs by a squadron of mosquitos circling overhead. Hatcher placed the smoking stub in an ashtray.

"Nope," he said, responding to Zim's question. "Everyone came home intact. But the guys did notice some skulls mounted on racks inside a couple of the huts. And they weren't monkey skulls."

Outside, an aircraft engine snarled to life as maintenance crews began their nightly labors.

Hatcher went on. "Flickinger drafted a couple of the Chinese colonels who'd been in the C-46 to be rice cooks, he held a daily sick call for everyone—including the natives—and led the survivors in calisthenics every morning." He paused and chuckled softly before continuing. "Apparently the natives thought that was hilarious, and they nearly died laughing. They were literally rolling around on the ground."

"Better to have happy headhunters than pissed off ones," I offered.

"Sevareid acted as historian and chaplain for the group," Hatcher continued. "And he said he was going to submit an article to the *Reader's Digest* about their adventures."

Hatcher polished off his beer and stood. "Okay, thanks for the juice. See you in the a.m."

He and Zim left together. I unfolded the message Hatcher had given me and read it.

TO: MAJOR RODGER SHEPHERD, 10TH WS DO, CHABUA AAF BASE

FROM: LT COL RICHARD ELLSWORTH, 10TH WS CC, HQ 10AF, NEW DELHI

SUBJECT: TRAVEL TO CHUNKING , CHINA

1. WILL ARRIVE CHABUA 1100 10 SEP 1943 TO PICK UP MAJ SHEPHERD.
2. DEPART CHABUA 1200 10 SEP 1943 FOR CHUNKING, CHINA.
3. ARRIVE CHUNKING, PROVISIONAL CAPITAL RC, 1700 10 SEP 1943
4. MEET WITH MGEN CLAIRE CHENNAULT, 14AF CC, AND GENERALISSIMO CHIANG KAI-SHEK, CHAIRMAN NGRC, 1300 11 SEP 1943.
5. TOPIC: INCREASED WEATHER SUPPORT REQUIREMENTS CBI THEATER
6. DEPART KUNMING FOR CHABUA O/A 12 SEP 1943

END

So in two days I would be heading for the wartime capital of China with Lieutenant Colonel Ellsworth to meet with two men whose fame had already landed them on the covers of *Time* and *Life* magazines.

I didn't know much about Chiang Kai-Shek other than that he was the chairman of the government of the Republic of China. And that his American-educated wife was apparently quite beautiful . . . and forcefully influential when it came to politics.

Everyone who flew, and most who didn't, had heard of General Claire Chennault. He'd retired from the Army in 1937 as a major and gone to China as an aviation advisor and trainer. In 1941, he was made a brigadier general in the Chinese Air Force and began recruiting pilots for the American Volunteer Group, the boys who became the legendary Flying Tigers. They flew P-40s, high-powered interceptor aircraft, with the snouts of fierce-looking sharks painted on their noses, and tigers with wings etched on their fuselages— courtesy of Walt Disney enterprises.

The US Army recalled Chennault to active duty in 1942. They made him a colonel, but within a year he'd pinned on two stars and become commanding general of the Fourteenth Air Force, of which the former Flying Tigers were now a part.

It seemed almost as though my upcoming trip to Chungking would make me part of history.

Right on schedule, two days later, Ellsworth set his C-47, *Betsy*, down at Chabua. He joined me where I waited for him in base ops.

"You'll be in the right-hand seat today," he said. "I'll be at the controls. Tex is catching some R and R in Ceylon. Let's get a weather briefing while they load the bird with some freight for Chungking."

"What's on the manifest? Nothing that explodes, I hope."

"Med supplies, mostly. Not much. Without turbochargers, the Gooney is kinda limited in its cargo load, especially if we have to climb rapidly."

In the weather section, we found Sergeant Jim Howard on duty, the same NCO I'd spoken with before my first trip to Kunming. We asked him if he'd received any recent reports on conditions over the Hump. Our route would take us over the southern reaches of the Himalayas to Kunming, then northeast another four hundred miles to Chungking.

"Yes, sirs," he said. "A couple of birds landed this morning and reported things were pretty rough over the mountains. Lots of turbulence, lots of clouds. IFR all the way. One of the guys—ex-Navy, I guess—said it was like being in a destroyer in hundred-foot seas."

"Guess we get to fly the Vomit Comet today," I said.

Ellsworth sighed. "That's why they pay us the big bucks." His words rang with cynicism. "The thing of it is, conditions aren't likely to get any better today. With daytime heating, the clouds are going to build even more."

"Maybe you could delay your trip," the sergeant suggested. "You know, it would be bad press to lose a couple of weather officers to, well, the weather." He issued a weak grin.

"Got a meeting scheduled with some stars," Ellsworth said. "I think we'd better show up."

The colonel and I walked back to *Betsy*. Sunshine flooded onto the base through a broken cloud deck. The humidity, as usual, grasped us in a soppy embrace. Our uniforms clung to us like newspapers to wet pavement.

To the east, over the First Ridge, piles of cumulus billowed skyward. Their tops, brilliant white in the morning sun, appeared as alabaster crowns sitting atop dark princes who threatened ill to those who challenged them.

"Flown the Hump before?" I asked. I hoped he had. It had become clear we had a rough journey ahead of us.

"I've got in a few trips. Not just over the Hump, but across the squadron's entire area of responsibility. We've got weather stations so remote the natives who live near them have never seen a white face. We have to ferry personnel, equipment, PX supplies, and mail into those places."

"Poor ol' *Betsy* must be getting tuckered out."

Ellsworth laughed. "Yeah. She's in the air almost every day, usually for five or six hours. Some of the guys have begun calling her TWA . . . Tenth Weather Airlines."

We climbed into *Betsy* and waited for the remainder of the supplies to be loaded.

"So have you approached General Chennault before about getting more weather troops in here?" I asked.

"We've traded messages. He's not at all happy about the idea of having to provide food and billeting to additional noncombatants. Nor is his buddy, Chiang Kai-shek. That's why I got this sit-down scheduled with them."

"What in the hell is wrong with Chennault? Is he stupid or something? Doesn't he understand that better weather support would help us get more supplies to his aviation operations?"

"One thing I've discovered, Rod, is that while general officers may be opinionated, intimidating, and outspoken, they aren't stupid. Dumb officers don't get to pin stars on their collars. All we can do is plead our case, make strong arguments, and hope they see the merits in them."

Slightly chastised, I nodded in agreement.

"Let's run through the checklist," Ellsworth said. "Time to be on our way to China."

We did the checklist, started the engines, and taxied into takeoff position. *Betsy* lifted off smoothly and made the standard circling climb out of Chabua. We punched into the rampart of adolescent cumulus clouds coming to life over the First Ridge. A few sharp jolts gave us an early warning this would not be a smooth journey.

A swirling grayness swallowed *Betsy* as she bounced around like a bug in a Bendix. Both Ellsworth and I clung to the controls, trying our damnedest to hold the plane in level flight. Impossible.

We'd catch an updraft and find ourselves pinned firmly to our seats as the C-47 leapt skyward. Then, almost before we could react, the bird would be hammered downward as if tumbling into an elevator shaft. Our safety harnesses would bite into our shoulders and thighs as they held us in place, preventing us from slamming our heads into the cockpit's ceiling.

"See if you can raise the Fort Hertz beacon," Ellsworth said over the interphone. "I've been trying to hold us on a steady heading, but we're jouncing around so much I'm not sure where the devil we are."

"Roger that." I searched for the Fort Hertz frequency for several minutes, but picked up nothing but static.

"No joy," I said.

"Seat of the pants, dead reckoning then," Ellsworth responded. He appeared relatively unperturbed by the situation, but I have to admit, I didn't share his composure.

Abruptly, the turbulence abated. But *Betsy* remained sheathed in clouds.

"Must be out over the Mali River Valley," Ellsworth said, then added, "but damned if I know exactly where."

"If there's a break in the clouds, maybe we'll be able to spot a landmark," I offered.

"Don't get your hopes up. We're gonna have to climb. I'm guessing things will get even rougher as we top the next two ranges. If the turbulence comes back—and I think we can count on it—we'll want to be up around twenty-five thousand feet."

Twenty-five thousand feet. Above the service ceiling for a Gooney Bird. I listened to the friendly growl of the Pratt & Whitneys. It sounded solid. But I knew the engines were no match for the monsters mounted on the C-46 that cranked out twenty-one-hundred horsepower apiece. They also sported superchargers that gave them a lot more oomph at altitude, something the Gooney Bird lacked.

I knew that at twenty-five thousand feet, summiting the Kumon Mountains and the Santsung Range that lay ahead of us, ol' *Betsy* would be gasping for breath and virtually unresponsive to any quick maneuvers we might wish to take.

We strapped on our oxygen masks. The initial inhalations of pure oxygen provided a cool, almost refreshing, counterpoint to the clammy rubber clamped over my mouth and nose. We forced the C-47 higher and higher as we continued to barrel eastward through the ashen gloom. Ice began to cling to the wings and props, but so far the deicers seemed up to their task.

"Into the snow zone," I commented.

"Here's my bit of useless information for the day," Ellsworth said. "Did you know Himalaya in Sanskrit means 'House of Snow?'"

"Ah, the inside dope. I'll remember that if we have to bail out and run into any Hindu scholars."

My comment elicited a chuckle from Ellsworth. I figured it might be the last one we'd have for a while.

Betsy began to wiggle and jiggle again as we approached the main Hump.

8

Airborne over The Hump
En route to Chungking, China

Daylight disappeared. Darkness as deep as a new moon night set in as *Betsy*, lurching from side to side, porpoised through obsidian clouds.

"Ride 'em, cowboy," Ellsworth shouted, clinging to the controls with grim determination.

With no preamble, the altimeter began to unwind like a line on a fishing reel with a thousand-pound marlin on the other end. Our C-47 became a lead sled plunging toward sawtooth mountain peaks that waited, unseen, to annihilate us.

Both Ellsworth and I pulled desperately on the yokes, fighting to get the plane's tail down and nose up. But the bird refused to respond. The needle on the rate-of-climb indicator lay comatose. Ellsworth yanked the throttles back to reduce power.

I wondered how many seconds we had to live. How many ticks of the clock we had left before *Betsy* joined the

Aluminum Trail. I honest-to-God closed my eyes. Not that I could see anything anyhow. I wondered for a fleeting moment if Trish would be happy to be with me again. Would she remember? Of course she would. The terror of dying fled. I had no qualms about "meeting my maker" for I knew Trish would be there to greet me. Sweet death.

The C-47 slammed into something. Not a rock pile. We bottomed out, pancaking into a slab of atmosphere, then rocketed skyward. But once more Ellsworth and I were only along for the ride. I tried to focus on the altimeter, but the convulsions rippling through the plane made it difficult. I thought I read eighteen or nineteen thousand feet. If so, depending on where we were—and we weren't sure—we'd perhaps flown below the level of tallest guardians of the main Hump.

My stomach rammed into my intestines as we shot heavenward. Straining, Ellsworth and I forced our yokes forward. To no avail. *Betsy* continued to accelerate upward like a cork released deep underwater. As cold as the interior of the plane had become, and despite my fleece-lined boots, wool blanket, and leather flight jacket, sweat poured off me as if I were in a steam bath. Effort and fear.

Then wham! Another gut punch battered the aircraft. Again we fell. Nothing we could do. A low howl thrummed through the cockpit as Ellsworth jammed on full power once more. Useless. We plunged. Down, down, down. My stomach clawed its way into my throat. I held on, wondering when, how, where this nightmare would end. The C-47 rattled, squeaked, and groaned. Why it didn't come apart, I have no idea. Perhaps it was just the toughest damn bird ever built.

The ride seemed endless. Ellsworth may have said something, yelled something once or twice, but even over the interphone I couldn't hear him above the din filling the cockpit. I don't know how long the battering went on. It seemed like hours, but I'm sure it was for only minutes. Maybe fifteen? I don't know.

At last the ride smoothed. Well, relatively speaking. We remained a ship in towering seas, but at least were able to control our flight.

Dense clouds continued to enshroud us. I had no sense of where the ground was, where the heavens were. The gyros had tumbled and the artificial horizon had gone all cattywampus, succumbing to the battering the plane had taken.

"We banking?" I asked Ellsworth.

He shrugged. "I don't think so."

"It feels like it."

"Any idea where we are?"

Now it became my turn to shrug. "At least we're in the air."

"That's the only good part."

"Lord, for all I know we could be flying inverted over Tibet."

"Don't think we're inverted. We could be over Tibet, though. Or Siam."

"I'll see if I can find a beacon." I searched through the frequencies once more. Nothing.

We flew on. At last the clouds thinned, the air smoothed, and I picked up a beacon.

"Li-Chiang," I said, unable to keep the excitement out of my voice. "Dead ahead."

"Li-Chiang? Really?"

I understood. "A little off course, aren't we?"

"A little? Maybe about forty miles north of where we should be."

And just a few miles south of a couple of Himalayan peaks that poked toward the stratosphere. Twenty-three thousand feet.

I cycled the caging knob and the artificial horizon came back to life.

Ellsworth glanced at me. "There's part of the problem." He nodded at the artificial horizon indicator.

We'd been flying in a tilted turn, toward the left, toward the north. But without the help of instruments, Ellsworth thought we'd been traveling straight and level. Vertigo. He leveled the wings and set *Betsy* on a course toward the southeast.

Finally, we punched out of the diminishing cloudiness. Below us, sunshine bathed the upland plain of China's Yunnan Province. I tuned in Kunming's radio beacon and we tracked that toward the big air base. Once there, we turned toward the northeast and Chungking.

"Four hundred miles to go," Ellsworth said.

"It seems like we've flown four thousand already."

The colonel radioed the tower at Kunming and reported the extreme turbulence we'd come through.

"Extreme?" I asked him.

"You didn't think it was extreme?"

"No. It was the next category up from extreme, whatever that is."

Chungking, China
Wartime capital

We set *Betsy* down, her joints creaking like an elderly dowager's, at the military airfield near Chungking. The city itself perched on a plateau squeezed between the Chialing and Yangtze Rivers that joined at the southern end of the plateau. Hills of terraced rice paddies rose on all sides of the city and flowed toward distant horizons across the vast, rolling topography of western China.

I'd read someplace, *Life* magazine maybe, that earlier in the war, with Japan bent on enslaving the entire nation, Chungking had been the most bombed place on Earth. Even now it appeared singularly unappealing, gray and colorless with stacks of rubble, and smothered in thick haze and smoke.

We deplaned, gave the mechanics a long list of items to be checked, and caught a ride in a jeep that bore us up a terraced hill toward the military headquarters.

"Were you worried back there," I asked Ellsworth, "over the Hump when all that turbulence slammed us?"

He didn't answer for a bit, then said, "Nah. Nothing I could have done about it. Why worry? It wouldn't have changed anything. Might as well enjoy the ride."

I gaped at him.

He flashed a sly smile and patted my arm. "I didn't say I wasn't scared."

The jeep pulled to a stop in front of a beat-up, wood-framed building with a red tile roof.

"The Generalissimo's staff headquarters," the private driving us announced.

We thanked the young man, got out of the vehicle, and stretched. Every muscle in my body, and apparently a few I didn't know I had, ached. The struggle and tension of our violent flight from Assam to China had come home to roost. I issued a load groan.

"Flyboys?" said a crisp, almost commanding voice from behind us.

I turned slowly, as did Colonel Ellsworth.

A man I instantly recognized, but didn't know, stood there. Weatherworn and angular with graying, close-cropped hair and round, wire-rimmed spectacles, he seemed both forbidding and full of vitality. It was none other than Lieutenant General Joseph Stilwell—Vinegar Joe—commander of all US forces in the CBI Theater. He'd been on the cover of *Life* magazine the previous year.

He'd gained fame with the American public when, at the age of fifty-nine, he'd led a group of Americans, British, and Chinese out of the Burmese jungle to India as the Japs closed in behind them. Wearing a battered campaign hat and carrying an ancient Springfield rifle rather than an officer's typical sidearm, he'd set a blistering pace of one hundred and five paces per minute. It became known as the Stilwell Stride. Many of the combat soldiers he led struggled to keep up.

Ellsworth and I popped to attention and saluted. Stilwell snapped off a smart salute in return.

"Yes, sir," Ellsworth said, responding to the general's question about being flyboys.

"Meeting with the Peanut?" Stilwell growled. I'd heard that Peanut was the unflattering nickname he used for Chiang Kai-shek.

"And General Chennault," Ellsworth said.

"That old bastard?" Stilwell responded. "Belongs in a retirement home."

Since I thought Chennault to be about ten years younger than Stilwell, I gathered they probably didn't get along.

"Discussing additional air support?" Stilwell snapped.

"Not exactly, sir," Ellsworth answered. "We're from the Tenth Weather Squadron. We're going to discuss getting more manpower authorized so we can provide the theater with better service."

Stilwell rolled his eyes and shook his head, seemingly in disgust. "Jesus, Joseph, and Mary. You damned air corps guys just don't get it, do you? It's not flying machines and weather guessers that are gonna win this goddamned war. It's gonna be ground-pounders and grunts, just like every other shitty conflict in history. Tell that to Fair Claire and Peanut, and you'll be doing our country a real service."

At that, Stilwell pivoted and strode away from us, muttering under his breath.

Recalling General Chennault's and Chiang Kai-shek's pre-existing opposition to additional weather manpower, I asked Ellsworth, "Do you have the sense this meeting is not going to go well?"

"Geez, why on earth would I think that?"

He attempted to brush the wrinkles and folds from his uniform, then headed toward the entrance to the building.

Inside, a dank, musty odor filled a small reception area manned by a Chinese soldier and an American MP. We presented our credentials to the MP who accepted them, checked them against a document on a clipboard, then asked us to follow him.

We trooped down a long hallway lined on both sides with tiny offices. About three quarters of the way down the hall, the MP ushered us into a conference room containing a sprawling mahogany table surrounded by cushioned straight-back chairs.

Brigadier General Claire Chennault, leather-faced and swarthy, sat at one end of the table. Again, here was an American hero who'd graced the cover of *Life* magazine the previous year.

At the other end sat Generalissimo Chiang Kai-shek, diminutive and avuncular-looking with a shaved head. He nodded and smiled as we entered.

Several other US Army staff officers sat at the table between General Chennault and the Generalissimo.

"Gentlemen, welcome," Chennault said. "Please, take a seat. Help yourself to the *Youtiaos*. There's tea and water, too."

The *Youtiaos* looked like deep-fried breadsticks with the texture of doughnuts. Ellsworth and I each reached for one. We hadn't eaten since breakfast.

General Chennault waited patiently for us as we downed the *Youtiaos* and sipped tea that bore the pleasant aroma of jasmine.

When we'd finished, Chennault spoke. His voice carried traces of a Southern or Texan accent. He seemed courtly, but at the same time I sensed he was a man who didn't put up with nonsense and was used to getting his own way.

"Colonel Ellsworth, Major Shepherd, I appreciate your flying here from Assam. I know that it's a long, arduous journey. But I hope you haven't made the trip with any illusions my previously stated position on approving additional equipment and manpower in support of weather operations might be swayed. It's something for which we absolutely cannot provide additional logistical backing."

"Sir," Ellsworth said, "if you would allow me to present our case, I think you might see that by approving our request for more men and equipment, both safety and tonnage delivered to the Chinese effort could be vastly improved."

Chennault held us in his gaze, his vertically seamed face not reflecting whether he held us in contempt or favor.

He remained silent for a short while, then said, "I truly believe you'd be wasting your time. But I'm not an unreasonable man and will certainly hear you out. I respect the fact you've come over nine hundred miles to lay out your argument. Please proceed."

"Thank you, sir." Colonel Ellsworth took a final swig of his tea, then began.

He laid out clearly and concisely, I thought, how additional men—observers, forecasters, briefers—and equipment

—radios, pilot balloons, theodolites—could pay huge dividends in improving the flow through the Hump lifeline.

A translator whispered into Chiang Kai-shek's ear as Ellsworth spoke.

After over half an hour of presenting his thoughtful analysis and prognosis, Ellsworth concluded, "Weather is the single greatest cause of fluctuations in the movement of air traffic between India and China. The Tenth Weather Squadron can't change that. But with additional men and equipment we can, without question, improve the position we're in now by telling pilots when and where the worst weather may occur. Fewer lives will be lost. More tonnage will be delivered."

Chennault remained silent and expressionless after Ellsworth finished. He seemed to be mulling over the argument the colonel had presented. I thought perhaps my boss had gotten through to Chennault, that he'd managed to turn a floodlight on illuminating the positive aspects of improved weather support to CBI operations. I thought he had done a bang-up job of presenting a military cost-benefit analysis.

Chennault nibbled on a *Youtiaos* and took a long drink of water, then wiped his mouth with a cloth napkin.

"Outstanding presentation, Colonel," he said. "I appreciate the thought and effort you and your staff expended on it. But I hope you appreciate my position, too. We're trying to hold off over three million Japs here in China. Every single cubic foot of cargo—combat supplies—we can cram into a transport flying from India to China is a matter of life and death."

I knew immediately where Chennault's rebuttal was headed. We'd lost the argument.

"No offense, Colonel Ellsworth," Chennault went on, "but the additional balloon blowers you've requested would take up vital space on Hump aircraft. And once they got here, the

Chinese would have to raise more rice to feed them. As I'm certain you're aware, no food is airlifted into China."

"If I may, General—" Ellsworth said, but Chennault held up his hand to cut him off.

"Between you and the signal corps," Chennault went on, "five hundred additional men have been requested to augment activities in my area. Let me be blunt. I've found that I can operate a combat group, including auxiliaries, with one hundred twenty-five men. Five hundred additional support troops would rob me of four groups. I don't intend to be robbed of four groups. Thank you for your time, gentlemen."

Chennault stood. The rest of us stood. General Chennault and Chiang Kai-shek departed the room. The meeting had concluded.

"You think he'll ever see the light?" I said to Ellsworth as we left the building.

"He might. It may take a while for the value of weather support to be fully understood and realized, but I think it will be. We've planted the seed. It takes time for concepts to take root, blossom, and bear fruit."

"You have a hell of a lot more patience than I do, Dick."

"I have no choice. I'm not going to win a face-to-face battle with a flag officer. But I believe in what we're offering and am willing to let things play out. We might well prevail in the longer run."

We opted to remain overnight in Chungking, not wanting to once again challenge the violent weather we'd flown through earlier in the day getting here. Besides, we knew the maintenance crews could use the extra time repairing the "battle damage" *Betsy* had suffered in flying over the Hump.

Before taking off for Chabua the following morning, we were handed a teletype message at base ops. It wasn't good news.

9

Chungking, China
to Chabua, India

Without saying a word, Ellsworth handed me a copy of the message.

It said that a C-46 bound for Kunming from Chabua yesterday had failed to make it. No one had heard from it. No distress signals had been received from the aircraft. The message directed that on our return from Chungking, once we were on the Kunming to Chabua leg, we should keep an eye out for any wreckage. Tail number 8806.

I handed the copy back to Ellsworth. "You know, considering what the weather was like yesterday, it's a wonder they aren't asking crews to keep an eye out for the remains of *Betsy*."

"I know," Ellsworth said quietly.

"You think there's any chance the guys bailed out?"

Ellsworth shook his head. "Not in the kind of turbulence that was out there yesterday. An airborne battleship might not have survived that."

We both knew, I think, that what had happened was that the crew had gotten lost and disoriented and slammed into one of those cumulo-granites that lurk on the Hump.

"I suppose it's unlikely we'll spot anything?"

"Virtually no chance," Ellsworth answered. "Most of the time we can't even see the ground when we're flying the Hump. And, assuming the pilots got lost, they probably weren't anywhere near the usual route between Chabua and Kunming when they crashed."

I hoped whoever had gone down, it wasn't someone I knew. I understood the Grim Reaper waits for all of us, lurking in the icy mountains, skulking through the steaming jungles. But it's easier to hold onto the "it won't happen to me" illusion if the scythe cuts down someone you don't know rather than a guy you've palled around with or flown with.

We lifted off from the grayness and bleakness of Chungking into an unblemished sky brushed with only the thin, white streamers of cirrus far above us. The air seemed strangely smooth, as though resting and recuperating from yesterday's violence. We climbed to twelve thousand feet, the engines purring like big cats, and winged our way southwestward toward Kunming.

At Kunming, we banked to the west-northwest and headed toward Chabua. The ride became bumpier, but nothing approaching the ferocity of what we'd experienced the previous day. Cumulus, like burgeoning cauliflowers, sprouted in the sky and thickened as we climbed toward the main Hump.

The spectacular scenery transitioned from the rolling, pastoral upland of Yunnan Province to the verdant, forested foothills of the southern reach of the Himalayas. Then came the snaggletooth peaks of the main Hump, the storied roof of the world, that waited to snatch your breath away with their beauty, or usher you into eternity if you gave them a chance.

As we lifted higher and higher to clear the big ridges, cloudiness swallowed us and hid the earth. We saw no sign of a crashed C-46, yet we knew without a doubt that another tragic milepost had been added to the Aluminum Trail.

Chabua, Assam, India
US Army Air Forces base

We touched down at Chabua in the late afternoon. I went directly to base ops to see who had been flying tail number 8806.

The tote board told the story. Tail number 8806, a C-46 piloted by Captain Pete Zimmerman, had departed Chabua the previous day at eleven hundred hours. It had never arrived in Kunming and never returned to Chabua.

Zim, my pal from the University of Washington, who loved poetry, who loved fishing, had flown off into the sky "where the dawn comes up like thunder" and met his fate in a land that William Blake might have written about in his poem "The Tyger." Maybe Burma. Maybe India. Zim had underlined the verse in the book he'd given me.

Tyger Tyger, burning bright,
  In the forests of the night;
  What immortal hand or eye,
  Could frame thy fearful symmetry?

. . .

I couldn't remember any of the poem's other passages except for:

When the stars threw down their spears
  And water'd heaven with their tears:
  Did he smile his work to see?
  Did he who made the Lamb make thee?

. . . *And watered heaven with their tears.* I sat on a bench against a wall, buried my face in my hands, and allowed silent sobs to convulse through my body. There would be no fishing trips for Zim and me after the war, no journeys to the wild, spectacular rivers of coastal Oregon. No salmon or steelhead battling us to avoid becoming pan-fried accompaniments to a cold beer or a whiskey on the rocks after our day was done. No camaraderie. No reminiscing about combat adventures and dead-eyed nurses. No welcome home by loved ones, family, or friends.

Zim would remain forever in a remote land, unburied, unmarked, and unsung. I squeezed my eyes shut and let their leakage drain down my cheeks. I sensed a presence next to me, an arm draping over my shoulder.

"You knew the crew?" Ellsworth said softly.

"The pilot, Pete Zimmerman," I answered, my voice raspy, fluted with emotion.

"Let's go grab our post-mission whiskeys. I'll sit with you awhile. We can talk."

"You need to get back to New Delhi, sir."

"I need to take care of my DO. Come on." With his hand on my upper arm, he stood and tugged me up. We headed toward the dispensary.

We each got our two shots of whiskey, but Ellsworth made

certain I got one of his. I'm not sure he even drank the one he had left. We sat in the hallway outside the dispensary on a couple of metal chairs. One of them, quite likely, the one I'd been slumped in when Captain Nurse and I had last traded words.

Ellsworth spoke to me, keeping his voice low and earnest. "Rod, you've been through a hell of a lot. More than most men your age. Losing your wife, now your pilot friend. I understand the wounds in your heart, how deep they must go, how much they must hurt. And I want you to know I truly admire you as a man, as an officer in the United States Army, and as a friend. I'm beyond proud to have you on my staff."

I nodded and downed my first belt of alcohol. It simultaneously burned and soothed me as it slid down my throat.

Ellsworth continued speaking. "Don't give up, Rod. Keep pushing forward, as difficult as it will be, as deep as your pain must cut. You're a good man, a valuable asset in this damned war. You've got way too much to contribute. As a pilot, the airlift over the Hump can't afford to lose you. Your experience, your skill, your courage. And most certainly the Tenth Weather Squadron can't afford to lose you. We've way too much to accomplish here. You're my right-hand man. I don't want to go into 'combat' without you watching my six. You with me, Major?"

He'd kept his voice soft and even-toned, his gaze locked on me. I nodded again. "Yes, sir," I managed to choke out. I swallowed my second shot.

"Get blitzed tonight," Ellsworth said. "Sleep until noon tomorrow. Then get up and tackle the world again. That's an order."

As he finished speaking, the door at the far end of the hallway, the entrance from outside, swung open. Someone walked in. Damned if it wasn't my old buddy, Captain Nurse, probably arriving for a night shift. As she strode by us, she cast a quick look at the shot glasses lined up on the floor by my chair. I couldn't read anything in her glance, neither understanding nor disapproval, but I sensed she wanted to say something. She didn't. Perhaps she was deterred by the presence of a lieutenant colonel.

She slowed her pace and continued toward the entrance to the main clinic.

"Now there's an attractive woman," Ellsworth noted, perhaps a bit too loudly.

"Not really," I said.

Captain Nurse stopped, pivoted, and stared back at me. Surprisingly, I read something akin to hurt in her eyes. Good, I thought. Karma can be such a bitch. Maybe it was the booze talking. Maybe not. I didn't care. I reached for my third shot and polished it off. The captain disappeared into the clinic.

Ellsworth patted me on the back, stood, and asked the medic for another ration of post-mission whiskey. "It been a tough day for the major here," the colonel explained. He handed me another shot, said goodbye, and departed.

I sat alone for a while, my head spinning, my thoughts jumbled, my emotions raw, and downed my final whiskey. Then, zig-zagging like a destroyer avoiding a sub, I wove my way back to my *basha* and crash-landed on my cot.

Two days later I was back on the flying schedule, tasked to ferry a load of fuel to Kunming. My assigned copilot, Second Lieutenant Roscoe Mullins, was fresh from the States. This would be his first trip over the Hump. I'd rather have had an experienced aviator in the right-hand seat, but I guess newbies had to get broken in somehow. Besides, experience hadn't saved Zim. So maybe it didn't make any damn difference in the end. Flying over the most dangerous terrain in the world, and through the worst weather on the planet, was just one big gamble anyhow. A roulette wheel of death. If you played the game long enough, your number would come up. Or sometimes, if you got "lucky" on your first spin, you wouldn't have to worry about playing again.

I could see apprehension scrawled across the lieutenant's face when he arrived. Between his palpable angst and the omnipresent humidity, he'd already sweated through his uniform. It looked like it had been yanked from the wash and not dried.

We introduced ourselves to each other and I briefed him on all the same stuff I'd been advised on prior to my first flight over the Hump. About using the template outlined on the floor of a warehouse to stack the cargo before loading it. About sitting on, not wearing, your parachute when flying. About having a heavy blanket to wrap around your legs at altitude.

"What's with the pre-stacking of the cargo?" he asked.

I explained to him it made loading the plane faster and more efficient, and that we wouldn't end up with any heavy cargo blocking the door in case we had to jettison stuff.

"Why would we have to jettison anything?"

"Lots of reasons. Engine failure, icing, low fuel, a need to climb to a higher altitude. Anything where a lighter payload would help keep us in the air. Today, since the cargo is nothing but fifty-five-gallon drums of avgas, there's probably no need to worry about cargo placement. It's all the same stuff."

"And the blanket?"

"To keep your legs warm."

"The heaters are busted?"

"Nope. We just don't use them. Especially with a load of high-octane fuel. They're open-flame heaters."

"Best to avoid becoming a twenty-five-ton Roman candle, I suppose," Mullins said. He caught on fast.

"Let's go do our walk-around while the cargo is being loaded," I said.

We headed toward the C-46 we'd be flying, tail number 7821. A shower had just passed over the base, and steam rose from the tarmac like mist on an English moor. At least I thought that's what it looked like. I'd seen English moors only in motion pictures.

We reached the bird.

"This is an old one," I said. A departing Gooney Bird drowned out the rest of my words as it lifted out of the steamy haze and climbed into a cloud-flecked sky.

"As I was saying," I went on, once the reverberations of the C-47's motors had dissipated, "this is an old bird." I pointed at the leading edge of the wings. "See, no deicing boots."

"Why?"

"They get cut to ribbons by the gravel and knife-edged rocks on the runways in China. Once they're shredded, they're removed. Best we avoid icing conditions."

Mullins sighed and rolled his eyes. The reality of flying the Hump had begun to sink in.

"And this old gal will probably leak like a sieve. Little holes always develop in the skin of these long-in-the-tooth birds, so if we hit rain, expect to get wet."

"I've heard one of the C-46's nicknames—one of many—is the Plumber's Nightmare."

"You'll find out why."

We finished our preflight inspection and climbed into the plane. It reeked of avgas fumes, spilled hydraulic fluid, and the accumulated fragrance of unwashed bodies. We settled into our seats and cranked the Pratt & Whitneys. Despite the dotage of the bird, the engines sounded robust. The instruments confirmed as much.

We took off into the cumulus-dotted sky and performed

the circling climb out of Chabua to gain altitude. I hoped to hell we wouldn't have to run a gauntlet like the one Colonel Ellsworth and I had faced on my previous trip to China.

I'd checked the weather before departing. The briefer told me incoming flights that morning had reported only occasional moderate turbulence over the main Hump with a bit of light icing in the clouds. After my violent journey to Chungking with Ellsworth, I figured "occasional moderate" and "light" would be a breeze.

We reached fifteen thousand feet, cleared the First Ridge, and leveled out. The only thing that bothered me was that I had to crank in about a thirty-degree drift correction to maintain our heading toward Kunming. That meant we'd encountered a flight-level wind of over a hundred miles per hour coming in over our right wing. It bothered me because a wind of that magnitude suggested things were happening in the atmosphere with a hell of a lot more vigor than anyone had anticipated.

But I decided there was nothing I could do about it at the moment. So I set the bird on autopilot and sat back to chat with Mullins on the interphone and point out to him as much of the geography and topography of the area as I could. He seemed an apt student and asked a lot of questions.

We neared the main Hump and I took the plane up to twenty-two thousand feet.

"Up ahead," I said, "those are the giants. First the Kumon Mountains, then the cavernous gorge of the Salween River, and finally the Santsung Range. The two mountain ranges are southward extensions of the Himalayas out of Tibet. You wouldn't want to ever wander too far north of where we are right now, or you'll bang into rock piles over four miles tall."

"Like the Rockies?" Mullins looked at me, wide-eyed.

"No. Higher."

I leaned forward in my seat, trying to get a better look at what lay in front of us. I suddenly didn't like it. Didn't like it at all. An obsidian wall of boiling thunderstorms lined the main Hump. Lightning sheeted from thunderhead to thunderhead, illuminating their flat, anvil tops in vivid oranges and whites. In a way, it was like catching a glimpse of the black flag of a pirate ship flapping on the horizon.

Dark poetry, I thought. A legacy, perhaps, of the world whose door Zim had opened for me.

10

_____

Airborne over The Hump
En route to Kunming, China

I angled Ol' Dumbo toward a gap in the bulwark of boiling clouds. My gut told me that might not necessarily be a good idea, but I figured since *Betsy* had survived her violent run through similar conditions a few days ago, a bird weighing over twenty thousand pounds more ought to stand an even better chance. I can't believe how wrong a person can be sometimes.

Even in the relatively cloud-free opening between the towering thunderstorms, a wind gust like the fist of God slammed into us. It hurled us sideways into a steep turn, directly into the maw of a seething, roiling mass of blackness.

We plunged, losing altitude so rapidly the altimeter spun like a whirling dervish. My stomach surged into my throat. Mullins and I fought back, attempting to gain altitude, applying full throttle to the big Pratt & Whitneys, but it turned out to be a useless endeavor. We bottomed out at fourteen thousand, far below the safe zone for summiting the Hump.

Then up we went, pinned in our seats. The C-46 shot heavenward, riding the rocketlike updraft of a savage thunderstorm. Again, Mullins and I could only hang on.

The brutal wallowing continued. The gyros and artificial horizon gave up the ghost. The needle on the rate-of-climb indicator flopped around like a rag doll in a bulldog's mouth. We were at twenty-one thousand feet one moment, twelve thousand the next. A forty-five-degree bank to the left one moment, the same to the right the next. Continuous lightning illuminated the cockpit. Despite his oxygen mask, I could see terror ingrained on Mullins's face. I'm sure he could see the same on mine.

Then things got really bad.

Another powerful gust virtually flipped us. Dirt and debris from the floor filled the cockpit. A loose E6B—a slide rule-like navigation tool—floated past me. A spare throat mike glued itself to the ceiling. A blanket, like an untethered kite, followed the mike. I bit halfway through my tongue as the plane tumbled. My safety harness bit into my body with viselike fierceness. Blood filled my throat.

The plane lurched to the right, slamming my head into the side window of the cockpit. Another loose object, maybe a clipboard or pen, sliced into my face. More blood. My head spun. I blinked, trying to rid myself of sudden double vision.

I wanted to lift the oxygen mask from my face and spit out the blood from my throat, but didn't dare move my arms from the controls. Not that I was able to control anything. The airspeed indicator dropped to forty miles per hour. I shoved the control wheel all the way forward to regain speed. Nothing happened. So we weren't really flying. We'd become a cork in a whirlpool.

What a shitty way to die, I thought. Riding an airborne coffin into a pile of granite. My breathing slowed. My heart rate dropped. I accepted my fate. I closed my eyes and listened to our cargo—fuel drums—breaking loose from their tie-downs in the cabin and slamming into the sides and top of the fuselage.

I knew it would be physically impossible for Mullins and me to bail out. And even if we could, we wouldn't survive in this weather or in the rugged terrain below that waited to consume us.

But then, a miracle.

I opened my eyes as our ride abruptly smoothed. My vision returned to normal. We appeared to be between cloud layers at twenty-one thousand feet. And flying. Upside down.

"Jesus," I yelled.

Mullins whooped something, too, but I couldn't understand it.

I applied full rudder and aileron, just like rolling out in a primary trainer. I brought Ol' Dumbo to right-side up. One of the engines sputtered. But that seemed a minor concern after what we'd just been through.

"We're headed in the wrong direction," Mullins said, his voice oddly steady.

I looked at the compass. Two hundred seventy degrees. Back toward Assam. But we'd passed the point of no return. China was closer.

"Let's get her pointed toward Kunming," I said, my words coming out slurred and painful in deference to my wounded tongue.

We turned the C-46 around and punched into the clouds once again. But this time the flight remained smooth with only the usual wiggles and jiggles. After our adventure of a few minutes ago, I felt as if we'd become becalmed. My head throbbed, but by God, I was alive. So was Mullins. Although I don't know why either of us should have been.

"Sorry about that, boss," Mullins said, and pointed at his crotch. Wet.

"Doesn't count," I said. "You do realize we both should be dead?"

He nodded without smiling.

Again, one of the engines coughed.

"What's that?" Mullins asked.

"Nothing good," I said.

I grabbed the Aldis lamp, flicked it on, and aimed it out the window at the wing and propeller on my side of the C-46. Ice had formed on the prop and around the carburetor scoops. A frosty rime also coated the leading edge of the wing.

The alcohol prop deicer seemed to be working fine. Ice flew off the blades and slammed into the fuselage just aft of the cockpit window. I could hear chunks thudding into the skin on the other side of the bird, too.

Ice on the wings presented a different problem. With no deicer boots, the buildup continued unabated and our airspeed began to drop.

Worst of all, if icing had stretched its frosty fingers into the carburetors, we were in truly deep shit. The engines would die and we'd cease being a flying machine.

"Got a fix on our location?" I asked Mullins.

"Not exactly, sir."

"Look, Lieutenant, *exactly* would be a really big help in this situation. We've gotta get to a lower altitude to shake this icing, but I'd rather not bump into something while we're doing that."

"I'm searching for a radio beacon, sir."

"Sorry. I know it's not your fault. After that trip through the washing machine back there, we're lucky to even have a compass working."

As if on damnable cue, the right engine cut out.

I feathered the prop, shut down the fuel flow, and cleaned up the aircraft the best I could. I got her flying straight and level. More or less.

I drew a deep breath. This trip seemed to be one we were destined not to complete.

"All right, Lieutenant," I said. "I'm going to restart the engine. I'll go to emergency-rich fuel mixture and full carburetor heat. Unfortunately, keeping the carb heat on in these birds is next to impossible. The handles and locking devices to keep the heat on are crap. You'll probably have to sit there and hold the handles in place."

"I'm ready, Major. Just say when."

I knew if we couldn't get to a lower altitude and out of the icing conditions quickly, we were doomed. We couldn't keep the engines on emergency-rich fuel and full carburetor heat and expect to coax any power out of them.

The smell of spilled avgas from the battered drums in the cabin mixed with biting cold that now filled the aircraft. I'm not sure if fear has an odor, but I know I detected the essence of it in the cockpit.

Before I could restart the dead engine, another updraft, one of exceptional violence, caught us by surprise and fired us like a cannonball out of the clouds and into the clear air on top. But then the other engine quit.

"Well, we're out of the icing," I said. Why not put a positive spin on things?

An eerie silence, except for the creaking and groaning of the airplane, engulfed us.

Mullins, his eyes suggesting he, too, had accepted our fate, shook his head in silent disbelief.

"Maybe one last chance," I said. "Try again to find a beacon."

Mullins ran through the frequencies once more. "Hey, hey, I got something," he yelled.

"Who?"

"Kunming. Strong signal. Gotta be close."

I flicked my gaze to the radio compass. "Got it," I said.

We had flown back into a thicket of clouds, but hadn't encountered any additional turbulence. I got the aircraft going straight and level once again. I wondered if I should try to restart the engines. But I had another idea.

"Okay," I said, "I don't wanna fool around trying to restart the engines now, because if I can't, we're going down. But we're close enough to Kunming, I think I can dead-stick us in."

"What!?"

"We should be on top of the field in a couple of minutes. The C-46 actually glides pretty well when it's cleaned up." I checked the altimeter. "We're only losing about five hundred feet per minute."

"And if we get popped by another gust?"

"Nothing I can do about it."

Absent the roar of the engines, I heard Mullins draw a deep breath as he sucked in a long draft of oxygen.

"Okay," he said, "dead-stick it is." We didn't even need the interphone to converse.

I held the plane on the radio compass heading for Kunming.

"The aerodrome's at sixty-two hundred feet," I said. "If we haven't broken out of the clouds by ten thousand, we bail out. We're over Chinese territory now, so friendlies will find us."

"Roger that."

We continued to lose altitude. We dropped below the freezing level. I could tell because water began dripping into the cockpit. It felt like we were sitting beneath a waterfall.

"Plumber's Nightmare," I said.

Mullins issued a hollow laugh.

At ten thousand five hundred feet we glided out of the clouds. Right over the airfield.

"You're still welcome to bail out," I said to Mullins. I decided to continue what I'd begun. Any aviator who couldn't dead-stick a plane onto a runway from directly above shouldn't be wearing wings.

"No, sir. I've come this far. I'm gonna finish things out."

"Call the tower. Declare an emergency."

He did.

The tower came back. "You're number three, seven-eight-two-one. There are two birds ahead of you in the pattern."

"No," I shot back, taking over from Mullins. "We're number one, like it or not. We don't have any engines. Get the others the hell out of the way."

The tower controller got the message and screamed for the other two aircraft to abort.

I set up the downwind leg and timed it to see how much altitude Ol' Dumbo lost in one minute. Then I would know when to make the turns that would lead me onto final approach. I rolled into the base leg about six miles out with plenty of altitude. I turned onto final with two thousand feet to spare and a speed of one hundred twenty miles per hour. Damned good aviating, I thought.

Except for one small problem. "Shit," I bellowed, so loud they probably heard me on the ground.

A thousand feet from the end of the runway, I realized I couldn't lower the landing gear. With the engines shut down, I had no hydraulic power. And there wasn't enough time left to extend the wheels manually.

I attempted to lose speed and altitude simultaneously, but again, without hydraulics, I found it impossible.

I reverted to my tried and true mantra when in deep trouble. "Shit!"

I passed over the end of the runway six hundred feet up. At the other end, I was still two hundred feet off the ground.

I banked the plane to the left.

"Big bump," I said as calmly as possible.

We hammered into a rice paddy about a half mile off the runway. We hit the spongy field at about seventy miles per hour. The plane spun a quarter turn and slid sideways through the paddy.

A deafening sound reverberated through the cockpit, something akin to a roaring waterfall. Then came a discordant symphony of popping rivets. Finally, a horrendous ripping noise rent the air as the right wing parted company with the fuselage and burst into flame.

Oddly, the bird mushed to a smooth stop.

Mullins and I released our harnesses and scrambled out the hatch over the left wing. We splashed through the rice paddy, running like bandits in the night, expecting the plane —with all the loose, leaking fuel drums in the cargo area—to explode like a five-hundred-pound bomb.

Nothing happened.

Mullins and I stood next to each other, panting heavily, as emergency vehicles arrived, including an ox-drawn cart full of coolies.

"Well," I said, catching my breath, "so that's what flying the Hump is like."

Mullins accepted my attempt at dark humor. "Mission successful, sir. They got their damn avgas."

"Except for what we spilled."

"We'll blame it on the weather." Mullins paused and stared at me. "Didn't I hear you have something to do with the Tenth Weather Squadron?"

My head felt like someone with a hammer was inside it trying to beat his way out. All I wanted to do was flop on a cot someplace with a cold washrag on my forehead. But Mullins had triggered an important thought.

"I'm the Tenth's DO," I mumbled. "I'll leave a memo for General Chennault in the morning and tell him what the hell happened. I'll bet we weren't the only bird that had problems. Maybe it'll dawn on him that better weather support might actually help."

A sudden, sinking feeling slammed into my gut. I knew without a doubt some American markers had been added to the Aluminum Trail today.

11

Chabua, Assam, India
US Army Air Forces base

Lieutenant Mullins and I caught a hop back to Chabua the following morning. We were ushered immediately into Major Hatcher's office. He appeared more harried than usual. A dead cigar rested in repose in the ashtray on his desk. The macaque monkey, the same one I'd seen on my first visit, sat quietly on the sill of an open window looking as dour as ever. Apparently, he—or she—and Hatcher had reached some sort of uneasy truce.

The major stared at me. "You look like shit. You get into a barroom brawl or something?"

"Or something," I said.

"Get the hell over to the hospital as soon as we're done here. This won't take long. Do you know how many fucking aircraft we lost yesterday?" A crimson tide arose on Hatcher's face.

"Nine," he went on. "And thirty crew and passengers missing or dead. Jesus."

Nine? And thirty?

Silence, except for the macaque gnawing on a bamboo stalk, permeated the small room.

Hatcher broke the quiet. "How in the hell did you guys survive? I know you lost your bird in Kunming. But you delivered the goods. How'd you do it? Only two other planes completed their mission yesterday. I heard you made a deadstick landing. True?"

Mullins chimed in. "Best damn flying I ever saw, sir. No power. No landing gear. No hydraulics. And Major Shepherd here manages to get Ol' Dumbo down in a rice paddy. He deserves a medal."

"I'll work on that," Hatcher responded. "But first I'm sending a message to Chennault and telling him to get off his goddamned ass and high horse and get us some more weather support." Hatcher slid his chair back and stood. "Now I've got a brief presentation to make."

He turned toward his closed office door and called out, "Gentlemen, enter if you would, please." Three junior officers from our flying group trooped in, solemn expressions on their faces.

"Stand, please," Hatcher said to me.

I did, but had no idea what the hell was going on. My head continued to pulsate.

"On behalf of the ATC at Chabua," Hatcher went on, "I would like to present you with the highest possible recognition of your exceptional aviation skills at Kunming, China, on 10 September 1943." He nodded at one of the junior officers, who stepped forward and handed Hatcher something.

"We didn't have a set of pilot's wings with a G stamped in the middle for glider pilot, so we cut one of our own badges in half." He pinned a sawed-in-half set of pilot's wings on my raggedy-ass, muddy, bloody uniform.

He extended his palm toward another of the junior officers, who handed him a paper airplane. It was painted gold and flecked with tiny golden flakes. "We'd like you to have this trophy as a memento of your valiant flight. It's the best we could do." He gave it to me.

Light applause, along with a chuckle or two, filled the room. The monkey skedaddled. Under any other circumstances this would have been a moment of great hilarity followed by a lot of drinking. But not after the loss of thirty men.

"Now get your butt over to the hospital," Hatcher growled. "Maybe that nurse with the big tits can fix you up."

Geez, I hoped not.

I headed to the hospital, marching to the beat of the drummer in my head. Bright sunshine lit the way, one of those rare September days that gave everyone hope the southwest monsoon might soon be in full retreat. October would still bring rainy days, but only half as many as September. By November, the rains would be gone, and the dry conditions of the "cool" season setting in. Cool is a relative term, meaning, at least in Assam, nighttime temperatures in the fifties instead of the seventies. Meaning also we'd be able to sleep comfortably without sweating through our skivvies.

I arrived at the reception desk of the main hospital, the 95th Station Hospital—not the dispensary. A young nurse greeted me, shook her head when she saw the condition of my face, and escorted me to a small exam room.

"One of our flight nurses will be in shortly to check you out," she said.

Flight nurse? "Not Captain Nurse, I hope."

"Who?"

"Never mind. Thank you, young lady."

She flashed me a young-lady smile and shut the door.

I sat in an uncomfortable chair and tilted my head back against the wall. I hoped whoever examined me would give me a handful of APC tablets—aspirin, phenacetin, and caffeine—tell me to take it easy for a few days, and send me back to my *basha*.

The door opened and in stepped you-know-who. Of course it had to be her. She whose last words to me were something about keeping my hands in my pockets and pecker in my pants.

My head spun, but I stood, jammed my hands into my pants pockets, and said, "See how well I can follow your advice."

"Hilarious," she shot back. "You know, you're a real shithead."

"Is that your final diagnosis or would you like to examine me first?"

"Get up on the table. Major."

"Yes, ma'am. Tell me, Captain, how often do you call superior officers 'shitheads,' or is that just your natural bedside manner?"

She glared at me, her icy blue eyes sending a chill up the back of my neck. What was it with this woman?

"Maybe a summary court-martial would teach me a lesson," she said, her words brittle and sharp. "What do you think?"

"I think my head hurts like hell and I'd like to get it fixed."

"Barroom brawl? The left side of your face is the color of an acorn squash."

"Thanks, I feel better already, Captain . . . name again?"

"Johannsen."

"I feel better already, Captain Johannsen. And it wasn't a barroom brawl."

"Do I care?"

"Apparently not."

She placed a blood pressure cuff on my arm and pumped it up.

"Okay, not a barroom brawl," she said. "What was it, then?"

"I want to be a stunt pilot when I get out of the Army. I tried some things. They didn't go well."

"You should be a standup comic."

She removed the cuff from my arm. "Your blood pressure's a little high."

"I wonder why."

"And I wonder why you're wearing pilot's wings that have been cut in half."

"Because it was determined I'm only half as good as most of the flyboys around here."

She clamped her lips together and again stared at me with those glacial eyes.

"I almost caught you, didn't I?" I said.

"Caught me what?"

"Cracking a little smile."

She retrieved a stethoscope from a cabinet. "I'd like to listen to your heart and lungs."

"It's my head that's giving me problems."

"Just breathe normally," she said. She put the ear tips of the scope into her ears, placed the chest piece over my heart, and rested her hand on my back. The effect astonished me. I suppose it had been so long since I'd felt the touch of a woman, I reacted with an innate male longing.

"I said breathe normally," Captain Johannsen snapped.

As much as the snippy personality of the nurse turned me off, how in the hell can you breathe normally when someone with a body like Rita Hayworth's and breath with the sweet, minty freshness of spring leans against your shoulder.

"I'm trying," I said, my voice catching.

"Try harder."

"Just for you, Captain."

"Why are you being such a difficult patient?"

"It just comes naturally around you, I guess."

After that exchange, a deadening silence filled the room as the nurse finished her exam with the stethoscope. My breathing returned to normal. I wondered how this physically attractive woman's grating personality had developed. Had she been in an abusive relationship with a man? Had a husband walked out on her? Or was she one of those women who just didn't like men, period? A dyke, or lesbian, or whatever the proper term was?

"A few more things, Major, sir," Johannsen said, her words clipped and icy. Her glare equally as frosty.

I didn't respond, just waited.

She asked me a bunch of silly questions, like did I know where I was, what day it was, who I had flown with on my last few flights. I had to make up a few of the answers. She went on and on. Had I been barfing? Once. Was I fatigued? Always. Was I irritable? Around you, yes.

She scratched a few notes on a pad, then said, "You need to be off flying status for a while."

"What?"

"Hearing problems, too?" She made another notation.

"I heard you just fine. What's this bullshit about not flying?"

"You've got a concussion. You shouldn't be piloting a plane."

"I'm perfectly fine. Give me some APCs and I'm outta here."

"You're not perfectly fine."

For a reason I couldn't divine, Captain Johannsen truly

had it in for me. Maybe all men. But I'd had all I could take of her and her crotchety, mean-spirited attitude.

"Tell you what, nurse," I barked, "how about letting a flight surgeon make that determination rather than some half-assed, pretend doctor."

She flung a final glare at me—I caught just a fleeting note of pain in it—and flounced out of the room, slamming the door. Maybe I'd gone too far with my verbal indictment of her, but I really didn't give a damn. She irritated the hell out of me.

In the end, I lost the battle. A flight surgeon—a young captain who went over the results of her examination with me —took me off flying status and told me to come back in a couple of weeks for re-evaluation.

"Can I get an appointment with you and not Nurse Nasty?"

"You'll be examined by whoever is available that day, Major. And by the way, you might just take it easy on Captain Johannsen. She's been through a lot."

"We all have. That doesn't give her cause to abandon civility and respect."

"I suppose you and her will have to work that out then, sir."

I slid off the exam table and stood. "I hope I never have to see her again, Doc."

He handed me a bottle of APCs. "Follow the instructions on the label. Now go back to your *basha* and get some sleep."

I did. Actually, I sailed off to the land of Wynken, Blynken, and Nod for twelve hours. I woke up in the evening, my head still feeling like a Sousa marching band was practicing in it, downed a couple more APCs, and zonked out again. When I finally came to, so to speak, bright sunlight filled the *basha* and I guessed it must be close to lunchtime. Apparently I'd been out of it for close to twenty-four hours. But at least my head had stopped feeling like a ripe melon about to explode. I pulled on the same khakis I'd worn to Kunming and back, and plodded off to the mess hall.

The air felt as humid as ever, but the sun seemed to have battled the usual cloudiness to a draw, and now shared the sky with stacks of cumulus. I took it as another reminder that the southwest monsoon was growing old and tired.

I lingered in the mess hall downing several cups of coffee and wading through three helpings of powdered eggs, hard toast, and mystery meat. They actually seemed palatable. And the coffee, though laced with chicory, tasted decent enough to restore me to life.

Finished, I headed toward base ops. As I approached the ops building, I encountered a full bird colonel accompanied by two light colonels. Strangers to me. They certainly weren't combat troops. Their uniforms looked as though they'd just come off a rack at a stateside PX—they bore an almost blinding sheen of newness and displayed creases so sharp they could have carved a steak. The three officers seemed as out of place in Assam as a rabbi in Mecca.

As I approached them, I snapped off a salute. It was then I realized I didn't have any headgear on.

The colonel halted, as did his two minions. He didn't return my military courtesy, but instead stared at me with obvious distaste.

"Are you a soldier?" he snapped, his words detonating like a drill sergeant's.

"Yes, sir. Major Rod—"

"Why in the hell don't you dress like one, then? What the hell is wrong with you people around here? I've seen folks decked out more smartly at backwater county fairs."

I doubted the guy had ever been to a county fair, but guessed that wasn't up for debate.

"Sir, I just—"

He held up a hand signaling me to stop talking, and stepped closer to me. He leveled his gaze at my chest. His stare could have frosted an aircraft's wing with heavy icing. With a neatly groomed mustache and a confident, erect posture, I guessed he'd probably been a corporate executive in civilian life.

Then it dawned on me who he was. Colonel Ellsworth had warned me. He'd told me he'd heard a reserve officer and veteran pilot who'd been a vice president at TWA might be coming in to take charge of Hump operations.

The colonel fingered my pilot's wings, the one my buddies had cut in half. "What on God's little green earth is this?"

"It's hard to explain—"

"I'll bet it is, so don't bother."

Smirks appeared on the faces of the two lieutenant colonels standing behind him.

A jeep ground its way along the rutted road beside base ops. It slowed as it passed the spot where I was being braced and reamed out, its occupants likely wondering what the hell was going on. Quite frankly, I was, too. I was also getting a little pissed.

One of the light colonels stepped forward. "Perhaps it would help if I introduced the colonel."

"It might," I said, irritation threading my voice.

"This is Thomas O. Hardin. He's taking command of the India-China sector of Air Transport Command. He'll also be running Hump operations. Has he got experience? You bet. He's been flying for twenty years. In civilian life, he was general manager of American Airlines, and later, vice president of TWA. His most recent assignment in the Army Air Forces was as deputy commander of ATC's Middle East Wing in Africa."

"Colonel Hardin," I said, "allow me to apologize if I don't

live up to your military standards. But this isn't American Airlines or TWA out here."

"I know it isn't, Major—Rod something, you said?"

"Rod Shepherd."

"Well, Major Shepherd, this may not be American Airlines or TWA, but it sure as hell isn't some kind of boys' flying club, either. This is a military operation and it's going to be run like one. Uniforms will be laundered and pressed, headgear will be worn, pilot's wings will be in one piece, and boots will be shined. Flight schedules will be adhered to and this *will* become a round-the-clock enterprise."

"Night flying, sir?"

"Of course. You can fly at night, can't you, Major?"

"I can. But half the kids they're sending us can't. They have no experience at all flying on instruments."

Colonel Hardin's carved-in-stone expression didn't change. "Then there's going to be a lot of on-the-job training, isn't there?"

"People are going to get killed," I snapped.

"People *are* getting killed. Our mission is to get cargo to China."

Somehow, I wasn't getting through to this guy. "Every time someone gets killed, Colonel, the mission fails. If you send pilots over the Hump who can't fly on instruments, or have only minimal training, then it's highly likely the cargo will end up in a Burmese jungle or in the Himalayas. And you end up with blood on your hands."

For the first time, Hardin's expression changed. His complexion flushed and his eyes flashed with anger. "Don't ever tell me how I end up, Major." His voice rose several decibels. "I dispatch pilots to deliver the goods, not crash. That's what this unit is tasked to do, and by God, we're going to do it.

And we won't do it by becoming a fair weather air force. If I order you to fly, you fly. Got it?"

I clearly had walked out onto thin ice, but I was too irritated —well, maybe too stupid—to turn around. "No, sir, I don't 'got it.' For one thing, I don't answer directly to ATC. I'm the Tenth Weather Squadron's director of operations. I take my orders from Lieutenant Colonel Dick Ellsworth, the Tenth's commander."

"You will take any legal order from a superior officer, including me, Major. You got that?"

I had to admit, he nailed me on that point. "Yes, sir."

"And about the weather," Hardin went on, "it's not a factor. From what I've learned so far, weather forecasts around here have about as much credibility as the propaganda Tokyo Rose spews."

"Sir, if we had more weather personnel and more—"

"Not going to happen. Combat troops and pilots take priority in this theater. Not wet-finger-testing-the-wind guys."

"I'll let Colonel Ellsworth know," I said, perhaps with a little too much snippiness in my voice.

"You do that, Major Shepherd. Now, I suggest you head back to your *basha,* get a clean set of khakis, polish your boots, find your headgear, and pin on some real pilot's wings. Try at least to *look* like an Army officer."

"Yes, sir."

"And by the way, did someone take a battle axe to your head? I've seen rotted pumpkins that looked better. What on earth happened?"

"Banged my head against a wall, sir."

I stood tall, tendered the colonel a crisp salute, and departed before he could level another verbal volley at me.

But I didn't go back to my *basha.* I went in search of Major Hatcher. I wanted to find out what the hell was going on. Why had we suddenly been "blessed" with a Simon Legree as our commander? The trouble is, I sort of understood where Colonel Hardin was coming from. He had a job to do, a mission to accomplish, and we *were* in a war, not undergoing training. I guess I just didn't like the guy or his approach. Sure, pilots and crews were going to get killed, and had been getting killed, but Hardin seemed just too damn cavalier about that.

I reached Hatcher's office. His door stood slightly ajar, so I stepped in, my confusion and frustration perhaps getting me more worked up than I should have been.

But it wasn't Major Hatcher sitting behind Major Hatcher's desk. The officer sitting there, a lieutenant colonel I didn't recognize, snapped his head up and glared at me. "Oh, did I forget to remove the sign that said Please, Barge Right In Without Knocking?"

"I'm sorry, sir," I said, "I was expecting Major Hatcher to be—"

"Major Hatcher has been relieved of duty," the officer snapped.

I took an instant dislike to the guy, obviously one of Hardin's acolytes. I didn't care for his curt attitude, I didn't like that he was an outsider, and I was totally put off by the expression on his face. He looked like a bulldog who'd missed dinner.

"Relieved?" I said. I felt as if the wind had been knocked out of me.

"I hope you're not one of the pilots here. Hard of hearing will get you grounded."

The macaque monkey who'd become Hatcher's self-anointed, grumpy mascot sat in the open window watching the exchange between me and the colonel.

"I'm not hard of hearing. Just stunned."

"Stunned that a guy who wasn't doing his job doesn't have

that job anymore?"

What an asshole this guy was turning out to be.

"No. Surprised it happened so abruptly."

"Well, I'm sorry we couldn't have eased into it, Major. Sorry we couldn't have had a few happy hours and a dining-in at the officers club, and said some hip-hip-hoorays for Hatcher before pinning a medal on his chest and foisting him off on some other command."

I had to get away from this guy.

"Sorry," I repeated. "I meant no disrespect by bursting in."

"Don't repeat that mistake."

"Yes, sir. If I may, sir . . . a friendly suggestion."

He stared at me through his bulging bulldog eyes.

"The monkey"—I tilted my head toward the macaque in the window—"was one of Major Hatcher's favorites. If you offer him a small corner of your office as his own, he'll be your good buddy for life."

I saluted smartly, pivoted, and strode from the office before the bulldog asshole could see the depraved grin snaking across my face.

I remembered well Hatcher's words regarding the monkeys: "Don't ever let 'em inside. They'll rip things apart looking for food. And don't try to make friends with them. With those teeth they'd just as soon tear into your arm as a banana."

I found Hatcher at the makeshift officers club, the one we'd staked out at the far end of a *basha*. It looked as if he was working on his second or third beer.

"Hi, boss," I said.

He looked up. "Not anymore."

I sat. "What happened?"

He didn't say anything. Just sat staring at the wall. The

bellow of a C-46 taking off for Kunming or wherever echoed through the *basha*.

"I met Colonel Hardin," I said.

"You mean Colonel Hard On?" Hatcher took another swill of his beer.

I chuckled. "Mind if I grab one, too?"

"Not worried about having to fly today?"

"I'm off flying status for a while. Those quacks at the hospital think I've got a concussion."

"I'm sure that won't bother Colonel Hard On. He'll have you in the air regardless. He's planning a round-the-clock operation. He told me that while crews have to rest, planes don't."

"He doesn't get it, does he? That half the pilots we've got here have less time on instruments than do a lot of the WASPs ferrying planes in the States?"

"Maybe they should assign some of those women to ATC."

I shrugged, stood, and walked to the icebox and pulled out a beer. I returned to the table and sat across from Hatcher.

"So who's the guy in your office?" I asked.

"A Lieutenant Colonel Bert Shaeffer or Shipper or Skipper. I don't know."

"Seems like a genuine asshole."

"That's the impression I got."

"I suggested he make friends with your macaque buddy."

Hatcher laughed. "I hope that damn monkey bites his flopper off."

"So what did Hard On say to you? Why your abrupt dismissal?"

Again Hatcher fell silent, but spoke after taking another swallow of beer. "He thinks I was running a flying club here. Letting the guys choose their own days to fly, set their own schedules, stand down if the weather got shitty. But we got the job done."

"But I guess not in military fashion."

"Part of it, I suppose. I'll tell you this. Hard On's a driven SOB, a hell of a lot more concerned with tonnage delivered than lives lost."

"We're going to add a lot of crosses and Stars of David to the Aluminum Trail, aren't we?"

Hatcher merely nodded and moved his unfocused stare to the wall again.

12

Chabua, Assam, India
US Army Air Forces base

I finished my beer with Major Hatcher and returned to my *basha*. There, I stripped off my uniform, took a cold shower, and flopped onto my cot. I dozed off and awoke in the early evening. I found a semi-clean, semi-unwrinkled uniform and put it on. It sported mildew in a few spots, but I decided no one would notice. Everyone had mildewed uniforms.

I pinned a set of pilot's wings on my shirt—a set that hadn't been cut in half. I brushed the mud off my flight boots and mounted a search for my flight cap. I found it in the bottom drawer of a jury-rigged bamboo dresser, buried beneath the "nickel nasties" my old friend Zim had given me.

I didn't feel like eating anything, so plodded off to base ops with the intent of writing a complete after-action report about my near-death experience over the Himalayas. A salmon-and-turquoise-tinted sky hung over the base as the sun sank into the Indian subcontinent. Bats, searching for dinner, dove and darted through the dusk. The usual symphony of insects and creepy-crawly things began tuning up, preparing for the deafening forte chorus that would come with full darkness.

The ops building, except for the duty NCO, appeared deserted. I found a quiet flight planning room, sat at a table, slipped on my reading glasses, and began to write my report. I didn't use the glasses often, but I found they helped when I was tired.

I'd been writing for about half an hour when a floorboard creaked and I looked up. Lieutenant Colonel Bulldog Asshole stood in the doorway.

"Working late?" he said.

"Just catching up." I removed my glasses and stood. I noticed he had a bandage on his forearm. "What happened?"

"The goddamned monkey," he growled.

I struggled to keep from laughing. "I'm so sorry, Colonel. That must not have been Major Hatcher's buddy sitting in the window. They kinda all look alike, you know."

"I'm sure they do." He glared at me like a canine that had spotted prey.

For lack of anything else to say, I decided to introduce myself. "I didn't take the opportunity earlier to properly present myself. I'm Major Rod Shepherd. I'm detached here from Tenth Weather Squadron headquarters in New Delhi."

"You guys need new crystal balls. The ones you have now aren't worth a crap. Well, I'm Lieutenant Colonel Harold Shaver. As you probably figured out, I'll be running operations here from now on."

"You don't think Major Hatcher was doing a good job? Sir."

"I don't discuss personnel issues, Major. Besides, it was Colonel Hardin's call. If you have any questions about his decision, you need to take it up with him."

Colonel Shaver's gaze fell on the reading glasses I'd placed on the table in front of me.

"I gather you've logged a lot of hours over the Hump, Major?" Shaver said.

"I've only been flying the route for about a month, but I've racked up well over a hundred."

"Well, no more. I don't want any damn 'four-eyes' flying my airplanes."

"Sir?" I wasn't sure what I'd just heard.

He nodded at the glasses I'd placed on the table. "Pilots in this organization are going to be in tip-top physical condition. That means anyone who needs glasses isn't going to be on the flight roster."

"These are reading glasses, Colonel. I don't need them when I'm flying."

"Maybe you do, and just won't admit it."

"I can read the instruments just fine, sir."

"Yet you lost a crippled airplane at Kunming, if I heard correctly."

"That had nothing to do with reading instruments." *What the hell was with this guy?*

"Well, who knows? Maybe in rough weather if your eyesight had been better, you might have been able to spot something on the instrument panel before you got into trouble and lost both engines."

"For Chrissakes, Colonel. You can't read the damn instruments when you're bouncing around like a fart in a full gale."

"So you need glasses for reading or writing, but not for scanning the instruments when you're in the pilot's seat. Makes no sense to me. Stay away from my airplanes."

"Sir—"

"That's an order, Major Shepherd."

The bulldog asshole pivoted, strode out of the office, and left me standing there feeling as if I should have been issued a white cane instead of pilot's wings. Well, I knew what I had to do next, what would make it all better. I wadded up my after-action report, hurled it like a Dizzy Dean fastball into a trash can, and headed toward the makeshift officers club. I damn well hoped I'd find something stronger than beer there.

As I neared the *basha* that housed the club, I could hear Benny Goodman's "Stompin' at the Savoy" wafting out in tinny sound waves through the woven bamboo walls. Someone had obviously commandeered a phonograph.

I entered the club to find about half a dozen pilots gathered inside. They shouted greetings at me. "Hey, melon head." "What happens when you piss when you're flying inverted?" "The government dropped ten grand to make you a glider pilot?"

"I'm not any kind of a pilot anymore," I barked.

The room fell silent. The Goodman piece ground to an end.

"What the hell happened, Rod?" someone asked.

I sat down at a table and told them.

"The new guy took you off flying status cuz you wear reading glasses?" came a response. "That's bullshit."

"I know," I said. "We don't have enough experience here as it is. They're putting guys in left-hand seats who should be flying open-cockpit trainers, not military transports."

"Sounds like it's gonna be a race between the amount of tonnage delivered and the number of KIAs," Lieutenant Mullins, the guy I'd flown with most recently, said.

Someone slid a coffee cup half full of brown liquor in front of me. "Jim Beam, midnight requisitioned from a C-47 being loaded for Kunming," a voice said.

I downed most of it in one swallow.

"So, is this 24/7 flying business the new CBI wing commander's idea?" Mullins asked.

"You mean Colonel Hard On's?" I said. I'd grown fond of that name.

It drew a big laugh.

I finished off my first helping of Jim Beam. The cup was quickly refilled. Halfway.

"So what do you really think of Colonel Hardin?" someone said. I didn't know if the question was being asked tongue-in-cheek or not.

"I think he's going to get a lot of us . . . you . . . killed," I said. I had to remember I was no longer considered an aviator. At least not by the jerk who now occupied Hatcher's office.

"Maybe not," a senior captain I'd heard was a West Pointer responded. "Maybe what we need around here is some real military discipline, some order to the chaos and casualness that prevails. Doing things by the book might actually save lives *and* get increased tonnage delivered."

I took another long swill of the Jim Beam. "Military discipline and doing shit by the book *won't* save lives and increase supplies if you've got kids flying over the Hump who are gonna get lost in the first cumulus that swallows them."

"You *do* understand we're in a war, Major," the captain retorted, "and that we don't always have the luxury of filling the gaps with the best and the brightest?"

"What I understand, crapton, Captain"—the Jim Beam was beginning to do its thing—"is that if we don't have the breast . . . the best and the brightest, we're going to end up the deadest and the dumbest." I had no idea if that made any sense, but I'd reached the point I didn't give a damn.

I polished off my second cup of Jim and tapped the rim for a refill. It appeared magically along with a beer. "Clear your palate, Rod," someone said.

I gulped the beer, then went back to work on the Jim. I felt mellow, at peace, as if I could float from Assam back to

America by merely closing my eyes and forgetting the war, forgetting the killer mountain ranges and jungles, forgetting commanders who didn't put themselves in harm's way and merely set policies and goals and gave orders. Deep down, I suppose, I knew it had to be that way. That's how the military operated. But I also knew shit always flowed downhill.

A third refill landed in my cup and quickly disappeared down my throat. More and more flyers appeared in the little club. At least there appeared to be more. I wasn't sure. My vision had become fuzzy. We told tall stories and lies about our flying adventures. We became fighter aces in C-46s and C-47s.

I tried to stand once, but the room began twisting and turning like an airplane doing evasive maneuvers while the bank and turn indicator went crazy. I sat and went back to work on the booze.

I felt happy and pissed off and helpless. I laughed, slammed my fist on the table, and sang along with Tex Beneke and the Modernaires as they performed "Kalamazoo" with the Glenn Miller Orchestra on a hand-cranked record player perched on an empty ammo box.

I downed several more shots of Jim. At least I think it was several more. I honestly don't remember. I seemed to lose track of everything. I do remember a few of my buddies helping me back to my *basha*. We weaved and sang our way along dark, rutted streets, yelled at monkeys, cursed the Japs, and fell into mud puddles.

We eventually made it to the *basha*. My compatriots pushed me onto my cot, yanked off my boots, pulled the mosquito netting over me, and left. I lay there for a while, the darkness spiraling around me like rushing water.

Water? I realized I had to piss. I sat up, shakily, then stood and took a tentative step forward. Something grabbed me, entangled me. I yelled and spun. Heard a ripping sound. I fell, the damned mosquito netting coming down on top of me. I tried to untangle myself, but only managed to become more enmeshed in the net, like a blue bottle fly trapped in a spider's web.

I crawled along the floor, probably looking less like a fly than a moving compost pile. Then I forgot what I was doing and where I was going. The image of the ensnared fly reappeared. It suddenly dawned on me I was about to be eaten alive by a vicious, eight-legged bug. I thrashed violently in the web, trying desperately to free myself. I did an outstanding job, ending up even more tightly cocooned.

I screamed and hollered. No response. Had everyone else already been captured and eaten? Terror overwhelmed me. I slithered along the concreted pad until I reached the end of the *basha*. Now what?

That's when my savior appeared. In this case, it was a Very gun resting in a metal box sitting on the floor beside a storage locker. I wriggled over to it, grabbed the pistol with my netted hand and, hoping it contained a signal flare, cocked the hammer, aimed it—more or less—down the center of the *basha*, and squeezed the trigger.

A satisfying pop sounded. A flare round shot out of the little gun's short barrel and arced toward the opposite end of the building, hit something, deflected upward, and punched into the thatched roof. A white blossom erupted. The roof burst into flame. I was saved!

That's all I remember . . . until I awoke the following afternoon in my cot. I'd peed in my pants, and the mosquito netting had gone AWOL. There seemed to be activity at the far end of the *basha,* which, strangely, appeared bathed in bright sunlight. I changed pants and staggered toward the brightness, my head pulsating like an anvil being used by a brutal blacksmith. The out-of-place odor of burnt sagebrush filled the air.

At the end of the *basha*, I found Lieutenant Colonel Bulldog Asshole and several of Colonel Hard On's lackeys staring up at the sky through an open, burned-out roof. A group of pilots looked on. Most of them looked little better than I felt.

I knew I needed to be more respectful of senior officers, so vowed to quit thinking of Colonel Hardin's team in terms of denigrating nicknames. Even though I'd been removed from flying status by that bulldog asshole—okay, Lieutenant Colonel Shaver—I still represented the Tenth Weather Squadron and realized I thus had to display some decorum.

"Anybody know anything about what happened here?" Shaver growled.

Silence.

"Anybody care to *guess* what happened here?" Shaver said. His crinkled countenance had turned the color of a "dawn coming up like thunder." Images of Zim seemed to never leave my mind.

One of the pilots glanced at me, then turned to Shaver and said, "We think one of the cleaning ladies might have accidentally triggered a Very gun, sir. There were some stored in a case on the floor at the other end of the *basha*."

"Did you question the cleaning crew?" Shaver snapped.

"We don't speak Assamese, sir."

"I see. Does this happen often around here? Indians shooting off flare guns? Accidentally, of course."

"No, sir," someone else answered. "Never happened before."

"Right," Shaver said. "A rare mishap, then?"

"Yes, sir."

Shaver turned toward me. "You're looking a bit green around the gills, Major Shepherd. Tough night?"

"No tougher than a lot of them, Colonel," I responded.

"Okay. Well, perhaps as the senior officer of the *basha,* and seeing that you have no more flying duties, I'd like you to conduct an informal investigation and find out what the hell happened here."

"I will, sir."

"And get the damned roof fixed."

"Yes, sir."

Shaver stepped close to me and stared directly into my bloodshot eyes. "And make sure the fucking Very guns are stored securely so we don't have any more cleaning ladies trying to burn down our *basha*s."

He and his entourage about-faced and strode from the building.

A few snickers and chuckles—unheard, of course—arose from the assembled pilots and trailed them out the door.

"Well, at least the entire building didn't burn down," someone said.

"Too bad," someone else responded. "Would have taken care of the rats and snakes."

It was clear the guys had closed ranks around me, but I still remained tasked with conducting an "investigation."

"Okay," I said, "let's get this over with. Did anybody see or hear anything? Anything that could be labeled as eye-witness, irrefutable evidence about how this fire got started?"

The response: a lot of "No, sirs," and heads shaken in the negative. And quite a few grins.

"Great. Thank you, guys. That wraps up my investigation. Look, I'm sorry I can't help out with the sorties anymore, but I'll do whatever I can to make sure you all stay alive and safe."

Amid thank yous and back slaps, the group dispersed.

Lieutenant Mullins, who I noticed had been part of the assemblage, approached me.

"Here," he said, "we thought you could use this."

He handed me a package containing new mosquito netting.

13

Chabua, Assam, India
US Army Air Forces base
Early October 1943

September faded into October and the southwest monsoon grudgingly relaxed its grip on Assam. Rainy days became fewer and further between, and even the stifling humidity backed off ever so slightly.

Weather over the Hump became somewhat less treacherous—according to those who still flew the Chabua to Kunming route—but we continued losing airplanes and pilots. Colonel Hardin's push to keep planes in the air around the clock and deliver more tonnage to China came at a cost.

Having nothing else to do except administrative bullshit, I sat down one day and figured out that for every thousand tons of cargo we were getting into China we were losing three American aviators. But the tonnage was going up, and that, apparently, was all that mattered.

Lieutenant Mullins stomped into my space at base ops after a particularly perilous flight one afternoon and said,

"You know, Major, it's probably safer to fly a B-17 over Germany than it is to fly a C-46 over the goddamned Himalayas from one friendly nation to another."

I couldn't disagree. I wondered if the rest of the military still thought of ATC as standing for Allergic to Combat. At least in a fighter or bomber, you could fight back against the enemy. You didn't have that option against weather and topography. When your number was up, it was up.

As for myself, I felt like a traitorous Fifth Columnist for having to sit on my butt every day while my buddies flew the Hump. I spent a lot of time in the "o'club," helping deplete the beer rations. I stayed away from hard liquor, however, not wanting to become known as the Assam Arsonist.

I took a couple of days off—not that I really had anything to be off from—and visited a rest camp about fifteen miles north of Chabua on the Brahmaputra River at a village called Kobo. The camp's accommodations weren't much different from those at Chabua, but it did offer diversionary activities and a peaceful solitude not found at the airbase.

Native fishermen took me on a short trip in a dugout canoe. And I went for about an hour's ride on an Indian elephant. The beast had legs as tall as I was, and I struggled to get aboard the damn thing. It turned out that riding an elephant is like being on a small boat in slow-motion ocean swells. The elevated view was nice, but I actually got feeling a bit queasy. I decided I'd rather be flying an Ol' Dumbo than riding on a real Dumbo.

Back at Chabua one afternoon, having nothing else to do —it was too early for an o'club visit—I decided to trek to the hospital to see if I still had my so-called concussion. Not that it would make any difference. Colonel Shaver had made it clear I would no longer be flying, concussion or not.

I checked in with the head nurse, who told me to have a

seat. I waited about ten minutes. And then my favorite nurse showed up.

She rolled her eyes when she saw me. "This way," she said curtly, and stalked off down a hallway. I followed.

"Can't stay away from me?" I asked.

"When I saw your name on the roster, I asked for you specifically. Have a seat." She gestured at a chair in the exam room she'd led me to.

Without speaking, she checked my blood pressure, took my temperature, and listened to my heart and lungs.

"How have you been feeling, Major?" she asked, her words cold and hard.

"Fine."

"No more headaches?"

"No. Well, only when I drink too much."

"And set fire to *bashas*."

I stared at her.

"Rumor has it," she said without smiling.

"Scuttlebutt isn't always right, Captain."

"How about the scuttlebutt you were taken off flying status because you wear reading glasses?"

"Just finish your exam," I said.

"Don't you want to see a real doctor?"

"What difference would it make?"

She shrugged. "You seem okay to me. I'll get the flight surgeon to sign off on my evaluation. I think you're good to go . . . to fly."

"Fine. That'll make my day."

"One more thing, Major."

"What's that?"

"Something that will really make your day." She tendered me that polar stare she'd patented.

I waited.

"I've been reassigned. You won't have to put up with me anymore. And vice versa."

"There is a God after all," I said softly.

"I don't think so," she shot back at me.

"Well, with your sparkling personality, I'm sure you'll get along famously at your new duty station, Captain."

She fired another piercing glance at me, her blue eyes reflecting anger—and again maybe a hint of pain—wheeled, and strode from the room without saying we're done, goodbye, or good luck. Not that I should have expected that.

In a way, I thought I might miss her. She'd become a favorite target for my frustrations. But in another way, I knew I wouldn't pine for her negativity and cattiness. Beauty gone to waste.

So, no more Nurse Nasty. No more trips over the Hump. My life had become becalmed. I should have known better than to believe that. I'd sure as shit been wrong about things before. And this current evaluation of my situation would turn out to be the biggest "forecast bust" of my life.

Back at base ops, the duty officer handed me a message from Lieutenant Colonel Ellsworth saying he'd be arriving at Chabua tomorrow to bring me up to date on where Tenth Weather Squadron activities in the CBI Theater stood. I couldn't imagine the news would be necessarily good.

Ellsworth and *Betsy,* the "TWA" C-47, touched down at Chabua the following morning. The colonel and I found a quiet corner in the mess hall and sat there to talk while we sipped coffee, or at least what passed for coffee.

I told Ellsworth about my encounter with Colonel Hardin, the apparent concussion I'd received, and of being removed from flying status by the new commander at Chabua, Lieutenant Colonel Shaver. I resisted using my favorite nicknames, and I left out any mention of target practice with a Very gun.

Ellsworth took in the news with little reaction, other than to shake his head in apparent disgust.

"Well," he said, "you're technically still under my command, so I might as well get you back to headquarters in New Delhi. To formalize things, I'll have my staff cut you a new set of orders and send copies to Lieutenant Colonel Shaver. Should take about a week."

"Thank you, sir. I'm accomplishing nothing here."

"More coffee?" The colonel, without waiting for my answer, grabbed my cup and, along with his, went in search of refills.

He returned to where we sat, placed two mugs of fresh, steaming joe on the table, and said, "Now for the good news."

"I'm ready for some."

"I heard about your trip over the Hump, your concussion, and dead-sticking your bird into Kunming. You were lucky. You know we lost over two dozen men in that storm?"

"Yes, sir," I said quietly.

"Sometimes it takes a tragedy to bring positive change. That September violence may have been one such incident. I sent General Chennault a strongly worded message after the losses, and I know the previous boss here, Major Hatcher, did, too. If nothing else, the death toll from that storm caught everyone's attention, including Chennault's. He finally acceded to our request for more men and equipment. Effective immediately, the Tenth Weather Squadron is authorized an additional two hundred personnel plus enough meteorological and communications equipment to support them. I told him two hundred men weren't nearly enough, and he promised additional mandates would be approved before the end of the year."

"That's terrific, sir. Allow me to express my genuine admiration of you not giving up on that effort."

I knew a lot of men would have backed off in the face of a general officer's—in this case Chennault's—initial opposition to beefing up weather support. But I was coming to learn that Dick Ellsworth was not just any man.

"But," Ellsworth said, "—there's always a 'but,' isn't there? —we have another problem."

He slid a copy of a message across the table to me. It was from Colonel Thomas O. Hardin, commander, ATC CBI Wing, and addressed to Ellsworth.

"Uh-oh," I muttered.

"Yeah," Ellsworth said.

I read the missive in stunned disbelief. Several phrases jumped out at me. One was that the "weather situation is wholly unsatisfactory," meaning, of course, weather support. The other read, "weather service in this sector is the only thing that is worse than communications."

"Jesus," I muttered, "this guy may have been an airline ramrod in civilian life, but he's certainly a Denny Dimwit when it comes to knowing about the challenges here."

"It gets worse," Ellsworth said.

"It can't."

"He came out with an edict a few days ago that said, 'There is no weather on the Hump.'"

I almost choked on a swallow of coffee. "He said what?"

"There is no weather on the Hump."

I sat there with my mouth agape.

"I know it makes him sound looney," Ellsworth said, "but it's just his way of saying missions are going to be flown regardless of the weather."

"So why grouse about lack of weather support, then?"

Ellsworth issued a sad smile. "So when an airplane drives into a rock pile or nose dives into a Burmese jungle, it isn't his fault, it's ours."

"I trust you've launched a counterattack?"

"If I can take on a brigadier general, I can take on a full bird colonel. In the message Hardin sent me, he claimed I was to have visited him to discuss improving weather support, but that I hadn't yet contacted him."

"I suspect the only thing he really cares about improving is his image."

"Easy, Rod. Even though that's a possibility, we don't have any evidence that's the case. At least he cared enough to fire off a nasty-gram saying he thought we were doing a crappy job."

"Yeah, the guy is a sweetheart." I wiped my mouth with a napkin and sat back in my chair. "So did you respond to his allegations?"

A private pushing a mop over the mess hall floor worked his way past us, and Ellsworth waited until he was some distance away before responding to my question.

"Yes. I just gave him the facts. He'll do with them what he wants. I told him the India-China Wing had never properly informed the Tenth Weather Squadron of its requirements for weather support, that we were hamstrung by an acute shortage of personnel, transportation, and communications, and that he, himself, had never offered any constructive criticism for improving weather services."

"And he responded how?"

Ellsworth shook his head. "He didn't bother. As far as I can determine, he believes the best source of weather information is reports from the guys flying over the Hump."

"And we know how diligent they are about filing them."

"Yeah, I know. Apathetic might be a generous description."

I had the feeling that even after the squadron began to receive more men and equipment, Hardin would never become a fan of ours. Deep down, I harbored a suspicion that as long as he could blame airplane crashes and air crew losses on weather service shortcomings rather than on his foolish edict that "there is no weather on the Hump," he'd be perfectly happy in what he was doing—cracking the whip to get more and more tonnage delivered to General Chennault and Chiang Kai-shek.

Ellsworth and I continued our discussion by going over some administrative details regarding running the squadron. After we'd finished, Ellsworth stood and told me he had a jeep scheduled to run him over to Dinjan, the adjacent air base, to meet with the weather troops there.

"I'll get those orders cut for you as soon as I get back to New Delhi," he said. "In the meantime, I'd like for you to develop a plan on where and how we can best employ the influx of men and equipment we expect."

"Yes, sir," I said. "See you in a week." I wouldn't, but had no knowledge of that then.

Over the next few days, I went back to my routine of hanging out in base ops, working on the plan Ellsworth had requested, and helping out the weather guys however I could.

My orders dispatching me back to Tenth Weather Squadron headquarters arrived five days later. I made arrangements to catch a hop to New Delhi on a Gooney Bird.

Three days before the flight departed, I put the finishing touches on my initial draft of the plan I'd been tasked to develop, and policed up my work area.

"Preparing to escape purgatory, I see, Major."

I looked up. Lieutenant Colonel Shaver stood in the doorway, a bulldog scowl on his face as usual.

"Yes, sir," I responded. *You SOB.* "Not much I can do here."

"Actually, there is. One last mission. A special flight to Kunming."

"I'm no longer on flying status, sir, in case you'd forgotten."

"Why do you think I'd forget? I'm the one who removed you from the flying roster."

"Good lord, sir, do you believe in miracles? My eyesight has suddenly improved? Praise be to God!" I raised my arms toward heaven in mock tribute.

"Cut the smartass shit, Major, and listen up. At oh-nine-hundred tomorrow, you'll depart Chabua in a C-47 with a special passenger bound for Kunming."

"My flight out of here is scheduled in three days. Surely you've got other pilots, non-four-eyers, who could do the job?"

"We're fully tasked, Major. No other experienced pilots are available. This is a milk run. You'll fly solo with a light load of medical supplies. The Station Hospital here has been tasked to move to Kunming. Your passenger is the key coordinator for that move. You'll be back here the day after tomorrow and on your way to New Delhi the following day."

"You do understand, sir, there are no milk runs over the Hump?" I could see the bulldog asshole was in fine fettle, and that I was going to make one last journey to Kunming whether I liked it or not.

"Oh-nine-hundred takeoff. Tomorrow." Shaver whipped an about-face and stomped off down the hall.

"Who's the passenger?" I called after him.

I got no response. But I had a pretty damned good idea who it was.

14

Chabua, Assam, India
US Army Air Forces base
Mid-October 1943

The next morning dawned clear. The sun came up in a burst of light, popping over the First Ridge in a silent explosion. Like hushed thunder. I thought of Kipling. I thought of Zim. *Come you back, you British soldier; come you back to Mandalay!* Except Zim was an American soldier who would forever be in Mandalay. Or somewhere near there.

I walked out to the airplane I'd been tasked to fly, a weather-whipped Gooney Bird that looked as tired and beat-up as I felt. We'll make a great team, I thought. Its nose was dented and dinged as if it had encountered a hailstorm. A series of patched holes in its fuselage suggested it had been the victim of a Jap fighter or some damned accurate ground fire. And its scratched and peeling paint bore the clear message it already had flown too many missions.

"One more," I said to it quietly as I performed my walk-around, checking the control surfaces and tires, and looking for leaks. Despite the bird's battle-scarred appearance, it seemed flightworthy. I'd make my final call on that after I'd cranked the engines.

I walked to base ops and entered the weather office. A grizzled master sergeant greeted me.

"How's it look to Kunming today?" I asked.

"Good morning, Major," the sergeant said. "Actually, not bad at all. Only scattered cu and altocu, and some pretty good tail winds."

"How good?"

"At fifteen thousand feet, probably up in the sixty to seventy mile-per-hour range. Just one thing."

"Yes?"

He squinted at me and cocked his head. "You aren't planning on coming back today, are you?"

"No."

"Good. Because we got a couple of reports out of far northern India and Nepal early this morning of flight-level winds well over a hundred miles per hour. Looks like a nasty disturbance is barreling in this direction. Wouldn't want to be up in the air later today."

"But remember, Sergeant, there is no weather over the Hump."

"Just because a bird colonel puts lipstick on a pig doesn't mean it still ain't a three-hundred-pound porker, sir."

"Don't I know it." I thanked the sergeant and left.

I filled out my flight plan, turned it over to the ops officer, and walked back out to the C-47. Even with the southwest monsoon on the wane, haze and humidity still hung in the air, reminding me I was in northern Assam, not northern Idaho.

The loading of the plane appeared well underway and Lieutenant Colonel Shaver waited beside it. I slipped on my reading glasses.

"Very funny, Major," Shaver growled.

"Can't find my way to Kunming without them, sir."

He scowled at me. At least I think he scowled. It was difficult to tell the difference between that and his normal
expression.

"Your passenger will be along shortly," he said. "Go ahead
and start your preflight. I'll escort her onto the aircraft when
she arrives."

"Her?" I said, not totally surprised. At least now I was
virtually certain who it would be, my number-one fan of all
time.

"A Captain Johannsen," Shaver responded, "from the
Ninety-fifth. She's the senior flight nurse in the CBI Theater."

"The senior flight *witch*," I mumbled, and climbed into the
plane. I entered the cockpit and plopped into the right-hand
seat, almost laughing about the reality I'd be airlifting Nurse
Nasty to China. Well, I'd drop her ass in Kunming and that
would be that. I'd be in New Delhi in two days and she, I
hoped, would be forever in Kunming.

I began to run through my checklist.

About halfway through, Captain Johannsen stuck her
head into the cockpit.

"I checked the cargo tie downs," she said. "They look solid.
We ready to go? Major." Her last word came out in a semi-
sneer.

I turned to greet her. "Trouble with your broom? Broken
rudder? Bad hydraulics?"

"Yes," she snapped, "that's how I ended up in a C-47 with
an officer who's not qualified to sit in the pilot's seat." She'd
zeroed in on the fact I was perched in the copilot's position.

She disappeared back into the cabin. This was going to be
a wonderful trip.

After I completed the checklist, I called Clear to the

ground crew and went through the engine start procedure. On run-up, despite the age of the old gal—the plane, not the nurse—they sounded solid and the gauges indicated the same. I made a mental note to mention that to the maintenance guys when I got back. They busted their butts keeping these birds in the air and they never got enough credit.

I swiveled my head to look back into the cabin and make certain Nurse Nasty had belted herself in. She had. I taxied into takeoff position. The tower gave me clearance to go, and the C-47, with a light load, lifted off easily into the golden dawn. I didn't even have to make the usual circling climb to clear the First Ridge.

Airborne over The Hump
En route to Kunming, China

I settled into a one hundred and eighty-five mile per hour cruise at twelve thousand feet. Smooth sailing. It felt good to be in the air again, to be soaring over the tangled green ruggedness of northern Burma far below me. It lifted my spirits. Maybe too much.

Somewhat against my better judgment, I turned and motioned for Nurse Nasty—well, okay, Captain Johannsen— to come forward and sit in the pilot's seat. She hesitated, but moved into the cockpit—perhaps against her better judgment, too—and sat.

I indicated for her to slip on an oxygen mask and interphone set. She did.

"Let's declare a temporary truce," I said, "at least for the duration of the trip."

She looked at me, nodded, but didn't smile.

"I thought you might like to see the roof of the world," I

went on, "on a rare clear day from a pilot's viewpoint." I wondered why I was trying to make peace with her. I decided it was probably because I just felt so damn good being at the controls of an aircraft again. It made all seem right with the world. Even though I knew it wasn't.

"Okay," Captain Johannsen responded, "but may I ask a question?"

"Go ahead."

"Why am I sitting in the pilot's seat while you're in the copilot's chair?"

"Because I really don't know how to fly this thing and I thought you could read me the instruction manual, especially when we have to land."

She didn't crack a smile, just stared at me. Did I just break the truce?

"Sorry," I said. "It's because when you're flying this bird solo, it's easier to do it from the right-hand seat. All the controls can be reached from here, especially the cowl flaps."

She nodded, remaining a woman of few words.

I brought the Gooney Bird up to fourteen thousand feet as we approached the Kumon Mountains along the Burma-China border. The shark-toothed ridges, partially hidden beneath cotton-ball cumulus, appeared both beautiful and deadly. Beautiful in VFR conditions, deadly if you're lost and flying on instruments.

The plane began a jiggly dance interspersed with sudden jumps and tumbles. But the roar of the engines added a modicum of comfort to the flight as it became increasingly bumpy. Overall, however, the bounciness proved less pronounced than usual.

I did a quick nav check. We seemed to be making even better time than I expected with our ground speed over two hundred fifty miles per hour. That suggested we were being boosted along by a tailwind component of at least sixty-five miles per hour. All good.

I glanced over at Johannsen. Her gaze seemed focused on the rugged chain of mountains coming up.

"So what's going on with the Ninety-fifth?" I asked, wondering if one could actually have a conversation with the sullen nurse.

"We're moving to Kunming to replace and also assimilate, I guess, a small Army medical unit that's already there. I understand we'll end up being the only large Army hospital in China."

"What happens at Chabua?"

"The One-eleventh Station Hospital will replace the Ninety-fifth."

"Are you excited about going to China?"

She shrugged. I guessed that was the end of our immediate conversation.

We exited the crest of the Kumons and soared out over the Salween River, a silver thread snaking through a slender green valley far below us. The turbulence ceased and the flight became smooth. But only for a matter of minutes.

The Santsung Range loomed immediately in front of us, the giants, as Zim had told me the first time we flew over them. I took the Gooney Bird even higher, and once again it began to shimmy and shake. I aimed for a spot between two towering cumulus clouds and drove the bird through it over the knife-edged ridges of the range.

Again we bounced around vigorously, but only for a matter of minutes. Then we were out over the next river valley, more than three miles beneath us.

"That's the Mekong," I said, "on its way to French Indochina and the South China Sea."

"A long journey," Johannsen acknowledged.

"Like life itself, I suppose."

"Yes." She turned to look at me, a sad, perhaps wistful blankness in her eyes.

"We'll be landing in Kunming in a few minutes."

"Okay."

In short order, we were scooting over the Yunnan-Guizhou upland plateau, beginning our descent.

Kunming, China

Below us, clouds of dust lifted from the ground as a stiff breeze galloped over the land. Rows of Lombardy poplars, planted as windbreaks, bent before the gusts like praying monks.

I maneuvered the C-47 into the landing pattern.

Captain Johannsen remained in the pilot's seat.

"Keep your eyes open for Japs trying to sneak into the queue," I said.

She flashed me a quit-yanking-my-chain look.

I told her what had happened the first time Zim and I had landed here.

"Oh," she said, and began craning her neck to check our six and all other directions of the clock.

The working coolies scattered to either side of the runway as I crabbed the bird in for what I thought was a pretty smooth crosswind-landing on the PSP runway. The tires buzzed loudly over the pierced-steel planking as I taxied the old Gooney toward base operations. Once there, I stopped and shut down the engines.

Johannsen unfastened her seat belt, stood, and walked back into the cabin where she retrieved her bag. Without a word—a thank you, or saying nice trip or even goodbye—she unlatched the passenger door and deplaned. She spoke briefly to the ground crew, giving them instructions about what to do with the med supplies, I presumed, then strode toward the ops building.

I watched her go, as did the ground crew. I assumed that would be the last glimpse of her I would ever have—her back turned toward me, how apropos. What a strange, beautiful woman, I thought. I wondered if she would ever be—ever had been—happy.

I told the ground crew I'd be returning to Chabua tomorrow, and asked them to check a couple of minor items on the plane I'd noticed on the flight to Kunming.

As I walked toward base ops, a C-46 with the name *Overtime* emblazoned on its nose taxied by me. Great name, I thought, considering the long hours put in by Hump pilots. But we sure didn't get overtime pay.

A large wooden sign, one I'd seen many times before, at the entrance to base ops greeted me. In big block letters it proclaimed: YOU MADE IT AGAIN. GOOD WORK! I hoped it would be the last time I'd ever see it.

I checked in with the ops officer, then went to base weather to give them a PIREP, a pilot report on the weather.

"Thanks, Major," a lanky corporal manning the weather desk said. "You know, we've gotten two or three reports out of Assam and Bengal the last couple of hours of winds at ten thousand feet up to one hundred twenty-five miles per hour plus some pretty severe turbulence."

"I don't have to return until tomorrow," I responded, "so I hope by then that crap will have blown through."

"Roger that, sir."

Next on my agenda, getting some chow, then securing a bunk in a *basha* for the night. By this time tomorrow, I'd be back in Chabua. And by the end of the following day, I should be ensconced in the relative comfort of New Delhi. No more flying the Hump, no more senior officers referring to me as Four Eyes, and no more nurses treating me as if I had leprosy. It would be great to be working directly under Lieutenant Colonel Ellsworth again, an officer who genuinely cared about people, yet at the same time got his missions accomplished. He seemed to me the epitome of what a military officer should be.

By late afternoon, I'd settled into the *basha* assigned to me. I leafed through the latest *Saturday Evening Post* magazine, at least the latest one to reach China. It was only two months old. Eventually, I nodded off, the comfortable warmth of the day and a full stomach from a lunch with large helpings of rice and chicken doing a number on me.

I don't know how long I dozed, but I was abruptly awakened by someone calling my name.

"Major Shepherd, sir. Major Shepherd."

I forced open my eyes and looked up into the eyes of a pimply-faced private standing in front of me.

"Sorry, sir, but the general wants to see you."

"The general?"

"General Chennault, sir."

I groaned. I seriously doubted I was being summoned to attend an awards ceremony.

15

Kunming, China

I knocked on General Chennault's door in the headquarters building. "Enter," he responded. I stepped into his office and rendered a crisp salute. He returned it and nodded at a wooden chair in front of his desk. I sat.

"My apologies for requesting your presence on such short notice, Major Shepherd," the general said, a trace of Southern courtliness in his words. He stared hard at me. "We've met before, have we not?"

"Yes, sir. I was here with Lieutenant Colonel Ellsworth when we discussed weather support about five weeks ago."

"Ah, yes, the balloon blowers," he said, a flash of peevishness registering in his furrowed, swarthy countenance. "Well, I guess you made your point, got your additional men and material."

"I think the weather made its point, sir. We lost over two dozen men in that September storm."

He grunted. The sound he made reminded me of water being sucked down a drain. Once more he locked me in a stony gaze. "Won't happen again though, will it? Now that you weather guessers got more help."

"If, as Colonel Hardin says, 'there's no weather on the Hump,' more help won't make much difference, will it, sir?" As usual, my retort came too quickly. I'd missed another golden opportunity to keep my mouth shut. What I said probably made weather support sound superfluous.

"What Colonel Hardin meant," Chennault retorted, "is that wartime operations have to proceed regardless of atmospheric conditions. We're fighting a war, Major. So flight operations aren't limited to daylight, VFR conditions."

I wanted to point out once more the lack of experience and training many of the pilots we were getting had, but it seemed pointless to get into a debate with a flag officer. So I bit my tongue and said, "Yes, sir."

"All that aside, let me get to the crux of why I called you in here. We've got an emergency situation that requires an immediate medical evacuation back to Chabua. A senior officer, an Army colonel, was accompanying Chinese troops on a combat operation in southern Yunan Province when he tripped a Japanese booby trap. One of his legs was blown off. The other is badly damaged and he may lose that one, too . . . and his life unless we can get him to the hospital in Chabua right away."

I began to see a scenario unfolding I really didn't like. But I didn't say anything. Instead, I waited for General Chennault to finish.

"I know you just landed a few hours ago with Captain"— he leaned forward and looked at a sheet of paper on his desk —"Johannsen, but I'm tasking you and her to get the colonel, Alfred Willis, back to Chabua today. Captain Johannsen is a flight nurse, so that's fortuitous for Colonel Willis. She'll accompany you and attend to the colonel in-flight.

"As we speak, the colonel is being transported to your

aircraft. We've got the plane topped off with fuel already, so you should be good to go within an hour. Any questions?"

Yeah, a million.

"Ironic as this sounds, sir, did anyone bother to check the weather conditions?"

As if to emphasize my point, a gust of wind hurled a spray of dust and fine gravel against a window in the general's office.

"That's your job, Major Shepherd."

Sure it is.

"As a matter of fact, General, I checked it right after I landed."

He fixed me in a steely gaze, suggesting maybe he'd already heard enough from me.

Before I spoke again, I ran through some quick calculations in my head.

Satisfied with my back-of-the-envelope math, I said, "There're some powerful headwinds developing between here and Assam. Turbulence aside, and there'll be plenty of that, having enough fuel to get back to Chabua is going to be marginal. That's the best-case scenario."

"And the worst case, Major?"

"We run out of gas over the Hump."

"Then I advise you not to run out of gas, Major."

"Sir, if we could wait until tomorrow morning—"

"The doctor here said we don't have that luxury."

"I think it's just too big of a risk, sir. If we could—"

"I'm sorry if you misunderstood me, Major. I wasn't soliciting your opinion. I was giving you an order."

And that was that. "Yes, sir. I'll grab my flight bag, file my flight plan, and be on my way." I stood, saluted, and departed.

Well, I thought, my world had certainly turned to shit. I truly felt as if I had less than a fifty percent chance of making it back to Assam. Not only that, my "crew" would consist of the only woman I'd ever known who spoke fewer words than Buster Keaton in his silent movies, and had all the personality of a barnyard butterhorn.

I stopped by the weather office on my way to the flight planning room, kind of a pro forma move, since I knew nothing likely had changed in the past couple of hours. The same wiry corporal I'd spoken to earlier greeted me.

"Any more reports on the winds?" I asked.

"A C-46 landed after you did, Major, and the pilot said his ground speed had been well over three hundred fifty miles per hour on the final leg of his flight. Then a Gooney Bird with a full load took off for Assam but turned around after about an hour. Said he'd never make it against the headwinds."

"Wonderful," I mumbled.

"What? You aren't going to try it, are you, sir?"

"I've got my orders."

"Jesus."

At least I'd be traveling light. But that might not matter given the apparent strength of the flight-level winds. And, I thought, given the severe turbulence we were likely to encounter, it would be difficult to keep our medevac patient in his litter. At the very best, he'd likely be extremely uncomfortable.

I filed my plan and walked out to the bird. Dust and small pebbles pelted the old girl as wind gusts I guessed in excess of forty miles per hour ripped across the flat terrain of the airfield. I performed my walk-around, then climbed into the aircraft.

Captain Johannsen, a young flight surgeon, and a couple of orderlies were busy securing the patient to a traveling litter.

"No," I said sharply. In air ambulance configuration, the Gooney holds three tiers of litters rigged by bars and brackets to the top and sides of the plane. The patient was being placed in one of the mid-level positions.

The nurse and surgeon stopped their work and stared at me.

"Put him in the lower level," I said.

"It's easier for the nurse to attend to him if he's in a middle rack," the surgeon said.

"We're gonna get bounced around all to hell on this trip," I said. "If the colonel is on the bottom level, he won't have that far to fall if things start to break loose."

The nurse and surgeon looked at each other. Then the surgeon nodded and they went to work shifting the colonel to a lower position.

The orderlies stood by holding IV bottles, ready to fasten them in place once the patient was secured.

I headed toward the cockpit. The flight surgeon, who I guessed had only recently been commissioned, intercepted me. "We've got about six hours' worth of IV drips for the patient. You think that will be enough?"

"If we aren't down in Assam in six hours, we're down someplace else, and then it won't make any difference."

"Optimistic, aren't you?"

"I'm optimistic we'll be down."

"The colonel"—the surgeon nodded in the direction of the litter—"is in really bad shape. He needs to reach a well-equipped hospital. Soon."

"I know that. I'll do my damnedest to make sure he does. But there are certain things beyond my control."

"I understand. Godspeed, sir." He returned to the business of repositioning the patient.

I entered the cockpit and began my checklist run-through.

Fifteen minutes later, I was taxiing into takeoff position. Captain Johannsen peeked into the cockpit.

"I guess we're stuck with each other again," she shouted, making herself heard over the roar of the engines.

"Destiny," I yelled back.

"So the weather's going to be worse than it was coming here?"

"It'll be a trip you'll never forget." Deep down, I hoped we'd have the opportunity to never forget it.

She nodded and returned to the cabin.

I asked the tower for takeoff clearance and it was granted. The visibility dropped to near zero as dust and gravel flew over the runway, pelting the aircraft with the ferocity of a violent hailstorm.

I noticed even the coolies had hunkered down at the edges of the runway, likely unable to remain upright in the gale-force wind. Happily, none appeared in a sprinter's position, ready to dash in front of the airplane as it took off in an effort to make mincemeat of a bad-luck dragon. Or maybe we'd taken care of all the dragons, and now they rested in repose beneath the PSP. Or perhaps—perish the thought—some had managed to grab onto various transports and been airlifted to Assam. Just what we needed.

The Gooney Bird, with a light load and strong headwind, lifted off quickly. It rattled and shook as it fought its way into the air, doing battle with the turbulence springing from the rollicking winds as they swept over nearby hills and valleys and buildings.

Airborne over China
En route to Chabua, Assam, India

The brutal shuddering quieted as we reached ten thousand feet, but I noted our ground speed didn't seem much greater than an Army weapons carrier on a muddy road. Maybe if the headwind got no stronger than it was now, I could get the bird to Assam and dead-stick it into a base as it ran out of gas. But we'd have to climb to get over the Hump, and I knew the wind would become even stronger as we gained altitude.

I swiveled in my seat to see how Captain Johannsen and the colonel were doing. The colonel appeared comatose, but the captain was on her knees beside him, holding his hand and stroking his forehead to comfort him. She seemed to be speaking to him, but I had no idea what she might be saying. I saw genuine empathy and tenderness in her actions, something I'd never witnessed from her before.

Shaking blond curls from her eyes, she lifted her head to glance at me. For a change, she wasn't throwing me an icy glare. In fact, I thought I glimpsed a certain softness in her gaze. I nodded at her and went back to flying the airplane. She puzzled me. Who was she really? Why did she display such a hard edge toward me and other men, yet seem to become virtually angelic when it came to someone in pain and incapacitated? Was it merely her training kicking in? Or was it a revelation of her true self, something that someone or some event had forced her to bury?

A sharp jolt to the airplane yanked me out of my pseudo psychoanalysis state. I had much more important things to attend to. Like figuring out exactly where we were and precisely how fast we were going. The airspeed indicator showed two hundred miles per hour, so we should have been over Yunnanyi, typically about an hour out of Kunming, by now. The flight-level visibility remained decent, so I should have been able to spot the Chinese town.

Yet no sign of it came into view. Up ahead, a ten-thousand-foot ridge loomed, a ridge well east of Yunnanyi. That suggested our ground speed was somewhere near seventy miles per hour. The headwind was killing our progress toward Assam. We could still make it at that speed, but I knew without a doubt as we mounted the Hump, the westerly wind, the gale slamming its fist into our nose, would grow even more powerful.

I turned back toward Nurse Johannsen and signaled her to put on her oxygen mask and get one on the colonel. I pulled mine over my face and began a climb toward twelve thousand feet in order to clear the ridge ahead of us.

After another half hour, Yunnanyi hove into view. I called the tower there and told them we were a C-47 medevac en route to Chabua, heading three hundred degrees mag. At least if we went down, search aircraft would have our last known position, time, and heading.

I took the aircraft higher, toward twenty thousand feet, hoping that would give us ample clearance going over the Santsung Range, "the giants." If it got rough, I might have to push it even higher. But the service ceiling on a Gooney Bird was twenty-three thousand, so I wouldn't have a lot of room left. Besides, the headwind at that altitude could push us back to Kunming.

As we soared out over the Mekong Valley, the horizon ahead of us morphed into blackness. I knew what that meant. I turned to Johannsen, lifted my oxygen mask, and yelled, "Strap in, it's gonna get rough."

We punched into the inky clouds and the plane began to dance, leap, and bounce. I couldn't see a damn thing. I'd become a night flyer, my surroundings illuminated only by sporadic flashes of lightning.

A severe updraft caught us, launching us on a rocket ride toward the stratosphere—well, at least well above the service ceiling of a C-47. Then the rocket fizzled and we plunged, becoming a dive bomber instead of a military transport. All I could do was hang on to the yoke. I had no control over the aircraft. None. You'd think I would have gotten used to that by now, given how often that had occurred flying over the Hump, but for a pilot, it's always unnerving having no command of an airplane.

I watched the altimeter unwind with the speed of a sweep second hand. We dropped five thousand feet in less than a minute. We weren't flying, we were passengers on a roller coaster where the ride could terminate on a Himalayan peak.

We slammed into the bottom of an air pocket and my stomach made an escape attempt through my throat. The plane rolled violently from side to side, then shot heavenward again. I chanced a glance at the nurse. She lay prone on the floor, gripping a vertical support post with one hand and holding the other on the colonel, trying to keep him in the litter. Blood dripped from a cut on her chin. The tethered IV bottles swung back and forth like pealing church bells. I wondered why they didn't shatter as they constantly slammed into each other.

I knew we couldn't remain aloft much longer in these conditions, especially with the headwind slowing our ability to fly out of the mess. But since I held no sway over the aircraft, there was nothing I could do to get us out.

Abruptly, we punched out of the storm and into clear air. Above us, bright sunshine. Below, a thick, flannel undercast. I could see nothing beneath us save snow-capped peaks jutting out of the clouds like canine teeth. The altimeter indicated twenty-two thousand feet, the airspeed indicator three hundred thirty miles per hour. Good grief. I double-checked the compass. At least we remained headed toward India.

But our ground speed, my God, our ground speed. I watched the peaks poking out of the undercast. Their positions relative to us seemed to change with all the speed of a slug leaving a silver trail through a summer garden. Our airspeed may have been that of a fighter aircraft, but our groundspeed I guessed was closer to that of a tank.

I ran through some quick calculations in my head. There was no way we were going to reach Chabua.

16

Airborne over the Hump
En route to Chabua, Assam, India

The air smoothed out, though the Gooney continued to wiggle and squeak like a pig in a poke. The engines, thank God, maintained a robust growl. I motioned for Captain Johannsen to come forward and sit in the pilot's seat. She did so and slipped on an interphone set.

"We're in trouble," I said.

"Yes?" She looked at me and I could read neither fear nor concern in her eyes.

"There's no way we can make it to Chabua before running out of fuel. If we try, we'll crash. The headwind is eating us alive."

She stared out at the white and gray montage—mountain peaks and solid undercast—that lay before us. "So what do you suggest?"

"Return to Kunming. We've still got enough gas to make it back. But we'll have to fly into that maelstrom again, the one we just came through."

"No."

"No? You do understand that's our best chance of staying alive?"

"The colonel will die without immediate skilled medical attention. He can't get that in Kunming. That's why we're out here."

"I understand that, Captain. But it's pretty simple math. Yes, he may not make it—and that pains me—if we turn around. But two of us will. If we continue toward Chabua, I can pretty much guarantee none of us will survive. So the no-shit bottom line is that two of us live or all three of us die. Take your choice."

Captain Johannsen fell silent. The aircraft continued to shudder and clatter as it clawed its way forward through the savage headwind. Far ahead of us, I spotted yet another phalanx of blackness. More storms lying in wait for us over the crest of the towering Kumon Mountains, the guardians of the Burma border.

Finally Johannsen spoke. "No other options? None?"

"One," I said.

"Tell me."

"We go south, try to fly out of the core of the strongest winds and drop to a lower altitude. Less fuel burn."

"Well," she snapped at me, "why didn't you do that in the first place?"

"Japs."

"Japs?"

"The Japs control the skies over most of Burma. There's a big airbase at Myitkyina packed with Jap fighters just waiting for a slow-flying, unarmed transport to stumble into their midst. There'd be a feeding frenzy. That's why we stick to this northern route, hugging the Himalayas."

"But we'd have a chance if we turned south?"

Not much of one.

"We'd have a much better chance if we turned around," I retorted. But I knew our mission hadn't been to fly from Kunming to Kunming.

"Maybe the Jap fighters won't be up," Johannsen suggested. "Maybe they'll be standing down because of the weather, not expecting any American aircraft to be flying."

"Maybe Lana Turner will send me a love letter."

"Maybe you should have stuck with flying a desk in Chabua," she snapped.

Nurse Nasty was back. Whatever thaw I might have glimpsed in her demeanor had quickly refrozen. Man, was she difficult to like.

"Maybe you should have gotten your broom repaired," I barked.

She began to remove her interphone set.

"Hold on," I said. "My assignment is to get the colonel to a hospital. We'll go south and I'll do my damnedest to reach Chabua. But the odds are against us."

"You said that from the get-go. But no one ever guaranteed the odds would be in our favor when we signed up for the military."

She had a point.

"Two roads diverged in a wood and I—I took the one less traveled," I said.

"What the hell are you talking about?"

"Poetry. Robert Frost. I had a friend who—oh, the hell with it. Go back and take care of our patient. But if I may make one suggestion, it's that you strap on your parachute now. There may not be time to do it if the Japs catch us."

She didn't acknowledge my recommendation, and moved back into the cabin to watch over Colonel Willis.

I took my suggestion, however, and pulled my 'chute from

beneath my seat and struggled into it. My intent was to get us to Chabua alive, but I also understood the reality of the situation.

The cloud cover below parted briefly and I spotted a green valley threaded by a twisting streak of silver, the Salween River. I turned south, tracking the river and remaining between two towering mountain ranges, the Santsungs and Kumons. Once I got far enough south, I'd head west and try to weave my way through various mountain passes without having to climb back to higher altitudes. I also hoped that by heading south, I'd be flying away from the core of strongest winds.

The bird continued to shake like a person suffering from severe Parkinson's, but the violent battering we'd taken earlier didn't return. I continued south for about half an hour, then banked the Gooney west, toward Burma . . . and toward the enemy.

My idea of snaking through gaps in the mountains didn't pan out well. Thick clouds returned and forced me to climb higher than I'd planned—to avoid peaks I couldn't see—and back into a more powerful headwind.

Airborne over Burma
En route to Chabua, Assam, India

After over an hour of bouncing westward, we shot out of the clouds and roared out over the rugged green topography of Burma. Below us lay a thick, tangled rainforest infested with snakes, tigers, headhunters, and Japs. All kinds of incentives to remain airborne. All I had to do now was avoid hitting something, running out of gas, or getting smoked by a Jap fighter.

I found a river valley and scooted along at about three

thousand feet. As long as the visibility remained good and the clouds didn't close their jaws over us again, I'd be able to hug the terrain and hope any Jap planes that might be up wouldn't spot us. I noted our ground speed had picked up markedly, so we seemed to have escaped the vicious headwinds that had plagued us since we lifted off from Kunming. Maybe we had a chance, I thought, just maybe. Although I knew the moment that notion flitted through my mind, I was asking fate to bite me in the butt.

I turned to see how the nurse and patient were doing. Captain Johannsen sat on the floor beside him, monitoring his pulse. I decided I could use her help so I beckoned her into the cockpit again.

Once she'd donned her headset, I told her what I wanted.

"I need an extra pair of eyes up here," I said. "If you could keep watch out the left side, that might help save our bacon. But feel free to go back and check on the colonel whenever you need to."

"What am I looking for?"

"Airplanes."

"How can I tell if they're good guys or bad guys?"

"There are no good guys around here. No American fighters, no British fighters. The Japs rule the skies over most of Burma, except for the far north where we should be. Down here we're an antelope in lion country."

"Maybe we should have painted a red cross on the plane."

"You think that would make any difference to the Japs . . . besides giving them an aiming point?"

She shrugged.

"A few months ago," I continued, "a Jap sub torpedoed a clearly marked Aussie hospital ship off Queensland. Over two hundred and fifty lives lost. The Japs play by their own rules, and they're far different from ours."

"I'll keep my eyes open," she said, her response soft and maybe a bit shaky.

The river I followed soon joined another flowing from the north. I guessed it was the Mali. To the west sat another range of mountains, no offspring of the Himalayas for sure, but still I estimated they crested at around ten or twelve thousand feet. Stacks of billowing, white cumulus shrouded the peaks, so once again I'd have to climb and fly by instruments.

That's good news and bad news. The good news being that in the clouds enemy aircraft couldn't see us. The bad, on the climb into the clouds we'd be more visible, and once at altitude, the stronger headwinds would come into play again.

We flew away from the river and I began our climb. The engines still sounded hardy and the fuel gauge indicated we probably had just enough gas to make it to Assam. So the big challenge now was not getting caught by the enemy.

"See anything?" I asked my "partner" in the pilot's seat.

"I'll let you know if I do."

I'm sure you will. Always the conversationalist. But at least she'd stopped throwing daggers at me.

Then the fate I'd worried about earlier did jump up and bite us in the ass. I buzzed over a road lined with a Japanese truck convoy before I realized it. *Shit.* I'm sure the roundels on our wings and fuselage, with the big white stars and horizontal bars, looked nothing like a red ball, the rising sun, or whatever in the hell the Jap roundel was supposed to represent.

"Japs?" the captain asked, her eyes widening a bit.

"You bet."

"Will they report us?"

"Maybe they have crappy radios."

"So that's a yes?"

"Better go check on our patient. We'll be in the clouds up

ahead of us in a few minutes, but we're likely to have a greeting committee waiting for us on the other side."

She moved back into the cabin to take care of Colonel Willis.

I took the Gooney up to twelve thousand feet, just to be safe, and drilled into the side of a towering cumulus. Once again the ride became rough, and the old Gooney Bird bounced around like a fishing boat in stormy seas. I hated to do it, because it would prolong our turbulent ride, but I banked the plane to the north, wanting to stay in the cloud as long as possible.

When I turned west again, I wanted it to be well north of where our trajectory upon entering the clouds suggested we might pop out. Of course, the Japs, assuming they'd be lying in wait for us, might be thinking the same thing. But I had to at least try.

My arms began to ache and the safety harness bit into my shoulders as the jouncing continued. Enough is enough, I decided. I motioned Johannsen back into the left-hand seat.

"I'm going to turn west," I said. "Maybe my evasive maneuver helped a bit, but I suspect the Japs may well be waiting for us once we exit our little hidey-hole here."

She nodded.

We burst back into bright sunlight. I didn't spot any other planes in the vicinity and pushed the C-47 into a steep dive, back toward the verdant jungle canopy. I settled into a nap-of-the-earth flight, skimming just above the dense, tangled rainforest and scattering hundreds of colorful birds that shot from the tops of the trees as a huge roaring predator thundered overhead.

"Uh-oh," Johannsen exclaimed.

"What?"

"A plane."

"Where?"

"Far ahead, off to the left."

"Give me a clock-face reading."

"What?"

"What's the bearing of the plane relative to us, using a watch face? Consider our nose pointed at twelve o'clock."

"Uh, it's at ten o'clock about forty degrees above the horizon."

"Good call." I looked and spotted the plane, a speck, flying away from us, maybe ten miles distant. I held the Gooney close to the treetops. Maybe we'd get lucky.

Nope. The speck banked and turned and appeared to be headed in our direction. We couldn't outrun a Jap fighter, but I wanted to get as close to Assam as I could before we came under attack. I jammed the throttles forward and the Gooney Bird responded, accelerating to over two hundred thirty miles per hour. Yes, we'd burn fuel more rapidly, but given the alternative . . .

"Still coming?" I asked Johannsen.

"Yes."

I willed the C-47 to move faster. It didn't help.

"He's starting a dive," the captain said. "It looks like a Zero."

"You know a Zero?" I couldn't keep surprise out of my voice.

"I've seen a few."

It probably wasn't a Zero. That was a naval aircraft. But the Jap army flew something similar. In all likelihood we were being pursued by a fighter with a top speed of over three hundred miles per hour and armed with two machine guns. As I recalled, they were slightly bigger than American thirty calibers.

All I had was a .45 handgun. That's not an air defense weapon. We were screwed.

"Go back and take care of the colonel," I said. "And put your 'chute on."

"What about the colonel?"

"What do you mean?"

"You don't think I'd bail out and leave him, do you?"

"Put your goddamn 'chute on," I yelled. I didn't need a debate right now.

She ripped off her headset and stalked back into the cabin.

The Jap fighter made a pass over the top of us, then rolled up and away from us. The pilot had identified us as an enemy aircraft. Now he'd come in for a kill. I spotted a second aircraft, undoubtedly the Jap's wingman, off to our right.

I dropped the Gooney even lower, to the point I was afraid I would decapitate trees. At the very least I could limit the Jap angles of attack. Though in the end, I knew it wouldn't make any difference.

Dead ahead, a tower of clouds beckoned me. But before I could even calculate how long it might take me to reach the temporary shelter, a splintering sound ripped through the cabin. Johannsen screamed.

I swiveled my head. Tubes of sunlight lit the interior of the aircraft, the fuselage of the C-47 now riddled with holes from machine gun fire. Johannsen appeared unhurt. But she still didn't have her parachute on, damn her.

The first Jap fighter we'd spotted had executed the attack. It climbed away from us. The second plane, the one on the right, now dove toward us.

We knifed into the cumulus. Gray mist cocooned us. But we'd pop out in no time. I rolled the aircraft to the right, hoping to punch out of the clouds at a point the Japs wouldn't expect us.

In an instant, we exited the grayness. Once again we became a duck in a shooting gallery. I glanced to both sides of the bird, then upward. No Japs. That didn't mean they'd vamoosed, only that they were biding their time, probably above and behind us. They knew we had nowhere to run.

They didn't bide their time for long. I caught the flash of tracers just outside the left-hand windscreen panel. Black smoke began trailing from the left-side engine. The rounds had found their mark, likely destroying the engine's oil tank and God knows what else.

Two thoughts sprang to mind. First, shut down the engine to prevent a full-blown fire. Second, gain some altitude so we could bail out.

I cut the fuel flow and killed the engine.

Even as I reacted, the second fighter came in for the kill, its machine gun fire tearing through the fuselage, into the cabin, and then shredding the cargo floor. How the rounds missed Johannsen and the colonel, I don't know. But I do know they found their way into the fuel tanks in the center wing section.

I yelled at Johannsen to get ready to jump.

She charged into the cockpit. "What the hell is the matter with you?" she screamed.

"We're going down." I flicked my head toward the still smoking but now non-functioning engine.

"You can't fly this thing on one engine?"

"Sure," I bellowed, "but not over the First Ridge which lies between us and Assam. And not with Jap fighters trying to blast us out of the sky. And not without gas. That last attack took out the fuel tanks."

She plopped into the pilot's seat and got on the interphone. "We've got a patient who can't jump."

"What the hell, Captain! You think I don't know that? You

think it doesn't tear my guts out to even *think* about doing what we have to?"

"I'm not leaving him."

"Why? What on earth can you accomplish by dying with him? Don't you fucking get it? I can't keep us airborne. I can't crash land in the jungle. We jump or we die." Of course, I couldn't guarantee we wouldn't die if we jumped, either. But I knew which option carried the better odds.

The Gooney Bird struggled to gain altitude. I knew the Japs would be back in a minute or two.

"I could order you to bail out," I said. "But that would be pointless. If you disobey, you'll be killed, so I couldn't court-martial you anyhow."

She remained mute, perhaps mulling over her options.

The bird wobbled up to about three thousand feet above the jungle canopy.

I made one last quick pitch to Johannsen.

"You can't help Colonel Willis or the war effort by dying. And that's what's going to happen if you don't jump!"

I wanted to say more, to grab her by the shoulders and shake some sense, some logic, into her, but time had run out. I put the plane on autopilot, unstrapped from my seat, checked to make sure my 'chute was secure, and moved back through the cabin toward the paratroop/passenger door.

PART II

THE JUNGLE

17

Northwest Burma

Sick to my stomach, I stopped by Colonel Willis's litter and knelt. He remained unconscious, unresponsive. I placed a hand on his head and said a brief prayer, wondering if such entreaties, especially in wartime, actually did any good. On the other hand, I supposed they couldn't hurt.

After I finished, I said, "I'm sorry, sir," knowing he probably couldn't hear me. "I don't know you, but I'm sure you're a good man who caught a bad break. What I'm having to do now slices me to the bone. I hope you—I hope God—will forgive me."

I stood. Next to me, Captain Johannsen struggled into her parachute. Tears glistened in her eyes.

"You win," she said.

"It wasn't a contest, Captain. Just a common sense decision to sacrifice one life instead of three."

I checked to make sure she had her 'chute firmly and correctly fastened. She did. She'd also strapped a medical kit onto one of the harnesses.

"We gotta go," I said. I snapped off a quick salute to Colonel Willis, my own eyes misting over—I hated what I was doing—and stepped toward the rear of the aircraft.

I unlatched the paratroop/passenger door. A rush of wind burst into the cabin. I stared down into the green hell flashing by beneath us. I'd never jumped before. My heart hammered at a rate I thought impossible.

I reached for Johannsen and moved her to the door. "Ladies first." I read fear in her eyes, but didn't have time to offer her encouraging words. Besides, I'm not sure I had any.

I placed her hand on the rip cord handle. "Jump, count to three, and pull this."

She didn't look at me, merely nodded. I prepared to give her a gentle shove, but before I could, she was gone.

I counted silently. I reached five. She still hadn't yanked the rip cord.

"Shit," I shouted, "pull it." Of course she couldn't hear me, my words torn away in the wind rush.

I couldn't wait any longer. I placed my hands on the door frame. I edged forward, then stopped. I noticed something I hadn't before. A sheathed machete mounted on the fuselage next to the door. I snatched it, jammed it into my parachute harness, and stepped off into the void.

I didn't bother to count, just yanked the damn handle. I felt a slight jerk and the silk canopy blossomed above me. I twisted and turned in the risers, trying to see if I could spot Johannsen. I couldn't. I didn't even know if she'd managed to open her 'chute. Damn, what a mess.

The roar of the Gooney Bird diminished, followed by the "thump" of an explosion as it plowed into a nearby ridge. I'd just sent a man to his death. I knew that would haunt me for the remainder of my life, but at the moment I didn't dwell on that. I had other concerns.

The Jap fighters screamed by overhead. Thank God they didn't bother strafing me. But they sure knew where I was landing.

And I landed in an instant. I sliced down through the broad-leafed canopy of the jungle, hoping I wouldn't end up impaled on the spike of a tree. I didn't, but crashed down into some sort of thorn bush with inch-long barbs.

I screamed in pain as the thorns ripped through my uniform like a meat grinder. At least the bush slowed my descent and I landed on my feet, splashing down into gooey mud several inches thick.

I slipped out of the parachute harness. The canopy hung suspended in tree branches above me. I'd heard tales from aircrew members who'd bailed out in the jungle that the 'chute canopy could be useful as a shelter or ground cover. I went to work yanking the thing down out of its entanglement. In a matter of minutes my cut and bleeding body—from the thorns—became braised in sweat. The mud sucked at my boots like quicksand.

Finally, the canopy came loose and drifted down into a soft, white pile at my feet. I cut the suspension lines with my trench knife, then stood there, panting. Strange sounds assaulted my ears from all directions. Squawking birds, howling monkeys, frogs, bugs, and who knows what else. Probably things waiting to eat me.

Strange. I'd been worried about dying on the side of a Himalayan rock pile. Now I was probably going to meet my demise in a tropical rainforest. God knows how far I was from civilization. Or even how far I was from Captain Johannsen, or in what direction. For that matter, I didn't even know if she was alive. But I knew I had to find out and, if she had survived, help her. As much as a pain in the ass as she'd been to me, I remained responsible for her, both as the aircraft commander and her superior officer.

My first step: orient myself. At this time of year the sun would be setting a bit south of due west. So what little sunlight made it through the top of the jungle should be casting tree shadows pointing toward the east-northeast. The plane had been heading roughly northwest. That meant Johannsen, since she'd jumped first, should be somewhere southeast of me. I pivoted, using shadows as my guide, to get myself facing, or so I hoped, southeast.

But the density of the jungle prevented me from picking out a distant landmark to aim at. I couldn't see more than thirty yards in any direction. Still, I had to move. I picked up the machete I'd stuck in my parachute harness, unsheathed it, gathered up the 'chute canopy in my other arm, and began hacking my way through Burma.

The cutting and slicing quickly became exhausting. It wasn't the kind of work I was used to. I don't know how long I flailed away at the virtually impenetrable undergrowth—thick bushes, heavy vines, bamboo—but I seemed to make very little progress. I finally gave up and collapsed against the trunk of a tree, allowing my butt to sink into the brown gumbo that constituted the rainforest floor. The cacophony of jungle noises increased as I ceased thrashing my way through the dense tropical growth.

I drew in great gulps of air, sweat draining down my skin in tiny rivulets. My muscles throbbed in stinging rebuke to my efforts. Complete exhaustion lurked only moments away. So did defeat. I pulled my knees toward my chest and rested my head on them.

"Keep going, you bastard, keep going," I whispered to myself. I sensed sunset must be only an hour or two off, and I had to use what little daylight remained to search for my favorite nurse. I wobbled to my feet, took some ineffectual swings with the machete at what appeared to be new-growth bamboo, and staggered off in what I hoped was the correct direction.

After about fifteen minutes, I caught my first break of the day: a trail of some sort. Probably a game trail, but I didn't care. I was so damned muddy, sweaty, and bloody, I couldn't imagine anything wanting to chow down on me—even a tiger might consider me a health hazard.

The trail, happily, seemed to run northwest-southeast. I struck out toward the southeast, having only to chop away huge leaves and small tree branches that leaned over the track here and there.

I paused every few minutes to rest and listen, though I doubted Johannsen, assuming she'd made it down safely, would be calling out. I doubted she'd risk being "rescued" by Japs.

After another hour of beating my way along the trail, discouragement began to wrap itself around me in an unfriendly bear hug. I spotted no signs of a parachute, but given the limited visibility in the rainforest, I probably shouldn't have expected to. Nor should I have expected her to land near the path to begin with.

Time was not in my favor. Darkness would soon cloak the jungle, and I'd have to shut down my search. I had to take a risk. I had to start yelling for her. I realized I wasn't just going to stumble upon her. I had to gamble she would hear me before any Japs did—assuming she could hear me at all.

I drew in a chest full of air and hollered, "Captain Johannsen, it's Major Shepherd. Can you hear me?" Nothing but the screech of startled birds came in response.

I tried again. "Captain Johannsen, let me know your presence!"

Screech, squawk, squeal. *Damn.*

I continued to plod along the trail, swampy goo sucking at my boots. I'd stop and yell every few minutes, but received no answer. At least nothing growled at me or shot at me. For the first time, I actually hoped to hear Nurse Nasty's prickly voice calling out, pissing off the birds and all the other critters who called this Godforsaken place home.

The forest fell into deep shadow as the sun slid toward the horizon.

Once more I bellowed into the tenebrous greenery, "Nurse Johannsen. Where are you?"

"Keep it down, will you," came a distant, muffled response. "There may be Japs nearby."

I heaved a sigh of relief . . . and surprise.

"Don't worry, they'll be more interested in you than me," I yelled back. Gotta love that woman. "Where are you?"

"Over here."

"That doesn't help. I can't see more than three feet." Her voice seemed to be coming from my right.

"I'm stuck in a tree."

"You're safe, then. Nothing can get you."

"There are ants and bugs all over me. Please. I need your help."

"That's a first." I began slashing my way through the jungle, trying to move in the direction of her voice.

"I can hear you cutting," she yelled. "You're getting closer."

"So are the Japs."

"Stop it," she screamed, "I'm scared enough already."

Another ten minutes of hacking brought me to the base of what I guessed must be a massive teak tree with soft, scaly bark and big leathery leaves. Captain Johannsen dangled about ten feet above me, her parachute entangled in the branches of the tree.

"Good to see you," I said, genuinely meaning it.

"The bugs are eating me alive," she answered, a tinge of desperation in her voice. "Can you get me down. I can't reach the latches on my parachute harness."

"Use your knife. Cut the straps."

"I don't have a knife."

Jesus.

I drew a deep breath. Frustration. "I can't climb the tree."

"Please."

"If I toss *my* knife up to you, can you catch it?"

"I'll try."

I took out my trench knife.

"Don't grab it by the blade. I'll try to pitch it up to you handle first. If you can't snatch it by its handle, let it drop and we'll try again."

"Okay."

It took six tries before we perfected the technique, but she finally caught it. Safely.

"Now, cut yourself loose and I'll try to cushion your fall," I said.

"I'm going to drop my medical pouch to you first," she answered. "Then me."

"I can hardly wait."

She dropped the medical kit, which I fumbled.

"That doesn't bode well for me," she said in her usual snippy manner.

"Try not to be too supportive."

"Ready?" She sawed away at the harness.

"Try to give me a warning just before you make the last—"

She plunged from her hanging place before I could finish my request. I managed to wrap my arms around her just as her feet hit the ground and we collapsed into the muddy soil together. She ended up on top of me. We might as well have been two hogs rolling around in a sty. It was that romantic.

"You look like shit," she said.

"You got a few claw marks on your mug, too."

We separated.

"What happened?" she asked me, staring at my face and arms. "The cuts and scratches?"

"I think I landed in a cactus."

"This is a rainforest."

"Then it was a rainforest cactus."

"Quit being a jerk. This is serious. We're out here alone, probably in enemy territory. Some of those cuts are pretty deep. I need to get them cleaned up and covered, otherwise they'll get infected."

"Sorry," I said. "I know this is serious. But my cuts can wait. We need to get some shelter. It's almost dark."

To punctuate the urgency of our circumstance, the rumble of thunder reverberated through the jungle.

"And it's probably going to rain," I added.

I went to work slashing at some bamboo. I had no experience in survival techniques, but I'd heard of guys being able to construct jury-rigged tents using bamboo poles and parachute canopies. My arms felt as if they weighed five hundred pounds each. I don't know how I kept moving them, but I did. To Captain Johannsen's credit, she pitched in by unfolding and untangling my parachute canopy, preparing it to deploy over the poles . . . assuming I could get three or four sturdy ones cut.

I ended up with two. I found a relatively dry patch of ground near a giant hardwood of some sort, and jammed the poles into the soft surface. As the last vestiges of daylight disappeared and a stygian blackness advanced, I managed to get the canopy draped over the bamboo stakes. Then I collapsed with my back against the tree.

Johannsen lowered herself beside me. "Kind of a mess you got us into. But thanks for coming back for me."

A mess I *got us into?* Her remark pissed me off, but I was too tired to return fire. Like it or not, I was stuck with her. I knew I'd be the constant object of her ire until we managed to extricate ourselves from this fix—if we could—so I decided I'd better get used to it.

I don't know how quickly I fell asleep, but guessed it was within a minute or two. I awoke after a few hours to the flicker of lightning and grumble of thunder. A dull roar, like ocean surf, seemed to be marching toward us through the forest. Then it hit. A deafening tropical downpour. The landscape became awash in rushing water. Waterfalls cascading off leaves. Flash floods burbling through gullies. Lakes forming at our feet. Streams of cold water spilling from the parachute canopy.

"You might have had better luck stringing a fish net over us," Johannsen snapped.

"Two canopies might have worked better than one, but somebody left hers in a tree," I retorted.

Within a few minutes, we were both shivering and miserable.

I reached toward her. "It would help if we shared our body heat."

"Wrap your arms around yourself," she responded, and sat alone in the downpour, cold and shaking.

Exhaustion again overwhelmed me and almost immediately I floated off into a desert land where warm sunshine bathed me and voluptuous women fed me grapes and cherries. I hoped I'd died and gone to heaven.

But I awoke in the same green hell I'd landed in yesterday

—monkeys howling, frogs burping, insects whining, and everything saturated and dripping from last night's gully washer. Johannsen leaned against me, snoring softly.

I remained still, trying not to disturb her. Stiffness and aches permeated every inch of my body, and I attempted to stretch various parts not in contact with hers.

Sleep had mollified my exhaustion, but I became aware of something else. I was damned hungry. My stomach growled loudly, joining the discordant symphony of rainforest creatures. I considered loading my .45 with birdshot rounds, but decided Japs would likely be more of a threat than hunger.

Johannsen's scream jerked me from my musings.

I snatched my weapon from its shoulder holster.

18

The northern Burma rainforest

With both hands, I swung my handgun in an arc in front of me. "What?" I said in a loud whisper.

"Ewww, ewww," Johannsen exclaimed. "Get them off me. Oh, my God, they're eating me. Please, please." Her voice reflected pure panic.

I turned and saw her staring at her arms while she held them straight out in front of her. Then she turned her head toward me and screamed again.

"You've got them, too."

My shirt sleeves, tattered and ripped, had slid back from my forearms, which were dotted with slimy-looking worms or slugs.

"Jesus." I holstered my weapon and swiped at the worm-like creatures, each about an inch or so long. Some were bigger, however. And I quickly realized why. They'd become engorged on my blood. Leeches. I couldn't just brush them off. They'd latched onto me with tiny, powerful suckers.

I managed to pull a few of the disgusting things off me, but the goo on their tubular bodies made them difficult to grip.

"They're leeches," I said. "We have to pull them off."

Johannsen settled down, and like the trained nurse she was, went to work. We found we had the slimy little vampires not only on our arms but on our legs and ankles, as well. I pulled up what was left of my shirt. Yep, on my chest, too. I got those off.

"Nurse, if you would, please, take a look at my back." I turned my back toward her.

I felt her pull several of the blood-sucking creatures off me.

"Now you," I said.

She fired a reproachful glare at me.

"Look, Captain," I said, "I want to pull some leeches off you, not try to feel you up, okay?"

She didn't say anything, but swiveled her back toward me and lifted her blouse. I removed several of the critters from her—I couldn't help but notice—very smooth skin.

"Thanks," she muttered.

"I'll turn my head and look away now, if you've got some on your, uh, chest you'd like to remove."

"Yes."

I kept my word and didn't peek. Although as well-endowed as she was, the thought crossed my mind. I was a natural male pig, I suppose, even in the midst of dire circumstances.

"Thank you," she said softly. "I think I'd better attend to your cuts and scratches next. Do you have any water?"

"Small canteen. Go easy on it. It's all we've got."

"We can get more water. I've got purification tablets."

She went to work on my "battle wounds," cleaning them

up, dusting them with sulfa powder, and even slapping a small dressing on a couple. I nodded my gratitude.

"Now what?" she asked.

"We gotta move. I'm guessing the Japs are looking for us. Headhunters may be, too. If—"

"Headhunters?" she interrupted. "Is this another one of your little flyboy jokes?" Irritation threaded her words.

I sighed. "No, Captain, it's not. We've been told there are a few tribes around here that still practice headhunting. But as far as I know, our guys have never encountered any. In fact, most of the natives have been helpful to Americans."

"Most?"

"I'm sorry I mentioned it. Look, let's worry about the Japs, not headhunters. Headhunters don't carry guns."

"How would we tell if a tribe are headhunters or not?"

Please. Stop. "I don't know, Captain Johannsen. They probably stare at your head or something. Don't get wrapped around the axle about it. Gather up your stuff and let's get going."

I grabbed the parachute and we set off along the trail, this time toward the northwest, toward Assam and hopefully away from the Japs. Our clothes, soaked from the previous night's rain, clung to us like damp washrags. The only saving grace, if you could call it that, is that they dried quickly as an unrelenting tropical sun beat down on us.

The leeches turned out to be just as unrelenting. They lay in wait for us, hanging from trees, hiding in the mud, or sitting on plant leaves with the upper half of their bodies waving around like tiny cobras waiting to strike.

We learned quickly to halt every fifteen minutes or so and pluck the damn worms off of us. At least off the visible parts of our anatomies. I'm sure a few of the slimy critters had managed to squeeze through microscopic openings in our clothing and clamp onto body parts unseen. Maybe body parts unmentionable.

The mud seemed as ubiquitous as the leeches. Every step became an effort, as the gooey soil proved determined to suck the boots from our feet. Eventually we reached a small rise, an open field of shrubs and thick, waist-high grass. Trenches and fox holes dotted the area. A few rusted rifles lay here and there. I bent to examine them.

"Japanese," I said. "A battle was fought here."

"So we're probably still in enemy territory?" Johannsen said. She moved her gaze over the surrounding jungle.

"Well, there's no sign of an Allied presence here, so that would be my guess."

"We need to keep moving, then."

"You're going to make a good soldier, Captain Johannsen."

She actually cracked a small smile. I almost chuckled, but didn't. She'd probably take it the wrong way.

We pressed on, back into the depths of the rainforest.

"You got anything to eat?" I asked.

"No. You?"

"Nothing. And my stomach is angry. It's making scary noises."

"We can make it without food for several days," she said. "But we gotta keep drinking water."

"I wonder if leeches are a source of protein," I said.

"Yeah, they'd be real happy inside your tummy."

That shut me up for a while.

At some point after midday, we reached a small stream. We refilled the canteen and dropped in a couple of purification tablets. Even though the water was laced with mud and probably other stuff we didn't want to know about, the tablets would render it safe to drink.

"You think walking in the stream would be easier?" Johannsen said.

"It might be." But I wasn't sure. The stream bed could be layered in mud.

"Let's find out." The nurse stepped into the water, took several halting steps, then looked back at me. "I'm stuck."

"Get out," I snapped. "Now."

"I can't. Oh, crap, it's like quicksand."

"Don't move."

"I'm sinking. The mud's sucking me down."

"Don't panic. Stay still. It's not going to swallow you. Let me think."

I grabbed my machete, found a small stand of bamboo, and hacked off an eight-foot branch. I darted back to the water and extended the stick to Johannsen. She grabbed it, I tugged it, but all I managed to do was yank it from her grasp. She remained firmly embedded in the mud.

"Plan B," I said.

"What's that?"

"I don't know. Yet. But I'll come up with something."

"Yes. Please."

I sat on the edge of the stream and stared at her. "Me Tarzan, you Jane," I said after a while.

"That's cute. That's your Plan B?"

"Yep." I arose and tramped back into the jungle.

I came out with a long, sturdy vine and tossed one end of it to her. "It's leech free," I said. "I de-leeched it. Wrap it around your waist and tie a non-slip knot in it."

"I'm not sure I know how to do that."

Give me strength. "They didn't teach you to tie knots in nursing school?"

"They taught us quick-release knots. They also said we'd be flying in airplanes, not stuck in quicksand in a Burmese jungle," she snapped. But I detected just a flicker of dark humor in her voice.

"I understand. Okay, here we go. Pull the vine around your waist. Then wind the loose end around the long end and back underneath itself."

She did.

"Good. Now stick the loose end back through the loop you've created."

"I can't. Too short."

"Pull more of it around your waist. Give yourself some slack."

She managed that and we repeated the procedure. This time she completed it.

"Good. Pull it as tight as you can."

I didn't know what kind of knot I'd created, but it seemed to hold.

"Okay, I'm going to tug you out. Don't move your feet too much until I get you closer to the stream's edge." It turned out not to be an easy process. It took time, but it worked. She finally staggered out of the water with dark mud caked to the top of her ankles.

"Thank you, Tarzan," she said.

"That's Major Tarzan to you, Captain Jane."

She didn't laugh.

"Were you ever a member of the Blackfeet Indian Tribe?" I asked.

She glanced down at her feet. This time she laughed. A breakthrough.

"It's good to hear you laugh, you know," I said.

She nodded, but didn't smile. I guessed I'd probably pissed her off by making her laugh. I splashed some water from the stream onto her pants and flushed off most of the mud.

"Next?" she said.

I looked at the sky. Clouds had puffed up all around us, but it didn't look like any of them were building into thunderstorms. "It's getting late. I'm guessing it won't rain tonight, so let's find a place we can use the parachute canopy as a tarp and maybe pull part of it over us as a cover."

We found a meadow of sorts on the side of a small hill and deployed part of the parachute as ground cover and rigged the other portion to serve as a silk blanket for us.

"There," I said as we finished, "our honeymoon bed. But I promise I'll keep my hands in my pockets."

"Yes," she said, "I know you will. You've been a gentleman."

"An officer and a gentleman, right?"

"You've looked out for me as an officer. And I do . . . well, I really . . . do appreciate that." She seemed to have difficulty saying the words and they came out haltingly.

"Thank you. Perhaps we could raise a white flag on our harsh words and acrimony until we get out of this mess."

"Okay," she answered.

The inky blackness of the jungle night swallowed us. The usual raucous sounds of evening—grunts, screeches, growls, squawks—filled the humid darkness. The whine of unseen mosquitoes joined the chorus. Johannsen and I swatted constantly at the invisible attackers, accidentally slapping each other from time to time since we honestly couldn't see one another, though we sat just inches apart.

"Better get under the silk," I suggested, "unless we want to end up as giant welts."

We slid beneath the makeshift blanket and within minutes each of us had fallen into a deep slumber, exhausted by the day's events.

I awoke sometime later, shivering. I hadn't thought that possible in the jungle, but perhaps we'd gained some altitude, and it was late in the season, both factors that could make the nights cooler.

"I'm freezing," Johannsen murmured, her voice slurred with sleep.

"Me, too," I said. I paused, then forged ahead into what I knew to be dangerous territory, at least with her. "It would help if we shared our body heat."

No response. Then I sensed her wiggling in my direction. She reached me, stopped, and rolled onto her side with her back toward me. I extended my arm and eased her against my chest. She stiffened slightly but didn't resist. She remained silent.

Within short order she relaxed and fell into the rhythmic breathing of sound sleep.

We remained fixed in that position until the first rays of dawn's sun crept over us.

"Sleep well?" I whispered.

She wriggled away from me and sat up. "I stayed warm."

"That was the idea."

"I'm gonna go pee."

"Don't go far. A few feet. I won't look."

She stood and moved away from me as I turned my back. The jungle sounded alive with birds and monkeys. And I guess it should have been. This was their home, not ours. I hoped they didn't mind us using their backyard as a latrine.

Johannsen returned. "I just remembered something," she said.

"Yes?"

"I stuffed a couple of D-rations in my medical kit before we left Kunming."

"Breakfast," I exclaimed.

"Have you tasted one?"

"No."

She smiled, retrieved her med kit, fished out a D-ration, and tossed it to me.

"Nicely packaged," I said. The wrapper read "Hershey's Tropical Chocolate."

"You'll want to wash it down with water."

"Chocolate is chocolate," I said.

"Not really."

"Doesn't matter. I'm starving." I unwrapped the bar, broke off a piece, handed it to Johannsen, then snapped off a chunk for me.

I chewed it. And chewed it. And chewed it. "I'll take some water," I finally managed to choke out. I noticed she'd taken only a nibble from her piece.

"Like it?" she asked.

"Yum. It should kill any parasites that've taken up residence in me."

She nodded.

It tasted slightly better than a boiled potato, only more vinegary.

"Maybe I'll leave the rest for the monkeys," I said.

"Don't you dare. It's all we've got. Besides, they wouldn't touch it."

I re-wrapped the remaining chocolate. I hoped it wouldn't eat through its packaging. We gathered up what little equipment we had and prepared to set off again. For where, I had no idea.

Before we left, I said, "I'd really like you to call me Rod from here on out. And I'd like to know you by something other than Captain Johannsen." I hoped to build on the little ceasefire we had agreed upon.

She didn't respond immediately, but finally said, "Genevieve. My friends call me Eve."

A breakthrough. "What would you like me to call you?"

"If you don't mind, Major, let's stick to our military forms of address."

So much for a breakthrough. But I couldn't argue against her wish. We remained in a military situation.

"No problem, Captain Johannsen. I respect your request. You ready to hit the bricks?"

"Where are we headed?"

I really didn't know. "North. Away from the Japs."

"You think they're hunting us?"

"I don't think so. I know so." I pointed south. On the other side of a distant ridge, a thin column of smoke spiraled into the still air.

"What's that?"

"A campfire."

"It could be natives."

"In that direction? Let's not assume that."

19

The northern Burma rainforest

We hiked back into the denser jungle at a rapid clip. As rapid, at least, as cutting through the tangled undergrowth on various game trails would allow. As usual, the work exhausted me, and with the typical cloudiness absent from the sky, the sun warmed the forest with fierce intensity. Even the animals and birds sounded lethargic.

I paused every fifteen or twenty minutes for a breather, and also so Captain Johannsen and I could pluck the leeches off each other.

But I felt as if we were running a losing race. The Japs, once they picked up our trail, would be able to follow it with ease. And they wouldn't have to hack and slice their way through the wilderness since I was doing that for them.

Eventually, we came to what appeared to be an old dirt road, probably cut by the Brits when they held Burma. It didn't appear to have been used recently, but would at least afford us a little faster movement, since I wouldn't have to slash my way along it foot by foot. Fallen trees blocked the way here and there, forcing us to scramble over them. And occasional thick tangles of vines had me swinging my machete to slice them away, but overall we made decent progress.

By midday, the captain began lagging.

"Tired?" I asked.

"Yeah. Burned out. I dunno what the problem is."

Previously, she'd been able to keep up with me just fine.

"Can we sit awhile?" she said. "I'm feeling dizzy."

"Sure. Let's find some shade." The heat had become unbearable. I didn't like the idea of stopping and giving the Japs a chance to gain on us, but I could see Eve was struggling. She clearly needed a break.

I'd been carrying the parachute like a backpack. I unfolded it and placed it on the ground, just off the road, as ground cover for Johannsen to rest on. I placed it in the shade and told Eve to sit. I gave her some water, but she took only a few sips.

"I need to find more water," I said, "the canteen's almost empty."

She nodded.

"How about a little chocolate?" I asked.

She shook her head. "Not feeling so good. A little nauseous."

She'd turned quite pale, and her breathing seemed rapid and shallow. I assumed the heat had gotten to her. I hoped it wasn't something worse, like malaria or typhoid. Since I had no medical training, I had no way of knowing.

Whatever it was, I knew our journey for the day had ended. My stomach knotted with concern. A small ripple of fear coursed through me. Not only would the Japs be able to close the gap between us more rapidly now, but I had a sick partner. Now there's irony, I thought—me caring for the nurse I'd locked horns with ever since I'd arrived in India.

"Lie down," I said. "Take it easy. I'm going to search for some water—a stream, a pool, anything."

"Are we still in China?" she murmured.

I placed my hand on her forehead—cool and clammy. "No. We're in Burma now. Relax. I'll be right back." *I hope.*

I moved back to the unused road, stood and listened, hoping to hear a stream, fearing to hear Japs. But only the normal rainforest chatter reached my ears. I walked slowly along the track, listening and looking. I didn't want to get too far from the captain.

My watchfulness was rewarded. Several small deer trotted across the road about thirty yards in front of me and disappeared into the brush. They moved downhill. I hoped they might be heading for water. I thought about shooting one for dinner, but knew I'd only be signaling the Japs of our whereabouts.

I followed the deer along a narrow game trail. As I tracked them deeper into the jungle, the path dwindled to a tunnel suitable only for gnomes. I dropped to my hands and knees and crawled. The trail became muddy, but led to a reward—a pool of brackish water, brown and red and topped in algae and lily pads. The deer drank on the far side of the pond. One of them lifted its head, spotted me, and issued something that sounded like a cross between a bark and a scream. Startled, I dropped my canteen. The deer fled.

I retrieved the canteen and filled it with water. Slipping and sliding, I scrambled back to the road. I marked the game trail—hard to spot—with a pair of tiny branches I jammed into the ground like posts marking a gate.

Johannsen appeared virtually comatose when I got back to her. I felt her pulse. Weak and rapid. Using my shirttail as a filter, I dumped the water over her head. She flinched, but showed no signs of awareness. I headed back to the pond for a refill.

I repeated this several times. To the final canteen, I added purification tablets. We'd need something to drink.

Sweat dripped off my skin. My body felt as if it were on fire. I collapsed beside the nurse. The last thing I needed was for me to fall victim to whatever had knocked Johannsen off her feet. Heat, I hoped. She could recover from that.

One thing I noticed, she looked like hell. Her blond hair, stringy and muddy. Her skin, encrusted with welts, scratches, and mud. Her uniform, ripped and stained. So much for her Rita Hayworth image. But I'm sure I looked no different. If rescuers ever reached us, or vice versa, we likely would be ignored as denizens of the forest, indigenous natives.

It became clear we could go no farther today. I picked a few leeches off Johannsen, shaved a few bits of chocolate off the boiled potato bar, swallowed them, and tried to figure out what to do next. If the captain didn't recover, there wasn't much I could do. I'd already sent one individual to his death— not that I'd had much of a choice, but it gnawed at my conscience like a mouse nibbling away at a piece of cheese— and I knew I wouldn't abandon another person.

I dozed off. When I came to, I found Johannsen staring at me. Color had returned to her cheeks.

"Welcome back to the world," I said.

"Sorry," she said. "I think it was heat exhaustion." She held her gaze on me.

"I didn't know what it was. Something to do with the heat I hoped, but wasn't sure. I didn't have a nurse around to help me."

She issued a weak smile. "You did the right thing." She paused. "Thank you." The words came out in a virtual whisper. Again she seemed to struggle to say thanks. She continued to speak. "If you hadn't done something . . . to help me . . . if you'd pushed me to go on, it could have gotten much worse. Heat exhaustion in and of itself isn't necessarily dangerous. But if we'd let it continue, it could have morphed into something much worse."

"Heat stroke," I said. I guess I might have learned a bit in my first aid courses after all.

"Yes. And sometimes that can be, well, fatal." She lowered her gaze.

"I didn't want to lose my partner."

She ignored my attempt to tighten our bond, such as it was. Instead she said, "It's a good thing you aren't a beautician." She brushed a few muddy strands of hair out of her eyes.

"I thought about becoming one after the war is over."

"Four eyes or not, you should probably stick to being a pilot."

"I just lost an airplane."

"But not us."

"We aren't home free yet."

She sat up, but I could see she remained weak. "I feel better," she said, "but still a little woozy . . . and just a bit queasy."

"Why don't you try a little of the upchuck chocolate? You can wash it down with the water. It's about the same color as the chocolate, but the purification tablets should have had time to do their thing."

She gave me the evil eye, although I got the impression it was more of a mock rebuke than the previous ones she'd fired at me. "Your bedside manner leaves a lot to be desired, Tarzan. I'll skip the chocolate but try a little water."

"You slipped up, Jane. You didn't address me as *Major* Tarzan."

We passed the next hour in relative silence, the only sounds being the jungle musicians turning up for their night-time concert.

As a purple dusk morphed into blackness, Johannsen spoke. "You asked me a strange question once," she said.

"Yes?" I had no idea what it might have been.

"At the dispensary in Chabua one night. Maybe you'd had a little too much post-mission refreshment. I don't know." She kept her voice low and soft. Different from the strident tones she'd so often spoken to me in.

"Go ahead," I said, still puzzled.

"You asked me if I'd ever been a brunette, or ever been to Pennsylvania."

"Oh." Unbidden memories. Of Trish in her last days. I said nothing further.

"What was all that about?" Johannsen asked.

"Like you said, probably too many post-mission whiskeys."

"No . . . there was something. Something in your eyes."

I was glad she couldn't see them now, in the rainforest darkness. She would have seen the same thing. A misty, melancholic remembrance of my wife. Fearing my voice would betray me, I fell silent. I allowed the nighttime discordant symphony of the jungle creatures to fill the void.

"Major?" Johannsen spoke softly.

I didn't answer.

"I'm sorry," she said. "I . . . I didn't mean to pry."

"No," I responded, trying to manage the huskiness I was afraid would tinge my words. "It's okay. We're kinda all each other's got at the moment. Maybe I need someone to talk to. A woman."

"Not an Ice Queen?" Her voice, surprisingly, remained subdued.

"I apologize for referring to you that way. It was uncalled for."

"I'm not so sure. Maybe we're both toting baggage we need help with."

I drew a deep breath, not necessarily a fragrant one. Mud, decay, body odors, perhaps mixed with a bit of despair.

"My wife," I said. "It was about my wife, Trish." I paused, then added in choked tones, "My late wife."

I told Eve the story about the nurse who wasn't, the dark-haired nurse from Pennsylvania who'd sat all night with Trish in Letterman. Except there was no dark-haired nurse from Pennsylvania. Only the reality that the hourglass for Trish's time on earth had but a few tips left.

I finished the tale and allowed my head to droop against my chest. In the blackness.

Johannsen said nothing, but I thought I heard her stifle a sob.

"Captain?" I said quietly.

"Eve," she said. "Please call me Eve."

"Okay."

"I didn't know," she whispered. "I didn't know about . . . about your wife."

"Of course not."

"But I know your pain." Again, a choked-back sob.

"You, too?" I asked. "Do you want to talk about it?"

"No." Pause. "Yes."

"Please, tell me whatever you'd like. It will stay just between you and me."

A loud growl reverberated through the darkness. I flinched.

"Oh, my," Eve said, "what was that?"

"I don't know. A tiger, maybe."

"Close?"

"I don't think so. Relax. I don't think they'd growl if they were stalking something." I had no idea, of course, but didn't want to frighten Eve. I allowed my hand to drift to the .45 in my shoulder holster. Not that it would do any good against a big cat.

We remained quiet for several minutes, but the growl didn't recur. And the forest noises didn't change. I guessed we were okay.

"Go ahead, Eve," I said, "talk to me. Please."

She drew a long, quiet breath, then began. "I had a fiancé, a Navy ensign. He was assigned to the *West Virginia* at Pearl. He died in the attack." She let loose a heavy sob, this time not trying to hold it back.

"That's okay, take your time." I waited. I had no idea how I might console her.

She sucked in another long, slow gulp of air, then continued. "On the day of the attack, I was pulling a shift at Tripler General Hospital. The casualties came streaming in. Nurses and medics, both Army and Navy, worked side by side with civilian nurses and doctors. We couldn't keep up.

"We ran short of instruments, sutures, bandages. Doctors doing surgery passed scissors back and forth from one table to another. Good grief, we used cleaning rags as face masks and didn't have enough gloves. It was appalling."

"I can't imagine," I said, holding my voice low, at what I hoped was a comforting level.

"My fiancé, Will, was one of the casualties. I held Will's hand as he passed away on an operating gurney."

She stopped talking, lost in her sad memories, I supposed.

"I'm sorry," I said. What else could I say? We sat in silence for quite some time, each adrift in the storm-tossed sea of loss.

Eve broke the silence between us. "And I plead guilty to the Ice Queen label," she whispered. "There were too many officers, after Will passed, eager to offer me 'six inches of comfort,' if you know what I mean."

I did, but kept my mouth shut.

"Finally, a senior Army officer, assuming I was 'pussy on the hoof,' or whatever you guys call it, forced himself on me. Told me it's what I needed and would be forever grateful." ˋ

"He raped you?"

"Yes."

"Well, shit. Did you report him?"

"Are you kidding me? Accuse a field-grade officer of rape. Who'd believe a nurse? His word against mine. Besides, I wanted to keep my job. I can't *fight* the Japanese, but I can do my part to help the war effort. Anyhow, that's how I became a bitter, cynical witch."

"You're a captain in the United States Army," I said crisply, correcting her. "A very capable one."

"Yes?"

"As long as you're on my crew, you aren't a bitter, cynical witch. You're all I've got. You're my partner. And I don't team up with witches. Okay?"

She didn't respond verbally. But, in a strange turn of events, I felt her reach for my hand. I grasped it. She leaned against me. We fell asleep that way. But there was nothing romantic or sexual in our closeness—just a pair of wounded souls searching for peace.

I woke up before she did and crept away in the golden-gray light that precedes sunrise. I peed, then stepped back onto the rutted road to return to the pond and refill the canteen.

I hadn't taken more than a few steps when I spotted something and pulled up short, my heart hammering a million beats per minute. I reached slowly for my .45 and thumbed off the safety.

20

The northern Burma rainforest

A tiger, eyeing me, crouched in the morning mist near the entrance to the game trail leading to the pond. The huge striped beast made no move in my direction. I hoped he—she? —might be more thirsty than hungry. The only motion was the animal's tail, twitching slowly, almost casually, in the thin, gray light. The only sound: my own rapid breathing. The birds and monkeys, likely fearing for their own safety, had fallen silent, not willing to reveal their presence to the tiger.

I slowly brought the Colt to bear on the cat, though I knew I could never stop him if he decided on breakfast before beverage. Besides, he remained just beyond the effective range of my pistol, about forty yards from me.

I should have thought of a funny line, like "nice kitty," but I was too damn scared. I held the .45 in a two-handed grip, but my arms still quivered ever so slightly.

We watched one another for ten or fifteen seconds, my heart beating like a runaway metronome.

Without warning, the tiger stood.

I reflexively pulled the trigger, my arms jerking skyward from the gun's recoil as it fired.

A brilliantly colored bird tumbled from a tree ten feet over the tiger's head.

The tiger, like a ghost, disappeared into the forest.

Great. So I'd scared the tiger, shot a bird, and alerted every damn Jap within ten miles of us.

I sprinted back to where Eve waited.

"What—"

"Grab your stuff. We gotta go. I just sent an audiogram to the Japs."

She looked at me askance, but did as I commanded.

"I'll explain later. You feeling okay?"

"I'll make it. Partner." She flashed me a smile that carried more amiability than I'd ever seen from her.

We set off along the road at a vigorous clip.

"Go ahead of me. Keep moving. I'm gonna scoot down to the pond and refill the canteen. I didn't get around to doing that earlier."

I caught up with her in about five minutes.

"Water," I said, "drink lots of water. Keep yourself hydrated."

Fortunately, a few puffy clouds already dotted the sky, suggesting a return to the more normal cloudiness and maybe a thunderboomer or two by afternoon. I decided a soaking downpour would be preferable to the enervating heat of scorching tropical sunshine.

We trudged ahead.

"What happened earlier?" Eve asked. "The gunshot?"

"Tyger, tyger, burning bright," I responded.

"That sounds like a line from a poem I once read in college."

Eve stumbled over a tree root in the road, but kept upright

and continued moving.

"By William Blake. It's in a book my buddy Zim gave me."

"Zim?"

I told her about Zim. His love of poetry. His love of fishing. His death.

"Another loss," she said gently.

"Yes," I answered. I didn't wish to dwell upon it, so I changed the subject. "And this morning, I met the 'fearful symmetry' Blake wrote about in his poem."

"You met a tiger?" Surprise registered in her voice.

I related my adventure to her.

She laughed as I finished the tale. "You shot a bird?"

"'Fraid so."

"My great white hunter."

"The birds don't think so."

We plodded on, the old road gaining in elevation as it circled the periphery of a hill.

"You mentioned college, Eve," I said. "Where did you go?"

"Montana State in Bozeman. I was in the School of Nursing."

"Did you grow up in Montana?"

"No, Minneapolis. But there weren't any places near there to get a good education in nursing."

"My hometown, Coeur d'Alene, Idaho, isn't that far from Bozeman."

"Where'd you learn how to fly?"

"Randolph Field in San Antonio. Then the Army let me get behind the controls of a C-47 at Long Beach Army Air Field in California. And before you say it, yes, I probably need a refresher course."

"I wasn't going to say anything."

"Sure you weren't." For the first time, I began to feel comfortable with Nurse Nasty . . . Eve.

We halted for lunch—more chocolate potato shavings—then pushed on. Thickening clouds held the sunshine at bay, so I no longer worried about heat-related problems. But sweat poured off both of us in never-ending streams, so I made sure we kept downing the chloriney water.

By mid-afternoon, I slowed, not because of heat or humidity but because my feet hurt.

"You're limping," Eve said. "Let me take a look at your feet."

"No, we have to keep moving."

"If your feet get damaged, we aren't going to be moving at all. Listen to me, Major. I get to be the boss now. It's a medical issue."

So we halted in a small grassy patch abutting the road. I pulled off my boots and damp socks and allowed Eve to examine my feet. They didn't look good—swollen and blotchy. The soles, layered in pale, wrinkled skin, itched and tingled. Blisters dotted my heels.

"Trench foot," Eve said. "Not good. Look, I know the Japanese are looking for us, but we need to stop, build a fire, and dry out your socks and feet. Otherwise, you're going to be battling gangrene."

I knew she was right, but stopping terrified me, not that I would tell her.

"I'm going to go search for sticks and twigs," she said, "something to get a fire started with."

"Wait." I felt in my pants pocket to make sure my cigarette lighter hadn't abandoned me. I found it, clicked it several times, and a tiny orange flame appeared. "Okay, go search. You want my .45?" I extended it to her.

She waved it off. "Not my calling. I patch people up, not put holes in them."

"You might feel differently if somebody were trying to put a hole in you."

"I won't go far. I'll be back shortly." She glided into the rainforest.

While I waited for her return, I picked a few leeches off me, brushed away some very large ants, and swatted at mosquitoes and fleas. I listened to the sounds around me, seeing if I could detect anything other than the typical jungle clamor. Once I thought I heard some distant shouts and maybe a gunshot, but wasn't sure. Perhaps I was trying too hard to hear something that didn't belong. Still, I had the unnerving sense we were being watched. But again, I wasn't sure. How could I be when my vision was limited to no more than a few dozen yards and the chatter of animals and birds overwhelmed everything else? More likely, it was my imagination gnawing on latent fears, attempting to awaken them and plunge me into a frenzy of irrational actions. I rested the .45 on my lap. I felt so damn helpless.

Time seemed to crawl. Eve didn't return. I didn't like it. I holstered my weapon and reached for my socks. I needed to find her.

"What are you doing?" Her voice startled me. She'd approached from the opposite direction she'd departed toward. She carried an armful of tiny branches and dry bamboo stalks.

"Getting ready to search for you. I was worried."

"How nice. But I can take care of myself, Major. Just because I'm a woman doesn't mean I'm incapable of doing some heavy lifting once in a while."

"Forgive me for being worried. This isn't exactly summer picnic territory."

She dropped the kindling in front of me. "I know. Sorry."

"How about we just look out for each other without

reading something more into it than we're a team trying to survive in hostile territory?"

"Fair enough."

"You look a bit frazzled. How'd it go?"

She looked away from me. "I was scared."

"Because?"

"Shadows."

"What kind of shadows?"

"Just dark forms I thought I saw moving in the trees. Animals probably."

"Probably." But I shared her apprehensions. I decided not to mention mine, however.

We got a smoky little fire going, and Eve set out to retrieve bigger chunks of wood. She returned more quickly this time. In a few minutes, we had a bigger blaze popping and crackling and emitting genuine heat.

Eve stripped off her boots and socks, too. We draped our socks over short bamboo stakes and placed them as close to the fire as we dared. Following her instructions, I moved my feet closer to the flames to get them dried out and warmed up.

"Do it carefully," she cautioned. "Too fast and they'll turn red and hurt. Let it happen gradually."

She fed me some aspirin from the med kit, along with an atabrine tablet, the anti-malaria drug. She took one, too. Nice to have a nurse as your teammate.

The far-off roll of thunder suggested rain would soon be stalking us. Eve managed to get our trusty ol' parachute rigged as ground cover and a tent in our cramped "camping ground" and we prepared to spend the night. I didn't like being so close to the road, as unused as it might be, but I fully understood I had to get my feet in better shape before we pressed on.

We kept stoking the fire with short bamboo stalks and it continued to emit just enough heat to warm my feet and dry our socks. My feet ached as they warmed, but additional aspirin tablets helped alleviate the pain.

"What are you going to do after the war?" I asked.

"Find a job in a hospital, I guess," Eve said. "Someplace not in the tropics. And you?"

"Apparently you didn't like my idea of me becoming a beautician."

"I couldn't recommend you."

"Well, then, I don't know. I've never really thought about it." In truth, I hadn't. After Trish died, my future seemed to have, also. Maybe I assumed the war would take care of everything, that there wouldn't be a future for me to be concerned with, that Major Rod Shepherd, United States Army Air Forces, would be just a memory, another KIA.

At some point, I fell asleep. I remember rain pattering down, but not much. Thunder echoed through the jungle like far-off artillery blasts, the rolling thumps leaping over valleys and bouncing off hilltops, but it seemed more soothing than frightening.

I thought I heard Eve stir in the darkness once, but she settled down quickly and resumed her silent sleep.

Dawn crept into our little encampment slowly, heavy clouds holding the sunlight in check and, along with the dense rainforest canopy, preventing daylight from reaching the jungle floor until after the sun had been about its business for several hours.

I sat up, rubbed my eyes, and looked for Eve.

Gone.

Gone? Why in the hell would she be gone?

Forgetting my feet hurt, I stood. "Eve," I yelled. "Captain Johannsen, where are you?"

No response. Okay, she went to gather more wood, I told myself. Relax.

Fifteen minutes passed. I hollered for Eve again. Nothing.

That's when I spotted drag marks, and numerous foot-prints, on the muddy road. Shit.

Japs? Headhunters?

Shit, shit, shit.

I pulled on my socks and boots and made sure I still had my .45. I noted that whoever had snatched Eve had copped her socks, boots, and med kit, too.

I scrambled to the road and examined the footprints. They hadn't been made by shoes or boots. Not Japs, then. Besides, if they had been made by Japs, I wouldn't be standing here examining them.

Without wasting time to retrieve the parachute, I set off, following the tracks. If they stayed on the road, I could give chase. If not . . .

The body snatchers hadn't remained on the road long. I shortly reached a trail that crossed the road at right angles, running up and down the hill—actually, a decent-sized mountain. Eve and her captors had apparently gone up.

The path, narrow and walled with heavy jungle growth on both sides, would be perfect for an ambush. Obviously, natives had grabbed Eve, but who's to say they weren't Jap sympathizers and had the slant-eyed little bastards lying in wait for me.

I drew my .45, held it at my side, thumbed off the safety, and moved as rapidly as I could along the track.

At least my socks had dried, but the blisters still pinched.

By late morning, I'd reached the top of the mountain and popped out into an area that boasted only a thin stand of scrubby trees. I looked in all directions, but could see only the tops of other hills. Clouds, like gray rivers, poured through gaps and tumbled down hillsides, spilling into the valleys below and hiding them beneath thick, slate-colored blankets.

I felt as if I were the only being on earth. Even the sounds of the jungle seemed subdued up here.

There were no signs of humans—nurses, headhunters, or Japs.

I sat and buried my face in my hands. Lost.

21

The northern Burma rainforest

I don't know how many minutes I sat on the hilltop, but I knew I couldn't remain there long. Three trails descended the mountain. One I'd just come up. That left the other two as options on which to continue my search. There were no clues as to which one Eve and her captors had taken. At least no clues obvious to me. The ground had dried, so no fresh footprints were visible. I attempted to spot recently broken twigs or trampled grass, but quickly realized my tracking skills were probably no better than Helen Keller's.

I needed a different approach, a different way to choose my course. So I opted to follow the path that seemed to point in a more northerly direction, simply because it led most directly away from the Japs, who were surely on my tail.

I'd come to the conclusion that the natives who'd snatched Eve likely weren't in cahoots with the Japs, otherwise I probably would have been fishing with Zim somewhere in the next world by now. On the other hand, I hated to think about why Eve might have been grabbed in the first place.

True, I hadn't heard of any of our guys ever being harmed by headhunters. But what if the sight of a blond-haired, white-skinned female brought our native friends visions of a never-before-seen trophy to be proudly displayed above a mantel, or wherever they preferred to exhibit lopped-off heads?

It seemed bad enough I had to dodge Japs, but now I might have to deal with pissed-off headhunters if I tried to take their prize from them. Assuming I ever found them.

Going downhill, not surprisingly, turned out to be a lot easier than moving in the other direction. One thing about the rainforest natives, they didn't bother cutting trails around the periphery of mountains. They apparently had decided the quickest way up and down hills were straight lines. No fooling around using the contours of the land to make ascents and descents easier. In fact, a couple of times I got moving a little too fast and stumbled over hidden roots and rocks in the trail, a wonderful way to aggravate sore feet.

Even going downhill, perspiration soaked my tattered uniform. It wasn't so much the heat as the suffocating jungle humidity that sapped my body of hydration . . . and energy. I swallowed the last drops of water from my canteen and realized I'd better find a refill for it pretty quickly.

I continued down the trail. Shortly, the sound of rushing water reached my ears. A stream, I assumed. I could hear it but not see it. The path swung to the left, away from the sound. I turned around and retraced my steps, looking for a break in the underbrush that might lead to the water. I found one, sort of. It appeared old, unused, and overgrown with vines and bushes. Time for the machete.

I hacked my way through the rainforest, slow progress. But I needed water. I stopped to wipe away the sweat sheathing my face. Another sound reached me, one I didn't recognize. It seemed a cross between a hiss and a growl. *What the hell?*

I crouched motionless. Listening. Searching.

Oh. My. God.

It stood—maybe not the correct term—less than six feet in front of me, hard to spot in the tangle of the jungle. Brown with a yellowish underside. Huge, its back half on the ground, its forward portion reared above me, and the hood on its head spread to the size of a small kite. A king cobra. I'd seen them in Calcutta. Snake charmers may have defanged them, but this guy could kill me in a flash.

I remained still, the only moving part of me, my chest, heaving in and out. I wondered if I could ease my hand to my .45. Maybe. But if I was wrong . . . Not worth the try, I decided. So I waited. Or more to the point, *we* waited, the king and I. Quite a while. He didn't strike and I didn't move. My leg muscles began to cramp. Bad enough. But I didn't like losing time, either. Whoever had snatched Eve was putting even more distance between me and them. And the Japs, I had to guess, were gaining ground.

Finally, the snake lowered itself from its en garde position and slithered away into the rainforest. I got my breathing under control and resumed my push toward the as yet unseen stream . . . very, very carefully.

After another ten minutes, I reached it. The water appeared clearer and fresher than most I'd encountered so far, but I still jammed a couple of purification tabs into the canteen.

I began my climb back toward the road, begrudging the time I'd lost. Of course, just when I thought things couldn't get any worse, they did. A Jap patrol had overtaken me. Like the stream, I heard them before I saw them. Five of them, striding along the road, canteens and swords jangling softly on their hips. They carried rifles and sidearms.

I lay prone on the side trail, hidden by jungle growth, and

watched the enemy soldiers move past. To be honest, I felt
utterly defeated. The Japs had caught up with me—I guessed I
hadn't been a difficult quarry to track—and I still didn't know
where Eve was, or even if I was following the right path to find
her. I lowered my face to the jungle mud. Might as well let the
ants and leeches have me. I didn't know what the hell else
to do.

But getting a Purple Heart for being eaten by bugs and
worms seemed a really bad idea. I realized I had to do something rather than lie in a rainforest. I considered backtracking,
climbing back up the mountain and taking the other trail
down, more toward the west, toward Assam. But who's to say
the Japs hadn't sent some scouts in that direction, too? And
besides, I still felt in my gut that Eve and her kidnappers had
taken the road I'd been following. I made up my mind. I
picked myself off the ground and headed north. If I had to face
both Japs and headhunters, so be it.

Late afternoon arrived, and once again thunder rolled over
the rugged, green landscape of the Burmese rainforest. The
clouds lowered and, like amorphous gray schooners, sailed
over the jungle canopy. Rain would surely follow. Anything to
make my life more miserable. But, I decided, it wasn't my life
that mattered. It was Eve's. She remained my command
responsibility. Not only that, but I felt a personal connection to
her. Not a romantic one, certainly, but one of shared loss.

In addition, she'd suffered at the hands of superior officers, one in particular who'd sullied the ideal of being an
officer *and* a gentleman. Perhaps I harbored some sort of
chivalrous fantasy that I could atone for that. More likely, I'd
just end up getting killed. But as Eve had once said, no one
ever guaranteed the odds would be in our favor when we
signed up for the military.

Big rain drops splattered down on me. I tilted my head

toward the sky and opened my mouth. Pure, fresh water flooded into it. I stood on the road like a statue, sucking in sustenance from the heavens.

The heaviest of the downpour skirted where I stood, however, and instead hammered into the jungle some distance to my right. Still, it muddied the track I was on and once again slowed my progress.

After the rain ceased, I figured there'd be only a couple of hours of daylight remaining. Then I'd be stranded in the blackness with no shelter. I began to think of my *basha* back in Chabua as a Ritz-Carlton hotel. I trudged on, hoping I wouldn't inadvertently come upon the Jap patrol from the rear. Or walk into an ambush. I tried to move silently, but squishing through mud isn't a particularly quiet endeavor.

I stopped and shaved a few more slices off the barely eatable Army Hersey bar for dinner and began munching. But I should have been scanning, not chewing. I realized too late I'd just partaken of my "last supper."

The Jap came up silently behind me. He rammed the business end of a rifle into the back of my neck and shouted something unintelligible. I slipped what was left of the chocolate into my shirt pocket and slowly raised my hands and placed them on top of my head.

Other Japs stepped from the forest, self-satisfied sneers on one or two of their faces. Their leader—whether an officer or not, I had no idea—stepped in front of me, a pistol in his hand, and yelled something at me.

"I don't speak Jap," I said, hoping my voice didn't betray my fear.

He yelled again, waved his pistol in my face, then stepped back and holstered it. He motioned another soldier forward, a big guy with a round face whose short-billed cloth cap appeared about three sizes too small. He stepped close to me, grinned, removed my .45, examined it with a practiced eye, then handed it to the guy in charge.

The boss man nodded, then spoke to the soldier in firm, even tones.

The soldier responded, "*Hai*," or something of the sort, and withdrew a sword from a scabbard on his waist. He tested the sharpness of its blade, about two feet long and curved, on his thumb. It drew blood. He wiped it off on his pants.

I had a pretty good idea what was coming. I stared at the Jap commander. Trying to keep my voice steady, I said, "I'm an American officer. I'm a prisoner of war. You can't just execute me."

The Jap merely shrugged.

"Geneva Convention," I said, enunciating the words clearly, slowly.

The Jap smiled and responded to me in Japanese, probably telling me he didn't understand, or that Japan had signed the Geneva Convention but never ratified it, which I had heard was true. So the stipulations of the convention would do me no good.

The commander motioned me onto my knees.

I remained standing. "How about a smoke?" I asked. "A last smoke?" I puffed out my lips as if exhaling smoke from a cigarette. Anything to prolong the advent of my death. Maybe delay it just long enough for Jesus's Second Coming. Something.

The Jap appeared puzzled. I slowly—very slowly— removed my right hand from my head and dropped it to my lips. I mimicked smoking a cigarette.

"Lucky Strike?" I said. "Chesterfield?" I felt sick to my stomach. I didn't want my life to end in a Burmese jungle.

The commander shrugged and conferred with a couple of his troops. One of them pulled a pack of Jap cigarettes from his damp shirt and handed it to the boss. The leader approached me, gave me the ciggy, then lit it once I had it between my lips. He stepped back, drew his sidearm, and waited as I took several long drags. My hand shook. The cigarette didn't taste much different from ours. Not that it mattered.

I took slow, deep inhalations as the cigarette burned down. I closed my eyes and tried to pray, though it seemed pointless at this stage, the last moments of my life on earth. I took a final pull from the cigarette and dropped the butt onto the sodden road.

I considered charging the guy with the gun. Why not go down fighting? I tensed, ready to launch myself. But too late. Someone to my rear grabbed my arms, pulled them behind me and, with a slim cord, knotted my wrists together. Next came my ankles. The Japs had done this before, I decided, and knew how to immobilize their victims.

The Jap in charge, using his pistol, once again motioned me to kneel. It would be futile to resist, I decided. I lowered my knees onto the ground. I felt like asking if the big guy's sword was sharp enough so that one swipe would do it, but I couldn't fit the words together.

The commander stepped forward and pushed my head down, exposing the back of my neck. He said something to my executioner in low tones. The leader moved back from me, and the guy with the sword positioned himself to my side. He rested the blade against my neck, lifted it, moved back a half step, then placed it on my neck again. Measuring.

He lifted it one last time. The commander began a count-down—I guess that's what it was—rhythmic Japanese words, firm but soft.

Oh, God.

22

The northern Burma rainforest

A soft grunt reached my ears. The executioner's sword hit me on the back, not from a downward stroke but more as if it had been dropped. I chanced a glance to my side. The big Jap had collapsed to the ground, an arrow—yes, an arrow—sticking out of his chest.

Someone near me yelled. I looked up. The patrol's leader staggered back from me, his hands clutching at his throat, clawing at a spear that jutted from his neck while bright red blood spurted from a deep wound the weapon had opened.

What the hell?

More shouting. Japanese. A couple of shots rang out as the remaining Jap soldiers fired at whoever had ambushed them. Arrows and one or two spears arced through the air and rained down around them. They turned and fled back up the trail. One of the little bastards actually had an arrow sticking out of his butt.

I kept my head down, having no idea what was going on.

Silence ensued.

Then one by one, small, brown men—the attackers—stepped from the surrounding forest. They appeared lithe and muscular—not the kind of muscles toned in a gym, but by hard jungle living. About a dozen in all, they wore only loin cloths and nothing on their feet. A couple of them bore what looked like crossbows, several carried spears, the rest, short knives. Piles of black hair, like little haystacks, wound around their heads. They seemed neither threatening nor friendly, so I had no idea if I'd just been rescued or captured. First thought: headhunters?

The answer came quickly. Yes. Using their short knives, obviously terrifyingly sharp, they went to work on the dead Japs, severing their heads from their bodies with quick, practiced strokes.

I turned my gaze away, unable to watch what I'm sure was a common tribal ritual. One of the men, the chief I assumed, approached me and motioned me to stand. He didn't offer me a hand up, just gestured. He appeared older than the others. Three feathers protruded from his thick hair, and he wore a necklace adorned with tiny, carved wooden heads—some animal, some human. Like campaign ribbons, I suppose.

I struggled to my feet. Difficult to do with both my hands and feet bound. The guy, almost a head shorter than me, stepped closer. He ran an appraising gaze over me, then looked directly into my eyes and said, "Jeye?" or something of the sort. I had no idea what he was asking. One thing I knew for sure, I didn't want to piss off these guys.

Having no other ideas, I said, "Thank you," and smiled.

He didn't acknowledge my gratitude, probably didn't even understand it. He turned and babbled something to the men around him. One of them stepped forward and untied me.

The native leader tried again. "Jeye?"

I shrugged. I decided on a different approach. I gestured at the silver wings pinned to my shirt. "Ah-mere-eh-can pie-lot," I said slowly, then pointed at the sky.

The chief looked up, then back at me. "Ahmoodicun?"

Close enough. "Yes, Ahmoodicum. Good guy."

The leader's expression—neutral—didn't change. He pointed at the wings I wore, then at himself.

I think I got it. I unpinned the wings from my shirt and handed them to him. A goodwill gift, I hoped.

For the first time, he smiled, a semi-toothless grin of gratitude. He held the wings aloft like an Olympic trophy. His troops let out grunts and "umms" and various other sounds of approval. I guessed I'd just scored a victory. I grinned back.

But I desperately needed to find out something else.

"Ahmoodicum woman?" I asked.

Blank stares in response.

"Woman? Female? Girl?"

More blank stares.

Time for some artwork. I picked up a twig and knelt in the mud. Using the twig, I sketched a stick figure that included long hair down to its shoulders. Then I drew two big circles on its chest area. Boobs. Maybe this is where being a well-endowed female might pay off.

I pointed at my crude drawing. "Woman," I said.

The little brown men gathered around and examined the artwork.

Several of them nodded, including the chief. "Woomun," he repeated.

"You have?" I asked.

He gave me a squinty-eyed glare, one I didn't know how to interpret.

He turned and walked away from me, heading down the road. His men followed, two of them transporting the severed heads that continued to ooze blood and trail connective tissue.

The bodies of the slain Japs remained sprawled on the ground, already attracting flies, ants, and a swarm of other carnivorous insects. Small animals peeked from the jungle, awaiting their turn at the dinner table for an unexpected feast.

The scene repelled me. I assumed that only the bones of the dead men would remain by morning. I stood, confused. I guess I'd saved my head, maybe ensured peace—thanks to my "gift"—with a potential enemy, but apparently hadn't made any real friends. Were these guys just going to leave me here?

No. I'd already made up my mind about that. I plucked my .45 from the dead Jap leader's belt, brushing away swarms of bugs in the process. I took his sidearm and sword, and snatched a rifle from the body of my would-be executioner. I set off after the headhunters, only to find them waiting for me. Apparently, they just assumed I had enough sense to follow them.

I did, but had trouble keeping up. They moved at a pace I found unimaginable, even though it was mostly downhill. Then the trail started up again. The next mountain. Soon the little headhunters disappeared from view, easily outdistancing me. I found myself alone in the jungle. Again—sweating, discouraged, and surrounded by grunts, yowls, and squawks. And of course, leeches. I stopped. I picked them off me, those I could reach, and wondered if I'd need a blood transfusion if and when I got back to civilization.

I trudged on, dragging my feet instead of lifting them. Exhaustion seemed to lurk behind every step, but I willed myself to keep moving. Eventually, the trail leveled. It became broader and a bit more well-trodden. I soon discovered why. More traffic.

Young children, totally naked, scurried alongside of me, laughing and giggling. Women moved along the trail, too, some carrying babies, others transporting wood in backpacks woven of leaves and fastened by a strap to their head. They were more fully clothed than the men with colorful skirts wrapped around their midsections, and strips of cloth, similar to the men's loincloths, swathing the upper portions of their bodies. They shot me curious stares, but went about their business. Obviously, I was nearing a village.

A boy, perhaps twelve years old, give or take a year, began walking alongside of me. He touched my hand. "G.I.?" he said.

I stopped. "You know English?"

"Little bit."

"From where?"

"G.I. here. Brit men, too."

"G.I. here now?" I decided I'd better keep my sentences simple.

"No."

"Recently?"

The boy cocked his head.

"Uh, he here but go?"

"Yes, he go. Big bird drop boxes. More G.I. come, take him."

A rescue party. Well, I now knew these guys were friendly, at least if you didn't have slanty eyes.

"No like Japs?"

The boy scowled. "Many Jap come. Kill men. Hurt women. Take food. Burn huts. Naga kill Japs, take heads."

Naga? So these were the Naga people I'd heard about. Headhunters. Ethnic to the hills of Assam and northwest Burma. They obviously loathed Japs and sought revenge. That's probably why I was saved. Not that the Naga had any great affinity for G.I.s, but that they hated Japs with a great passion.

And G.I.s? I realized that's what the chief had been trying to ask me when he kept repeating. "Jeye?" Learn as you go. But there remained something else I had to learn. Quickly.

"Woman here?" I asked.

"Many." The boy gestured at those walking by.

"No. G.I. woman. Special woman."

"Specshul?"

"Different. Hair like . . . sunshine."

The kid's eyes lit up. "Okay. She here."

At last, good news. "We go?"

"Okay. We go."

"You have name?" I asked. "Me Rod."

"Tommy," he said. Obviously, the Brits had got to him first.

He strode off in the direction of what I assumed would be his village. A ten-minute walk brought us there, a clearing on the rounded top of a mountain. About a score of houses or huts—I wasn't sure what they should be called—comprised the settlement. The women seemed busy with cooking fires and food preparation. Several were using large stones to pound rice. The men were gathered around a large pot full of water suspended over a fire pit. Tommy and I arrived just in time to see them drop the Jap heads into the pot. Not the kind of interment I expected Japanese soldiers had hoped for.

Two or three big, black water buffalo wandered around the village, and about a dozen animals that looked like large, ugly pigs wallowed in mud holes. I guess the Naga didn't lack for meat. Chickens strutted about, too, pecking at the ground. A few scrawny dogs lay listlessly in shady spots.

The houses sat on slender log pilings about ten feet tall. You accessed the huts via stairways constructed of notches that had been slashed into larger logs. I supposed the elevation of the homes kept them dry and made it difficult for enemies, if they had any, to sneak up on them.

I assumed there were enemies about, other than the Japs,

because I noticed a wooden platform that extended out from the mountain and offered a panoramic view of the landscape below. A Naga warrior with a spear appeared to be performing lookout duty. A primitive-looking drum sat on the platform next to him. For a fleeting moment, I wondered if the Nagas could be trained as weather observers. Maybe we could teach them how to operate Gibson Girl radio transmitters so they could relay their reports to us. But I had more immediate concerns.

Tommy led me to the head man, who turned out to be the guy I'd labeled "chief" earlier when the Nagas had ambushed the Japs. Tommy referred to him as King Kalakeya, then spoke to him in what I assumed was the Naga language. I heard my name, Rod, mentioned a couple of times, so I guessed I was being introduced.

The king, standing near the big pot where the Jap heads were boiling, listened respectfully. When Tommy had finished, the king grinned at me and said something in Naga.

"The king greets you," Tommy said.

I nodded at Kalakeya and said, "Glad to make your acquaintance. Thanks for saving my ass . . . my head." Tommy stared. "Tell him thank you," I said to Tommy.

A strange odor, sweet but repugnant, wafted from the boiling water. I hoped the king wouldn't offer me any soup.

He babbled something in Naga again.

"The king says you welcome here," Tommy translated. "You may stay many sunrises."

I wasn't interested in a prolonged visit. I wanted to get reunited with Eve and get the hell back to Chabua.

"Tommy, listen. Ask King Kalakeya about woman with hair like sunshine, okay?"

Tommy smiled and spoke to the king.

The king responded with a long speech. I watched

Tommy's smile gradually fade and morph into an expression of dismay. Something was wrong.

"The king invites you to his home," Tommy said.

No, he said more than that. "Where is woman?"

"Come," Tommy said, and marched off toward the biggest hut in the village, the king leading the way. I guessed if I was going to learn more about Eve, I had to go along.

The hut turned out to be surprisingly large inside with three rooms, front to back. The first room appeared to be sort of a living room or parlor. The next room was obviously a communal sleeping area with bamboo beds hanging from the ceiling like hammocks. The back room, I guessed, was a cooking and eating space. A small fire on sand or fine gravel flickered in the center of the room. The smoke rose through a series of crude bamboo shelves suspended from a thatched roof on vines. Some of the jury-rigged shelving held meat, and reminded me of how damned hungry I was. I just didn't want any soup.

The king seemed quite proud of a sort of "trophy case" near the rear of the room. My heart missed about half a dozen beats when I saw it. A wooden rack with skulls—animals, birds, and yes, humans. Some of the bird skulls were quite large with protruding beaks. Maybe vultures. On the wall next to the rack were the skulls of what appeared to be water buffalo, horns and all.

Both repulsed and fearful, I stepped closer to the rack to examine the human heads, some with fuzzy tufts of hair still clinging to their skulls. Surely the Nagas wouldn't have decapitated a woman who'd done them no harm. Surely. I scanned the display carefully, looking for a tuffet that might have belonged to a blond. I saw nothing that suggested that, although I didn't know if blond hair would retain its color after being boiled.

Jesus, I couldn't believe the situation I found myself in. In a headhunter's hut in a Burmese jungle, scanning a display case for a nurse's skull, and wondering in the back of my mind if the Japanese, bent on revenge, weren't mounting an even larger force to go Naga hunting. I was an Army Air Forces transport pilot and weather officer, for God's sake, not a damn National Geographic Society rainforest explorer. How on earth had I gotten here?

King Kalakeya gestured for me to sit on the floor on a mat of woven leaves. I did, and the king and Tommy joined me. I wanted to get right to the point. I wanted to know where Eve was, and how she was. But the king had other ideas. I decided I'd better adhere to his protocols if I didn't want to end up memorialized in his trophy case. But I remained impatient. And hungry.

Kalakeya—I began to think of him as Kally—produced a hollowed-out bamboo pole maybe two feet long and a couple of inches in diameter. He filled it with water, then added some ground-up brown stuff. I didn't want to know what it was.

He inserted one end of the pole in the fire and propped the other end on a forked stick. One of the women in the hut handed bamboo cups to us. I assumed Kally was brewing some sort of jungle tea.

He was. He poured a cupful for Tommy and me. I sipped, choked back a gag, and smiled. It tasted awful, like boiled tobacco mixed with sawdust. Tommy glanced at me, smacked his lips, and I followed suit . . . hoping I had lips left to smack. The king seemed pleased. Then my stomach growled, loudly, probably sounding akin to a hungry tiger on the prowl.

The king called out to the woman who'd delivered our cups. In short order, I had a large green leaf on my lap, heaped with smoldering meat. Roasted monkey. I could tell it was monkey. Let me just say the Naga don't bother with skinning and cleaning. They obviously just toss their daily special into the fire, whole, and let it sizzle. But I was so blasted hungry, it didn't faze me. I ripped off the monkey's fuzzy outer covering and chowed down. Best monkey I'd ever had. I let out a soft belch of appreciation after I'd finished. The king smiled and poured me more tea. Thank God he didn't offer any soup.

To add to the ambience of my Burmese dining, something soft and diaphanous sifted down on me from above. I looked up. Pieces of soot tumbled from the ceiling, where the fire's smoke had blackened the grass thatching. Part of urban living in Nagaland, I supposed.

I turned to Tommy. "Thank King Kally—Kalakeya—for my dinner. But ask about woman with sunshine hair. I her chief. Must know." I couldn't come up with a better explanation at the moment.

The young boy and the king engaged in an extended conversation. After they'd finished, Tommy turned to me. I could read trepidation in his eyes.

I nodded at him to go ahead, to tell me what the king had said. His first words hammered me with a gut punch. I just about lost my dinner.

23

The northern Burma rainforest
A Naga village

"Sunshine woman no here," Tommy said, averting his gaze from mine.

"What?" I exclaimed. How could she not be here? Tommy had seen her. She couldn't have arrived more than an hour or two before I did.

"She leave."

"Leave where? Go where?" Surely not on her own.

Tommy and I spent the next half hour in a pidgin English conversation intermixed with stick figure drawings in the sand near the fire. King Kally watched us with detached interest while he puffed on a shabby-looking pipe filled with what I assumed was opium.

I learned that Eve had been taken to a nearby village and given to the chief there as a "peace offering." Kally's tribe and this other village had been at war for quite some time, and the king thought that by offering a unique female, Eve, to the chief of the other tribe as a gift, hostilities would cease.

I hated to think what this opposition chief might have in mind for Eve. As a wife who would bear him special children? Her head as a distinctive trophy to be mounted on a stake outside his hut? Whatever it was, I knew I had to find her as rapidly as possible. She'd suffered enough trauma in her young life. She certainly didn't need this.

"You take me to village?" I asked Tommy.

He looked to the king, but with glazed eyes, Kally appeared to have drifted away from us, off to another world.

Tommy shrugged. "Maybe sunrise."

Tomorrow? "No. Now."

Tommy shook his head. "Dark. Danger. No walk."

He was right, of course. Besides, I was drained of energy. Everything hurt. I needed rest. Tommy ushered me to one of the suspended bamboo beds in the sleeping area. I clambered in. But the thing turned out to be damned uncomfortable, unforgivingly hard . . . and squeaky. Between that and wallowing in concern over Eve, sleep came and went in spurts. I awoke before dawn, unrefreshed.

I crept outside to pee. At least one thing seemed promising. Like high-altitude fireflies, a billion stars twinkled overhead in a pristine sky. Not a cloud to be seen. A refreshing breeze caressed the mountaintop. Perhaps the soggy southwest monsoon had at last retreated to its winter abode, allowing the dry northeast flow from the cool-season high pressure over Mongolia to grab a toehold in east Asia.

At least that's how my meteorological mind worked. On a more practical level, I knew clear weather would allow Blackie's Gang to get in the air and perhaps begin a search for the medevac C-47 that never reached Chabua. Of course, the search and rescue guys might find the crashed bird, but would have no idea that Eve and I had escaped. I'd need to find a way to signal them.

Right after I found Eve.

I walked to the lookout platform and sat there waiting for the sun to rise, to explode over Indochina and illuminate the sprawling Burmese rainforest below me. I thought of Zim and I thought of Eve and I thought of Trish. I thought what a waste war was. Whether you fought for good or evil, became the victor or the vanquished, the cost was always extreme on both sides.

And it didn't matter the size of the conflict. I was enmeshed in a world war in which millions would undoubtedly perish. But the only feud that mattered to me now was between two tribes of headhunters in an Asian jungle. It was hardly on the scale of a global fight, but unless I could somehow retrieve the "peace offering" one tribe had made to the other—and hopefully somehow replace it—the cost would still be extreme . . . to Eve, to me.

About an hour after sunrise, Tommy and I, accompanied by two Naga warriors bearing spears, set off for the village Eve had been taken to. I armed myself with my .45, and the Jap pistol and sword I had liberated, but didn't bother with the rifle since it had only a couple of rounds remaining in its magazine.

Whether Tommy had received the king's stamp of approval for this mission, I had no idea. I assumed he had, however, since I doubt he could have recruited the warriors on his own.

We moved at a quick pace, downhill for a while, then back up. Apparently these guys liked to build their towns on mountaintops. That made sense, I guess. Always easier to defend the high ground.

Somewhere near noon I heard the thrum of an aircraft. It didn't sound close, probably off to our north somewhere. I hoped it was one of Blackie's, out looking for my C-47. But it could have been a transport on a routine mission. If it was the search and rescue guys, they would, of course, have had no idea I'd flown well south, into Jap-controlled airspace. Even if they did, they wouldn't dare venture into what was basically enemy territory. But all that I'd worry about later. First, Eve.

We trudged on, swiping the usual sweat and leeches from our bodies. At least the humidity had relented, so the jungle air seemed less oppressive than before. By late afternoon, several men—I assumed from the village we were approaching—fell in behind us. They didn't threaten us, merely followed in silence, bows and arrows slung over their backs.

Like the Nagas I walked with, they were small and brown. But they appeared heavily tattooed. I wondered if that reflected their exploits in battle or how many enemy heads they'd been able to carry home from a raid on an enemy village. God, what a strange, primitive land.

I noticed the two warriors accompanying Tommy and me had become a bit more apprehensive, constantly peering into the forest and casting glances back over their shoulders. Keying off their increased alertness, I slipped my Colt out of its holster and held it near my right thigh. Tommy edged closer to me and brushed against my left hip.

We walked into the village near dusk. It appeared smaller than the one Tommy lived in, maybe a bit less vibrant and active. Surrounded by thick stands of trees, it also lacked the sweeping views of the surrounding landscape that Tommy's possessed.

The inhabitants viewed us with suspicion. No smiles or friendly waves. The children seemed withdrawn. Several scrawny dogs lay listlessly beneath huts. We reached the center of the village and stopped. No one approached us. I didn't see Eve.

Finally, a figure emerged from a hut that looked to be more elaborate than the rest. A heavily tattooed man with a weathered, acne-scarred face walked toward us. He appeared to have what looked like animal incisors or small tusks protruding from his earlobes. On his head of dark, scrambled hair perched what look like a US Army flight cap. I hoped to hell whoever had owned it still had *his* head. I swallowed hard. I kept my hand on my .45, but the guy headed in our direction carried no weapons.

He stopped in front of me and gave me a thorough once-over. Then he rolled out a raspy paragraph or two of words I didn't understand. Tommy translated.

"He say he chief. Sagara is name. He welcome you, but want to know why you come, umm . . . he no ask you to village."

I nodded at Chief Sagara and smiled. "Thank you," I said, and bowed slightly, having no idea if that meant anything to him.

I turned to Tommy. "Tell him I friend. Friend of King Kalakeya who gave him lady with sunshine hair to make peace."

Tommy did. The chief nodded and grinned, displaying more blackened, rotted teeth than good ones.

"Okay," I said to Tommy, "now tell him I friend of lady, want to visit."

Tommy spoke to the chief again, but this time received a frown in response.

I knew what that meant. I plucked my rank insignia, a major's bronze oak leaf, off the right collar of my shirt and handed it to the chief. "I friend," I said.

Tommy repeated my words to him.

The chief nodded, then pointed to the aviation branch badge on my left collar. A hard bargainer. I unpinned the badge and gave it to him.

Holding both emblems in the palm of a calloused hand, he turned them over and over, giving them a close examination. He lifted his head and spoke to Tommy.

"He say okay," Tommy said.

"Now?"

"Sunrise."

"No. Now." This two-bit chief was pissing me off.

"Chief say sunrise."

I startled both Tommy and Chief Sagara by snatching my major's insignia out of the chief's palm. "Now," I barked.

Tommy translated. The chief stared at me. I may have overstepped my bounds. I certainly wasn't on the home field here.

"Tell chief I meant no disrespect . . .uhh, no." Tommy wouldn't know that word. "Tell him he my friend." I handed my rank insignia back to him. "Tell him friend take care of friend and let me see woman. Now. She friend, too. She like queen."

What a bunch of hooey I had to feed this guy. At least I'd elevated Eve from Ice Queen to full queen. Then I realized I might have just stepped on my flopper. I may have made Eve even more valuable to this tinhorn boss by likening her to royalty.

The chief remained silent for a while, then spoke.

After he'd finished, Tommy turned to me. "He say okay. Now. Be short."

Quick, I assumed. I nodded my thanks to Chief Saggy—as I'd begun to think of him—and forced a smile. False gratitude.

He called out to someone unseen. In short order, a grizzled tribesman appeared and beckoned me to follow him.

We moved through the gloaming, accompanied by the chitter of insects, the squeals of monkeys, and even the high-pitched howling scream of a jackal somewhere in the distance. A smoky haze hung over the encampment, the smoke itself bearing the odors of Naga cooking—blackened meat and boiled rice.

The tribesman led me to a small hut that had seen better days. He waited while I mounted the crude stairs to the elevated entrance of the thatched dwelling. I stuck my head into the abode. Dark, no fire, no lighting. I waited a moment while my eyes adjusted.

I spotted a figure curled up in a fetal position on the floor.

"Eve," I called.

No response.

"Eve? Captain Johannsen?"

The figure twitched.

I approached whoever it was, reached out, and rested my hand on her—I hoped—shoulder.

The person flinched, then rolled over to face me.

"Oh, my God, Rod," Eve whispered, "is that you? Really you?"

Rod, not Major Shepherd? "Yes. Are you okay? Did they hurt you?"

"I didn't think . . . didn't think anyone would come . . . I was so frightened . . . so alone." Her words came out raspy and broken and coated in emotion.

"I'm here, Eve. Listen, everything will be okay. I'll take care of you. I'll get you out of here." I didn't have the slightest idea how, of course.

Eve stared. "Rod . . . I . . . Rod . . ." She burst into tears—honest-to-God nonstop sobbing.

Not knowing if it was a good idea, I reached out to her. She struggled to sit, then leaned forward into my embrace, her face buried in my stinking shirt, her tears coming in great torrents. I guess we'd abdicated military discipline.

Eventually, she ceased weeping, pushed away from me, and worked on composing herself. I waited, and asked again, "Are you okay?"

She nodded, wiped her eyes, and ran her fingers through her hair. In the dim light, she looked anything but queenly. She sat on a dirty bamboo mat. Her uniform was mud-stained and torn; her face cut and bruised; and her hair tangled and grimy. I'm sure I appeared no better. On the other hand, we may have looked pretty damned good to each other.

"I'm glad I got my team back," I said, keeping my voice low.

"Can we leave?" she asked.

"There are a few things I have to work out first." What the hell was I going to work out? Even with the small arsenal I carried, we'd quickly end up on the short end of any kind of armed conflict. One .45 and a Jap pistol weren't going to hold off three or four dozen Naga warriors slinging spears and launching arrows.

"Okay," she said. "Please."

"Have you eaten? Do you have water?"

"They gave me some kind of meat," she answered.

"Probably pork." *Probably monkey.*

She gestured at a rough-hewn wooden cup on the mat beside her. "Some water, too."

"You still have purification tablets?"

She nodded.

The warrior who had accompanied me to the hut called out. Time to leave, I guessed. Tommy called my name.

"All right," I said to Eve. "Let me go see what I can do about getting you out of here." I gave her a friendly pat on the shoulder. "I don't know how long it will take, so try to get some rest. Oh, and before I go, I'd like a couple of things. Your nurse's badge and your captain's bars."

"Why?" she said, puzzled.

"Plan A."

"Is there a Plan B?"

"There's barely a Plan A, Eve." I probably should have tried to sound more optimistic, but I think my optimism had been worn to the bone by the events of the last few days. And I really didn't have a *Plan* A. It was more of a vague concept.

I returned to Saggy's hut, but was told he was sleeping. One of the women in the hut suggested I get some rest by climbing into one of the bamboo hammocks. Great. While Chief Saggy snored away dreaming of sunshine-haired women, I got to toss and turn in a concrete bunk trying to add some substance to my half-assed idea to get Eve out of here while both of us retained our heads. And I thought flying the Hump had been dangerous.

I floated in and out of sleep and awoke near dawn to a couple of chickens clucking their way through the hut. My breakfast consisted of a bowl of rice mixed with several pieces of unidentifiable meat. Before I dug into it, I stepped outside and scanned the village grounds to make sure the dogs I'd seen last evening were all still around.

After I ate, with Tommy's help I went in search of the chief. We found him talking with about a dozen members of his tribe, both men and women. There seemed to be some sort of crisis. I sent Tommy closer to the group to find out what was going on.

When the conference broke up, I saw one of the men carrying away a yowling baby who appeared in extreme distress. Probably quite sick. The infant's cries stayed with me as the man disappeared into a hovel.

Tommy returned and explained to me that the baby's

mother had died and the father was unable to feed the child. Nurse him, I guess. I asked Tommy if there weren't other nursing mothers in the village—at least I think I got my question across—who could provide for the baby, but he shook his head no and looked sad. Such is life in a primitive land.

I asked Tommy to get me another meeting with Chief Saggy. He chased after the chief and managed to secure another sit-down with him for me. I thought I'd crafted enough of a scheme, as half-baked as it still was, to get Eve out of here. But Saggy would be the arbiter of that.

We met—me sitting, Tommy standing, Saggy squatting— on a patch of ground covered by a well-worn parachute. I suspected it might have been liberated from either the Americans or Brits. We sipped some more of that wretched tea these guys seemed to love, and I found myself again forcing a smile to overcome my gag reflex.

Chickens, dogs, and children sauntered about, eyeing us with curiosity—well, at least the dogs and children did. The chickens, I suspect, were just searching for something to peck at. The occasional wail of the sick, probably dying infant I'd seen earlier floated through the village on a mountain breeze and reminded me of the aboriginal environment in which I now existed.

I placed Eve's flight nurse's badge and her rank insignia on the blanket, pointed at them, then at Saggy. I spoke to Tommy. "Tell chief gift for him if he give me woman." I had learned the Nagas loved shiny metal trinkets. They seemed as valuable to them as gold nuggets might to Americans.

The chief smiled his crooked, rotten-toothed grin and shook his head, declining my offer . . . as I thought he might. But I'd come prepared to negotiate. I removed my belt, then the brass buckle from the belt, and set it on the blanket. I pointed at it, then at the chief.

He shook his head again. No deal. *Bastard.*

Next move, the Japanese sword I'd taken. The Naga appeared to have little interest in guns, apparently intimidated by them, but more primeval weapons—spears, crossbows, machetes—seemed to pique their interest.

I removed the sword—my ace-in-the-hole—from its sheath and placed it in front of Saggy. He bent his homely, scarred face forward and examined the weapon closely. Its steel blade sparkled in the midday sun, its razor-sharp edge drew blood as he ran his thumb over it, and a dark stain near its tip suggested its lethality.

The chief picked it up, held it aloft, and swung it around his head, perhaps decapitating imaginary enemies. He lowered it and placed it back on the blanket. He spoke to Tommy.

Tommy squatted beside me, disappointment etched on his face. "He say no."

I swallowed hard, stunned. "What? Why? The sword special, make him great warrior."

"He say sunshine woman like Naga princess," Tommy answered. "Bring him much power, like king of kings."

"But the sword. No other like it. Fit for king." I sensed my edge slipping away.

"Sword killed Nagas, he say. No want. Evil."

Great, since the weapon had belonged to a Jap, an enemy, Saggy viewed it as something wicked or dishonorable. Bad karma. My ace-in-the-hole had just fallen victim to its provenance, something I'd never considered.

Jesus, had I just lost Eve? I struggled to breathe, crushed by the sudden turn of events. I felt wrapped in the coils of a python. I lowered my head into my hands, trying to think, to stave off defeat. Would Eve and I have to battle our way out of here after all? Leaving her was not an option, not even a consideration. I made up my mind I would not surrender another soul to whatever lay beyond this world. Trish and Colonel Willis had been enough.

Maybe in the end we all fall victim to fate—maybe there is no divine composition. Perhaps our lives do nothing more than jounce around in a roulette wheel of ultimate destiny in which the house always has the edge.

The cry of the starving baby again reached my ears, adding to the emotional miasma that had engulfed me and now threatened to drown me. But it awakened something in me, too. It lit a candle in the dark tunnel of a black night.

Screw the roulette wheel and the house edge.

I turned to Tommy. "Bring man with sick baby to me. Baby, too. Ask chief to stay here. I promise to give him great power. Bigger power than king of kings. But he must give me woman with sunshine hair."

What is it that men craved even more than treasure and women? Power. With power you can get all the treasure and women you need or want.

I had an idea. If it worked, Saggy would be my buddy for life. If it didn't, I wouldn't have a life left.

24

The northern Burma rainforest
A Naga village

Tommy spoke to the chief, who kind of squinted at me. Puzzlement mixed with suspicion, I suppose.

After he'd finished, Tommy nodded at me, which I took to mean okay.

"One more thing, Tommy," I said. "Tell chief I need to visit woman with sunshine hair again. I will be quick."

Again the nod.

Tommy departed to fetch the man and the baby; I trotted off to Eve's hut.

I found her dozing on her bamboo mat. She seemed happy enough to see me. She sat up and flashed a weak smile.

I knelt beside her. "I've got a Plan B."

"What happened to Plan A?"

"It turned out to be the same caliber as all my other plans."

"Oh."

"Do you still have your med kit?"

She swiveled her head, searching. "In the corner there." She pointed.

I grabbed it, brushed dirt and a couple of spiders off it, then pawed through it, hoping to find what I needed. I should have checked earlier, before I boasted to the chief about giving him "bigger power than king of kings," but I hadn't—since I'd acted on impulse and adrenalin—and now prayed I wouldn't pay for that oversight.

I got lucky. The pouch contained what I needed.

"I'm going to borrow this, Eve," I said. I told her why and asked for some quick medical advice.

Her first response reflected the quality of my scheme. "Is there a Plan C?"

"Yeah," I said. "It would require you handling a Colt .45."

"Let's hope Plan B comes through, then."

"Your honest opinion?"

"If the baby is sick because of malnutrition, it might work. If it's sick for some other reason . . . " Her voice trailed off.

As I departed the hut, I again heard the distant roar of an airplane, a transport. It sounded closer than the one I'd heard yesterday. I had to believe it was searching for me and Eve. But I knew the guys wouldn't expend much more effort doing that unless they had some indication we were alive.

The sky remained clear except for cotton-ball puffs of cumulus here and there, so we had that going in our favor. But before I worried about how I might signal the Americans, I had to get Eve out of the clutches of Chief Saggy.

I returned to where the chief and Tommy waited, this time accompanied by the Naga man with the crying baby. Only the baby had ceased crying, and now hung listlessly in the man's arms. Its little tummy was distended and its eyes closed as it struggled to breathe. It reminded me of the starving kids I'd seen on the streets of Calcutta.

And I wanted to stop referring to the infant, a male, as "it."

"Does he have a name?" I asked Tommy.

Tommy spoke to the man, then told me the baby hadn't yet been named. He'd been born just a few days ago and his mother had died giving birth.

"Okay," I said, "I'm going to call him Pete." After my pal, Captain Pete Zimmerman.

"Peeet?" Tommy said.

"Yes. Is American name."

"Good name. Peeet be my brudder, then."

I nodded, a little choked up. Just what I needed. More pressure to salvage the life of a little Naga baby in a Burmese rainforest. A kid Tommy decided would be his brother.

I gestured for Tommy and Chief Sagara to join me in a private conversation. We stepped away from the man holding Pete. I had Tommy explain to Saggy that I had a plan to revive the baby and let the chief take all credit for it —an idea that he could tell his people was inspired by the gods and executed by him, a great leader of the Naga people.

I asked Tommy to tell the chief I would show him how to bring the infant back from the brink of death and thus be revered by his tribe as a leader with far greater power than any other chief or king. I laid my hand on Tommy's shoulder. "But tell him, before I do that, he must give me word of honor that Sunshine Lady mine."

Tommy addressed the chief and answered several of his questions, each time casting an apprehensive glance at me.

Chief Saggy fell silent, eyeing me with a mix of suspicion and wonderment . . . and maybe hope. At last he nodded and jammed a fist against his chest. I took that to be a sign of agreement, his pledge of honor. Now all I had to do was deliver. Quite frankly, I'd rather be trying to dead-stick a

Gooney Bird into Kunming than attempting what I was about to.

I retrieved Eve's medical pouch and my survival kit and came back to where Tommy and Saggy waited. We moved to a nearby cooking fire. I told Tommy to make certain the chief watched very carefully what I did, so he could later do it on his own.

Pete had begun crying again, though his wailing sounded labored and painful. His obvious suffering gave new urgency to what I was about to try. I thought about praying, but wasn't convinced of its efficacy. Besides, I thought, if God had really wanted Pete to live, He probably would have already addressed the issue.

I pulled a tin of evaporated milk from my survival pack. I asked Tommy to bring some water to a boil in one of the Nagas' crude bamboo cups. He did. Then I mixed in the appropriate amount of evaporated milk, and voilà, real milk. Sort of.

I retrieved what was left of the horrible Hershey and shaved a few shards of it into the milk. Voilà, chocolate milk. Of course, if my plan worked, the kid might grow up hating chocolate, but that wasn't a key consideration.

Placing the cup on the ground, I made sure Tommy and Saggy understood the milk must be allowed to cool before executing the next step. We waited several minutes as Pete continued to vocalize his extreme discomfort.

I pulled an eyedropper out of Eve's medical kit and filled it with my magic formula. Through a series of pantomimes I showed Chief Saggy how I expected him to feed Pete. If my idea worked, the chief would save the kid and become a great hero, I'd get Eve, and we'd get the hell out of here. If it didn't . . . well, no need to dwell on that.

I asked Tommy to gather the tribe. I handed Saggy the

eyedropper and we walked back to where Pete and his father waited. In a matter of a minute or two, we had a large audience, including a few of the dogs and two pigs.

Tommy explained to the tribe what was about to take place. Saggy kept glancing at me, his gnarled countenance etched in consternation and misgiving, but I knew he wouldn't pass up an opportunity to become almost god-like to his tribe.

I retrieved Pete from his father and cradled him in my arms. He continued to cry. I nodded at the chief, who stepped forward with the eyedropper and placed it on the child's parched lips. He squeezed a couple of drops of milk into Pete's mouth. Pete stopped crying and swallowed them.

The chief continued squeezing and Pete continued to swallow, drop after drop. I held Pete, rocking him gently, until he'd downed maybe a couple of thimblefuls. I didn't want to put too much into the kid for his first meal, so I gestured for Saggy to cease his efforts.

Pete fell asleep. The tribal men and women stared at their chief with wide-eyed wonderment, and he grinned so broadly I feared he might pop out a few more of his rotted teeth.

I handed Pete back to his dad, but daddy waved him off, pointing at the chief. I called Tommy over to intervene. I asked him to explain to the father that the baby was his, but that whenever he awoke crying, he could bring him to Saggy for a refill. I also suggested that they teach daddy how to feed Pete.

I gave them the remainder of my so-called chocolate and pawed around in Eve's medical pouch until I found another tin of evaporated milk. I hoped that by the time Saggy and daddy had exhausted the milk and Hersey bar, Pete would be eating whatever baby food Nagas raised their kids on. Probably not strained beets.

Saggy gave me a big hug—one I'd long remember since he smelled like he'd just climbed out of a sewer pipe. I told him we'd trade Christmas cards. He smiled again, a Cheshire Cat in need of dental work, and motioned for me to go get Eve. I did.

With Tommy and the two warriors who had accompanied us on our journey here, we set out for King Kalakeya's village. I wanted to get away from Chief Saggy's settlement as quickly as I could. I presumed little Pete might recover fully, but there were no assurances of that, so I wanted to put as much distance as I could between us and Saggy's guys as fast as possible.

Since it hadn't rained for a while, the trail was firm and easy to walk on. Even the leeches seemed to have dwindled in number, but we still had to stop every hour or so to pluck a few of the ugly worms from our bodies. And Eve needed to rest. She remained stiff and sore from being a "guest" of the Nagas, so would require extra time to get back into fighting fettle.

The tangled jungle around us, which had begun to seem like home, was alive with its usual squeals and squawks and howls. Even occasional growls resonated through the tenebrous forest, but they no longer bothered me. I guess I really had gone native.

I told Tommy to ask the two warriors to precede us on our hike back to King Kally's place, just in case there were any Japs out looking for us.

"Do you think there are?" Eve asked.

"I doubt it, since they have no idea where we are. But I don't want to stumble into a patrol just in case they've got guys out trying to find us. My bigger concern, though, is that they may be hunting for the Nagas."

"Why is that?" she said, huffing and puffing a bit.

I told her about the ambush and how Kally's boys had saved my bacon. I skipped the part about the severed heads.

Once more, the bellow of airplane engines cut through the rainforest clamor.

"That's our boys out looking for us," I said, "but unless we can signal them, they aren't going to carry on much longer."

"How do we let them know we're here?"

"The best way would be to build a big signal fire."

"Wouldn't that tip off the Japs, too?"

"Yep. It could become a race between them and Blackie's Gang."

"Blackie's Gang?"

"It's a thrown-together search and rescue group out of Dinjan, adjacent to Chabua. They've pulled more than a few guys out of the weeds here. But since they don't know we're even alive, they probably won't waste much more time looking for us."

"So, do we light a fire tonight, after we get back to this little guy's village?" She gestured at Tommy.

"No. We won't get there until it's almost dark. Blackie's boys will have ceased flying for the day by then. First thing tomorrow morning would be better. If the weather holds, smoke from a big fire should be easy to spot."

"By both Blackie's Gang and the Japanese."

"'Fraid so. One bunch wants to save us. The other wants to kill us."

Eve flashed me a sardonic smile as we strode along the jungle track. "My life has become so much more interesting since we became friends."

We made it back to the village without incident. After an enthusiastic "welcome home" by Kally and his boys, we hit the hammocks early. The following morning, we awakened before the sun did and, with the help of Tommy and several tribesmen, went to work constructing a huge stack of bamboo for our signal fire. After we'd finished, the pile looked big enough that I guessed when we lit it the flames might be visible in China.

The dawn sky morphed from deep black inset with glittering stars to a soft turquoise tinted in streaks of pink and orange. Fine conditions for flying. At least the weather seemed to be breaking in our favor.

With sweat pouring off me from my early morning labors, I accompanied a group of men to a nearby stream and bathed with them, as well as with a few water buffalo and a bunch of curious monkeys. Despite being in a tropical jungle, the water felt as chilly as a mountain stream in the Pacific Northwest. But I emerged feeling clean and refreshed for the first time in days.

Eve trooped off with some of the village women to do the same in a spot just downstream from us. And, yes, I did sneak a peek or two. I noticed some of the other men did, too, though I don't believe it was driven by anything sexual. I think they were just curious about a light-skinned, fair-haired woman. Kind of like seeing a lamb cavorting with tigers.

Back in the village, King Kally approached us and began asking Tommy questions. I heard the word "Japanee" several times. Tommy explained to me the king was afraid the fire would attract any Japs who might be out searching for us and the Nagas who'd helped us.

I didn't know how to honestly counter that concern, but I tried to put a positive spin on it.

"Tell King Kalakeya the fire will bring American airplane. Airplane has guns, can shoot Japs. More men come, too. Help fight Japs." A little bit of bullshit, but not entirely.

That aside, my response seemed to satisfy the king. So I sat by the stack of wood and listened for the sound of an American transport. I hoped Blackie's Gang had gotten up early and resumed its search. I prayed, metaphorically, that yesterday's hunt hadn't been its last hurrah. If the search had been abandoned, I had no idea how Eve and I were ever going to get out of here.

I wasn't even certain where we were. My best guess was somewhere in far northwest Burma. Since I hadn't seen or heard any Jap fighters over the past few days, I assumed we were out of range of their base at Myitkyina. We obviously had escaped Jap-occupied territory, but that didn't mean we were out of reach of roving patrols or any platoons that might have a hard-on for us or our Naga allies.

I supposed if we had to, we could just keep plugging westward until we reached Assam. But I had no idea how far that might be or what kind of topography we might have to negotiate. Maybe the Nagas would help, maybe not. I knew it would be a whole lot easier if we had some Army rescue guys on the ground to help get us back to India.

By midmorning, no sounds of aircraft had reached my ears, only the chatter of the natives and the usual hubbub from the jungle.

I spotted Eve and Tommy in earnest conversation near a cooking fire. Tommy seemed fascinated by her blond hair and light complexion. He reached out to touch her and she didn't flinch. In fact, she smiled and allowed him to stroke her hair. Apparently, the Ice Queen had melted in the Burmese rainforest. A different Eve Johannsen appeared to have arisen from the vapors. I'll be damned if I wasn't beginning to actually like her.

The morning dragged on. Eve eventually came over and sat by me.

"I see you've got a young suitor," I said.

"He's a good kid."

"They're good people . . . chopping off heads aside."

"We've stepped into a different culture," she said, "and

probably a different century . . . you know, a few hundred years in the past." She doodled in the dirt with her finger.

"I wonder what *they* think about *us*," I responded. "Americans and Japanese, fighting each other in a jungle thousands of miles from their homelands. Using bombs and hand grenades and flamethrowers to kill each other. To the Nagas, this is their universe. They have no world view or sense of anything larger. All they see are a couple of strange tribes messing up their backyard."

Eve laughed softly. "You've got a point. Maybe we really aren't that much different from folks who lived a few hundred years ago. It's just that we've found more efficient ways to lop off heads. We blow 'em off instead."

I sighed. "It's a brutal world."

"Not entirely." She leaned over and kissed me on the cheek.

Of all the things that had happened to me over the past few months, that was the most stupefying. Too dumbfounded to say anything, I merely stared at her in response.

"That was a thank you, not a come-on," she said, her voice low and a bit husky. Maybe the husky part was just my imagination, but the Captain Nurse I'd come to know and hate seemed to have taken leave of this earth.

She held her gaze on me for what seemed a little too long for a mere thank you, but again, maybe it was just my imagination poking a stick into the eye of loss and loneliness.

I started to speak. "Eve—"

She held up her hand to shush me. "Listen."

I did. Through the humid, cumulus-flecked morning floated the melodious roar of two big airplane engines. Blackie's Gang on the hunt. Or so I hoped. Anyhow, I was about to bet our lives on it.

25

The northern Burma rainforest
A Naga village

Using a flaming piece of bamboo from one of the cooking fires, Tommy and I ignited the signal fire. Tommy blew on the glowing kindling, and the stack of wood burst into dancing orange flames wrapped in columns of white and gray smoke. A busy breeze tilted the pirouetting pillars toward the west. Air pockets exploded and popped inside the flaming bamboo. It reminded me of Fourth of July celebrations back home— kids tossing firecrackers and cherry bombs at each other. Certainly not safe, but sort of practice, I suppose, for what was coming, though none of us ever imagined it—lobbing mortar shells and grenades at other human beings.

It didn't take long before we had a huge blaze filling the morning with sounds of a miniature firefight. A bi-colored billow of smoke shot skyward, something no respectable search party could miss. And that included the Japs.

I noticed King Kally had dispatched some of his warriors down the trails leading up to the village. I assumed he continued to worry about bad guys spotting the smoke and deciding they ought to check it out. I sure hoped there was an American Gooney Bird or Ol' Dumbo nearby.

The heavy murmur of big aircraft engines grew louder, closer. And then, yes! It was over us. Blackie, Captain John Porter himself, at the controls of his brightly painted Gooney, vomit yellow and Navy blue. On the nose of the bird was scrawled in skinny block letters *Somewhere I'll Find You.* He zoomed overhead and waggled the wings. I jumped up and down like a kid who'd just won a ballgame with a home run. Even Eve got excited, waving her arms over her head and screaming like a cheerleader.

Blackie, I'd come to learn through the grapevine, had a particular hatred of Japs. His brother had been killed attempting to take off in a plane when the little bastards attacked Pearl Harbor. That explained why Blackie always armed his C-47s with the handheld British Bren guns. Any chance he had to kill Japs he was going to grab.

The Gooney Bird roared out over the jungle, then banked and came back toward us. The copilot tossed a message tied to a yellow streamer out his window. It landed with a tiny eruption of dust square in the center of the village. Tommy darted over to retrieve it. Like a well-trained retriever with a downed pheasant, he carried it back to me, pride reflected in his grin. I ruffled his thick, dark hair. Kind of like I would have a black Lab's, I guess.

The message instructed us to identify ourselves. Usually that could be done by using parachute panels to indicate the tail number of the aircraft being searched for. But we didn't have any parachutes. I explained my dilemma to Eve and Tommy.

Tommy, I think, had met this challenge before. He indicated for me to wait while he ran off someplace. He returned in no time dragging long stalks of bamboo. He cut them into about three-foot lengths, then split them in half. He sprinted off to grab another load, and did the same: cut them, split them. The inside of the bamboo proved to be unsullied white. Perfect. Using the split stalks, white side up, we could lay out the tail number of our dearly departed C-47.

While we went about our work, Blackie flew a race track pattern out over the canopy of the rainforest. With Eve's help, Tommy and I placed the bamboo on the ground in the center of the village to "spell out" the tail number, four-seven-three. Once we finished, we waved at Blackie. He headed back to take a look. He thundered over the mountaintop village so low he blew patches of dried grass off some of the thatch-roofed homes. He climbed away, circled, and came back, this time with the rear passenger door yawned open.

I knew what was coming. I motioned the villagers out of the way. Tommy helped, sprinting around the tiny settlement yelling warnings.

The rescue packets, parachutes attached, flew out the Gooney Bird's door in quick succession. You didn't want to get hit by one, since they weighed about a hundred pounds each. Blackie's aim was a little too good with the first package. It plunged directly through the roof of one of the huts. Luckily, no one was inside. They were all outside watching the show. The second packet thudded down about three feet from a cooking fire. The 'chute collapsed into the fire and burst into flames. Several villagers grabbed the package and pulled it from danger.

The third delivery didn't fare as well as the first two. The wind caught it and blew it away from the mountaintop into the thick jungle below the village.

"Damnit," I exclaimed. "I sure as shit hope that wasn't the Gibson Girl." We needed the radio to communicate with our rescuers, to tell them in detail how we were, and for them to tell us where we were. More importantly, we needed to coordinate plans on how they were going to get us out of here.

"Tommy," I screamed, "take some boys, find package."

Like a little general, he soon had a team organized. They plunged into the rainforest to search for the errant rescue packet.

I rushed to the hut that now had a hole in its roof thanks to the bombing run of an American transport. The owner and his wife were already there, staring at the rescue packet on the floor of their living room and probably wondering if a giant bird had just pooped on their house.

Using my knife, I ripped open the package. It contained medical and food supplies—including some more of that lousy chocolate and two bottles of tea pellets—as well as a bag of trinkets. The trinkets were just what I needed to pay reparations to the Nagas who stood looking over my shoulder and now owned the only hut in the village with a window in the roof. I found a couple of shiny mason jar lids for the man, and a necklace strung with Coca-Cola bottle caps for the lady. To my surprise, they both seemed delighted with their compensation.

I went back outside and found that the packet that had almost become part of a Naga bonfire contained the Gibson Girl radio. I cranked it up and called Blackie.

"Blackie, Rod here. Thanks for dropping by. What took you so long?"

"Four Eyes! Great to hear your voice. What took us so long? You aren't anywhere near that airplane you dumped in the woods."

"Yeah. Lost my glasses. Bumped into a Jap fighter. So where am I, exactly?"

A pause ensued. Eve strolled over and squatted down

beside me. Now that she'd gotten cleaned up, I realized how emaciated and worn out she looked.

Blackie came back on the air. "Twenty-seven north, ninety-six point six east."

"That's a big help."

"You're in the middle of nowhere."

"Shit. I know that, Blackie. How far am I from Assam?"

"There's a road, of sorts, about twenty miles west of you. That'll lead you back to Assam, maybe another twenty miles or so. Hey, I thought you were a Hump pilot. What the hell are you doing in a Burmese jungle?"

"It's a long story."

"I'll bet it is. By the way, who's there with you. I thought I saw *two* guys in uniform waving at me."

"Not two guys. One flyboy, one nurse, a Captain Johannsen."

"Shut my mouth. Not that bitchy broad from Chabua?"

"She's right here beside me, Blackie."

"Oh. My apologies, ma'am."

"She's actually a nice lady. Just had a rough go of it."

Blackie continued to fly his C-47 in slow circles out over the rainforest. "Again, my apologies," he said. "Look, how are you guys physically? Need a doctor?"

"Mostly just cuts and bruises and insect bites. The leeches love us. Captain Johannsen is looking a bit wobbly, though, so it probably wouldn't hurt to have a doc make a house call."

"Can do."

Eve nudged me, hard, with her elbow. "I'm fine."

"We've got two or three days of hard travel ahead of us just to get to that road," I said to her. "Some medical attention wouldn't hurt either of us."

Over the radio, Blackie said, "What else do you need?"

"Clean uniforms, new boots, ammo for my .45, maybe a couple of Mis."

"You expecting trouble?"

"Mmm, not expecting. Just preparing. I think there may be some pissed off Japs hunting for us. The Nagas borrowed a few of their heads during our rescue."

"Damn. Tell you what, I think we'd better throw together a rifle squad and drop them in to say hello. They can lead you out of Nowhere and get you to that road. In the meantime, we can arrange for a truck to greet you and get you back to Chabua."

"How far will we be from Chabua once we get to the road?"

"You're looking at another eighty or a hundred miles. It's not a four-lane."

"Roger that. Time estimate for you to dump some help on us?"

"I think we're looking at early tomorrow. It'll take us a few hours to draft a flight surgeon and gather some guys with guns."

"How're you fixed for airplanes?"

"Yeah, almost forgot. We've got a special Gooney standing by to fly out here and deliver your welcome-home gifts tomorrow. And even better news—though it'll be a few weeks—we found a couple of shot-up B-25s in a salvage yard. We're gonna patch 'em up and put 'em to work. They'll give us a little more firepower and a little more range for our search and rescue trips."

"Good deal, Blackie. Thanks for dropping by."

"No problem, Four Eyes. I'm heading back to Chabua now."

"Give my regards to Lieutenant Colonel Shaver." *Lieutenant*

Colonel Bulldog Asshole. "Oh, and by the way, sad to say, we lost a soul."

"Who?"

"We had a medevac on board, a Colonel Alfred Willis out of Kunming. He was on the bird when it went down. We couldn't get him out." I felt Eve's hand come to rest on my shoulder.

"Sorry, Major. I'll report that. All for now. Your next guardian angel will be overhead shortly after sunup."

Blackie waggled his wings once more, then climbed and headed west, back toward Dinjan.

"Thanks for saying . . . nice words about me, Rod," Eve said softly, her hand remaining on my shoulder.

"They were heartfelt. You are a nice lady."

Again she pecked me on the cheek.

"Just a thank you?" I asked.

She smiled and withdrew her hand.

Tommy returned with his band and the rescue packet that had gone off course. We found more food and medical supplies in it. Also some blankets, toilet paper, and flashlights, along with a couple of old issues of *Life*.

As evening crept over the jungle, and the bats careened, and the animals and bugs struck up their night music, Eve and I sat by the dying signal fire, staring into the dwindling flames. Perhaps she, like I, found comfort and hope in the lingering warmth and brightness of the diminishing blaze.

She leaned unabashedly against my shoulder and took my hand.

"I hope you find happiness after this is all over," she whispered. "I'm sorry for all you've been through."

"No less than I am for what you've suffered, Eve. You're a good woman. I'm sorry life has been rough on you. It's not fair."

"I guess someone has to draw the short straw."

We fell silent for a while, allowing the sounds of the rainforest and the snap and crackle of the fire performing its last dance to wash over us.

I turned my head to look at Eve and found her staring at me. Our gazes locked. I bent toward her and kissed her on the lips. She didn't resist. Our tongues found each other's. How long we kissed, I don't know. But it was way beyond the allotted time for mere thank yous.

Eve spoke first, her words barely audible. "Thank you, Rod, for not leaving me. For coming back for me." Then a soft sob. "For saving me."

But I knew someone else had been saved, too.

We sat together, my arm draped over her shoulders, as the fire faded and the darkness deepened.

"After we get out of here, will you go back to flying?" Eve asked.

"No. I was supposed to be in New Delhi by now, working at my real job."

"Your real job?"

"I'm the director of operations for the Tenth Weather Squadron, the squadron that supports the ATC in-theater here. After Colonel Shaver yanked me off flying status—except, ahem, for a certain special mission to Kunming—there didn't seem to be much use for me at Chabua."

"You're a fine pilot." She snuggled closer to me.

"I lost an aircraft and an Army colonel."

"Not through negligence or incompetence."

"The Army won't see it that way. A loss is a loss. A fatality is a fatality. That's all that will show on my record."

"That gets back to the 'not fair' issue, doesn't it?"

"Lot of that going around, I hear. But you, what about you? Back to Kunming?"

"That's my assignment."

A final "pop" issued from the fire and the last of the flames sputtered and collapsed, leaving only a banana moon and a dusting of stars to illuminate two Army officers, male and female, nestled together on a mountaintop in Burma. A long way from New Delhi and a long way from Kunming.

"Aren't there any military hospitals in New Delhi?" I said.

"Why do you ask?"

I didn't answer. She knew.

We clung to each other without saying much for another hour, then trooped off to our respective huts to catch some sleep, though it turned out to be a singularly unsuccessful effort for me. The following morning, I arose again before the sun and slipped outside into a thin mist. I wondered what Blackie had meant by a "special" Gooney Bird. I wondered what was happening between Eve and me. I wondered if there were any Japs nearby. Yeah, the world is full of wonders.

The sun crept above the horizon to the east, swallowing the mist and slathering a scattering of wispy cirrus with fiery tones of crimson and peach. I wondered—there's that word again—if this would be the last time I'd see the dawn come up like thunder . . . "outer China."

From the west came a different kind of thunder. A beat-up Gooney Bird, hugging the rainforest canopy, roared over the mountaintop village. It ran out over the jungle, turned, and made another low pass over the hamlet. This time I caught the name scrawled on her nose, *Betsy*. Good Lord, it was Colonel Ellsworth's C-47.

The Gibson Girl crackled to life. "Hey, anybody awake down there?"

"They are now," I responded, unrestrained joy wrapping my words, though I doubt that was evident over the radio.

"Tex here, Rod. We got some goodies for you. But first, your boss would like to speak to you."

I waited until Colonel Ellsworth came on the air.

"Good to hear your voice, balloon blower," he said, "but I need you in New Delhi, not hanging out with monkeys and headhunters, okay?"

"Wasn't my idea, sir."

"I'm sure it wasn't. So let's get you and your flight nurse out of there."

My flight nurse? "Got any good ideas, Colonel?"

Tex slowed *Betsy* and began orbiting the mountaintop. The village came to life as the Nagas stepped from huts into the fresh morning air to see what was going on.

"We're going to drop a flight surgeon, a Lieutenant Colonel Archie Bonner, in on you to make sure you folks are ready for a brisk hike. He'll be followed by a squad of rescuers who will get you to that road. It's about a three-day trek from here. We've got truck transport set up from there back to Chabua."

"Roger that. That's wonderful. We're ready."

"Okay. The village gives us kind of a small target on that mountaintop, so we'll have to make three or four runs over it to make sure we don't send any of our guys rolling down the mountainside into the jungle."

"Got it. By the way, how's the weather business?"

A long pause followed my question.

"Your first mission after getting back to headquarters will be to pay a visit to Colonel Tom Hardin."

"The there's-no-weather-on-the-Hump guy?"

"You got it. I'm banking on you to get that straightened out."

"In that case, forget about the rescuers, sir."

Ellsworth laughed, then said, "Too late. Delivery on the way."

Tex had climbed higher to give the team's parachutes a chance to open. Two figures tumbled from *Betsy* as it made a slow pass over the village. One 'chute blossomed almost instantly, but the other was delayed as the guy in the harness appeared inverted. He struggled to right himself and did so at the last instant. The canopy opened, but not enough to keep him from thudding into the ground like a shot-put ball.

The villagers ran to extricate him from his 'chute. He stood, shakily, then took a tentative step or two.

"Owww, damn," he yelled.

I trotted over to him. "Major Rod Shepherd," I said, saluting. "You okay?"

"No, damn it. Sprained my ankle. Don't think it's broken, though. Forget the saluting shit. I'm Lieutenant Colonel Bonner. Just call me Archie."

"Flight surgeon?"

"Yeah. Ain't that great? I came here to help you folks, and I may be the one in need of help first." He snorted a sardonic laugh.

"First jump you've had trouble on?"

"First fucking jump period. I'm supposed to be a doctor, not a goddamned paratrooper."

The other jumper trotted over to us.

"I'm Sergeant Dewey," he said, "squad leader. Is the colonel okay?"

"Mainly embarrassed," Colonel Bonner growled.

Betsy rumbled overhead again and two more guys leapt out.

Eve arrived, purposely brushed against me—I doubt anyone noticed—introduced herself to the colonel, and went to work probing his ankle.

"They'll push some med supplies out of the plane on one

of these passes," Bonner said. "There are some compression bandages in there you can use."

"You'll have to stay off that foot for a while," Eve said, "and keep your ankle elevated."

"Well, that ain't gonna happen, is it?" Bonner grimaced.

"I suppose not," Eve responded. "We don't have any ice, either."

"War is hell. Just make sure you keep me stuffed with APC tabs, Captain, and I'll be fine."

Six rescuers with rifles and ammo, plus the colonel, ended up on the ground. The medical supplies, boxed in a small crate, landed safely, too.

I called Tex on the radio and told him we had one minor casualty, but that his mission had been successful.

"See you in New Delhi," he responded. "Your taxi awaits on Burmese Highway One." He made a good-bye run over the village and headed west. All seemed to be going well. But you should never think that in a war zone.

A pair of Naga warriors, from the group King Kally had dispatched to patrol the jungle trails below, raced into the village, yelling. I couldn't understand what they were saying, of course, but I caught the fear that tinged their voices and recognized at least one of the words they uttered, "Japanee."

26

The northern Burma rainforest
A Naga village

Tommy raced over to me, his eyes wide. "Japs come," he said. "Many many."

I knelt in front of him and rested a hand on his shoulder, hoping to calm him. "How many?"

"Many many." The words tumbled out.

"I know, Tommy, I know. But *how* many?" I spread the fingers on my hands and held them up, ten, in front of his face.

He shook his head. "More."

I tried ten plus five.

Again he shook his head.

I went to twenty, opening and closing my fingers twice. Even that didn't do it. I added five more.

"Yes, maybe."

So, it sounded like a Jap platoon. They'd probably spotted the smoke from yesterday's fire, then seen the C-47 making drops this morning.

As Tommy and I talked, the village men wasted no time in

grabbing their weapons—spears, knives, crossbows. They would be no match for the firepower of the Japs, of course, nor would the M1 carbines and .45s the rest of us carried.

Sergeant Dewey trotted over and I told him what Tommy had just related to me.

The sergeant rolled his eyes and muttered, "Always something." He had the appearance of a hardened veteran— muscular, swarthy, and scarred. "I fought these weasels on Guadalcanal. I know how to deal with them."

"We're outnumbered and outgunned."

"I didn't say we can beat them. Just that we can deal with them." He cast his gaze on Tommy. "This little buzzer your translator?"

"Good kid."

"Great. I'll tell you how I want to set up, then maybe you and he can get the message across to our buddies here."

"Okay. Hold on a minute."

I remembered we had an ace-in-the-hole, *Betsy*. Hopefully she hadn't flown out of radio range, and hopefully Tex and Colonel Ellsworth had Bren guns with them. I cranked the Gibson Girl and made a frantic call. I thought I got a response, but it came across broken and staticky, so I wasn't sure. I decided they had either heard me or hadn't. At the moment, other matters needed my attention, so I set the radio aside.

Tommy, Dewey, and I sat on the ground and I asked Dewey to sketch his plan in the dirt while he explained it. I thought it might help Tommy.

"The Japs will feint a frontal attack," he said, "probably moving right up the main trail toward the village. They'll yell and scream and fire every weapon they have. But their main goal will be to outflank us. Even though the jungle seems impenetrable, they know how to get through it. The bastards gained a little— actually, a lot—of experience on Guadal-canal, too."

Dewey grabbed a stick and made a crude drawing in the dried mud. "Village here." He pointed at a circle he'd sketched. "Japs here." He traced a straight line away from the circle, then scratched in a bunch of little stick figures.

Tommy watched in rapt attention, seeming to understand.

"What I want the Nagas to do," Dewey went on, "is to wait for the Japs on the main trail, fire a volley from their cross-bows, then get the hell out of Dodge, back into the jungle. They can't dig in and fight the Nips. They wouldn't stand a chance. I want them to skedaddle into the forest and protect our flanks. They'll have the home field advantage there and can give the Japs hell. I don't want enemy soldiers slithering into the village from places we don't expect."

"Sounds good," I said. "Tommy, run and get King Kalakeya and bring him here." I wanted to make sure the Naga commander had a good grasp of our plan.

Once the king arrived, we went over the scheme with him step by step with Tommy translating. The Nagas may be prim-itive, but they aren't dumb, and Kally caught on right away. Made sense, I guess. These guys had been fighting in this land for centuries. And I'm sure the king had visions of a few more buck-toothed trophies for his display rack.

Kally, his chest puffed out like a proud general, scurried off to direct his troops.

"We'll set up around the periphery of the village," Dewey said, "but focus on the entrance from the primary trail. We don't have heavy weapons, but we've got the high ground and can erect barriers we can hunker down behind. Does the lady know how to shoot?"

"She's a nurse."

"Okay, I'd like it better if she were infantry, but we might need a medic, too."

Betsy did not reappear like some avenging angel, so we'd end up with six guys bearing carbines and Lieutenant Colonel Bonner and myself with pistols to defend the village. The pistols, the .45s, wouldn't do much good unless the Japs got into our knickers, but they could make a lot of noise and make the bad guys think we had a lot more firepower than we really possessed. And, of course, we had headhunters watching our flanks.

What could go wrong?

We went to work throwing together some jury-rigged barricades consisting mostly of stacks of bamboo. Eve and Tommy and a few other village youngsters pitched in. The Naga women brought us water and some kind of gooey rice to snack on.

By noon, we'd finished constructing our defensive positions, such as they were. About the same time, the jungle fell silent. No squawks or yowls or chitters. An odd stillness for midday. It was as if the birds and animals sensed danger, that something was afoot in the forest that shouldn't be. An eerie hush permeated the village. Several of the rescuers/riflemen puffed on cigarettes and whispered to one another.

I leaned against a bamboo battlement, my .45 at the ready. Eve ducked down beside me.

"This is bad, isn't it?" she said, keeping her voice low.

"It ain't good."

"Are you scared?"

"I'd rather be in a Gooney Bird flying over the Hump in a storm than squatting here with a lousy .45."

"Kind of out of your element."

"Yeah. How in the hell did I end up here? I'm supposed to be soaring over the roof of the world, threading my way through snow-capped Himalayan peaks, and thumbing my nose at gravel shufflers and ground pounders."

"Yet here you are—"

"—in a Burmese rainforest, hunkered down like an infantry grunt, headhunters from the eighteenth century for allies, waiting for an attack by Jap jungle fighters. How's that for irony?"

"Hard to beat. Except maybe if you're a nurse from a tropical paradise, like Hawaii."

"Ain't war wonderful?"

She gave me a sad smile infused with pain, loss, and sadness—and perhaps just a trace of hope.

Our gazes locked, the iciness in her blue eyes absent, replaced by a softness that seemed to border on longing. I reached for her hand.

"When this is all over," I said, "this whole damn war, would . . ." I ran out of words. Or maybe courage.

"Yes?"

Seize the moment. "Would you consider, well, being my gal?"

She didn't answer right away. I guess I'd blown it.

"No," she finally said.

I released her hand.

"I won't consider it," she continued. "Can't I just *be* your gal."

"Genevieve Johannsen," I whispered, "you little bitch."

She laughed, a genuine chortle that tinkled with merriment.

That's when the first gun blasts echoed through the dense rainforest. From below came the high-pitched yells of Naga warriors and the furious screams of Jap soldiers. The battle had been joined. But just as quickly, the tumult ceased. Again a foreboding silence crept over the hills. The headhunters had done their bit, carried out a hit-and-run attack, then scurried into the jungle to guard our flanks.

We waited. Eve burrowed into my shoulder. I felt her breathing—short, shallow breaths.

"Keep your head down," I cautioned.

"You don't have to remind me."

As Sergeant Dewey had predicted, the Jap assault came straight up the main trail with a lot of wild gunfire and yelling. But as Dewey had also said, it seemed designed more to intimidate than actually gain ground.

"Don't waste ammo, boys," he shouted, "just fire enough to let 'em know we're ready to fight. They're gonna try to outflank us."

We opened measured fire at the Japs but, as Dewey had suggested, we didn't squander our rounds. I hoped our headhunter buddies were up to the task they'd been given. I had to guess they were. After all, they were defending their homes. I didn't envy the Japs. Even though they may have fought on Godforsaken islands in the South Pacific, I couldn't imagine that prepares you for slithering on your belly through the mud in a jungle infested with leeches, snakes, and little brown men ready to part your head from your neck.

I suspected that might well be happening when piercing screams suffused with terror and agony rippled from the rainforest, sounds that sent waves of palpable chills coursing through my body.

We continued to shoot at the Japs, presumably without hitting any, since they hadn't bothered to show themselves. The firing on both sides gradually dwindled until only occasional shots and yells punctuated the afternoon heat.

Dewey combat-crawled over to my position. "I think they've figured out they can't outflank us, so they're probably trying to come up with another plan."

That turned out to be an assault right up the gut, this time accompanied by a light machine gun. The machine gun raked our positions and one of the riflemen caught a round in the chest. We fired back with everything we had—not much—as the first of the slant-eyed weasels rushed into the village.

Someone yelled for a medic. Eve stared at me, her eyes as big as silver dollars, but she didn't hesitate. She grabbed her medical kit and ran in a squat toward the wounded soldier. Colonel Bonner was already there, ripping off the guy's shirt.

Bullets continued to fly with Jap rounds thudding and zinging into our bamboo barricades. As quiet as the day had been, the sound and fury of men trying to kill one another now filled the air to the extent that communication became impossible except by screaming your lungs out.

Another of our guys got hit, but kept firing. Bonner left Eve with the soldier who'd gone down, picked up a rifle, and emptied a clip at a pair of Japs who'd made it into the village waving swords like they were some sort of invincible warriors. They weren't. Our guys with the MIs dropped them in their tracks. But others kept coming. I sensed the balance of the fight beginning to tilt in the wrong direction.

That's when a C-47, not *Betsy* but Blackie's *Somewhere We'll Find You*, popped back onto the scene. The Gooney Bird thundered over the village, turned, and came back. It banked to the left and slowed as it passed over the firefight. Blackie, out the cockpit window, and a crew chief, from the rear passenger door, opened up on the Japs with Bren guns.

The firepower of the Brens seemed more potent than what the Japs could deliver with their light machine gun. Chunks of tropical leaves and bamboo shoots sprayed through the air, and geysers of dirt and mud erupted where the shells ripped into the enemy positions. I guessed the Brens probably fired bigger bullets than what the Jap weapon did.

Somewhere We'll Find You's pass was over in a matter of seconds, but it came back for a second run. The Japs fired a few perfunctory shots in its direction, but most of the attacking patrol melted back into the forest.

I heard Blackie calling me on the Gibson Girl. "Sorry we're late to the party."

I darted over to where I'd left the radio. "I didn't know if you guys got my message or not," I said, thankful they'd showed up at all.

"Colonel Ellsworth gave us a heads-up. He heard your call for help but didn't have any weapons on board. He radioed in and we were in the air before he landed."

"Stick around. I'm sure the fun isn't over."

"Roger that."

Sergeant Dewey trotted over to me.

"Think the Japs will beat feet?" I asked.

"I doubt it. They don't give up easily. I think we can count on them coming up with another plan. But they know we've got air cover and little brown guys staking out the woods, so their options are pretty damn limited."

For the next half hour, nothing happened. Blackie orbited out over the jungle, and Eve and Doc Bonner worked on the wounded riflemen. A couple of Naga warriors slipped in from the jungle bearing the heads of four Japs. We'd taken out three or four of the attackers near the village, so the bad guys had to be down to less than twenty now.

I grabbed a smoke and kept a close watch on the trail, but no enemy reappeared.

"I don't like this," Dewey said. "Normally these rat bastards are a little noisier than this. You know, throwing insults at us, calling us names, just to whip up their own courage if nothing else."

"You think they're trying a sneak attack?"

"Not really. The Nagas would nail 'em." Dewey brushed away the sweat and dirt caked on his face with a swipe of his arm. "But I sure as shit know they're up to something."

Now Dewey had me worried. I called Blackie on the radio. "You guys see anything out there? It's been weirdly quiet down here."

"No, but we'll do a recon run and see if we can spot anything."

I gave him two quick clicks on the radio as acknowledgement.

The Gooney Bird lumbered around the perimeter of the village, then called back. "Can't see any kind of activity, no motion at all down there. Maybe they caught a slow boat back to Tokyo."

I glanced at Dewey. He shook his head. "They aren't quitters. They'll be back."

I thanked Blackie. He said he'd make a run every ten minutes or so to see if he could spot anything.

Eve and Doc Bonner appeared to be finishing up with the wounded soldiers, so I walked over to where they were. Eve looked up at me and did something I'd never seen her do, grinned ear to ear. In that smile I caught a sense of accomplishment, of hope, of caring about a life again. I squatted down beside her.

"My gal," I whispered. "Nice work."

Still grinning, she jabbed me with her elbow. I'll have to admit, I liked having her as "my gal."

But sometimes life can be exceedingly cruel and turn on you with the fierceness of a mother grizzly guarding her cubs. Or maybe happiness is merely incompatible with war. Or perhaps it is just not meant for certain mortals, period.

A strange "thunk" reverberated through the jungle.

Sergeant Dewey recognized the sound immediately. "Down," he bellowed. "Mortar!"

The shell exploded near the far edge of the village, sending an eruption of dirt, mud, and chickens into the air.

Two more rounds followed in quick succession. A clan of screeching monkeys scrambled through the village and dove down the far side of the mountain. A water buffalo, streaming blood from a wound in its side and bawling in pain, charged into the wooden pilings supporting a hut and brought it crashing down. A Naga woman, crying in agony, staggered out of the smoking aftermath of one of the shells, clutching at a gaping wound in her abdomen.

Eve spotted her immediately and rose to rush to her aid.

"Eve, no," I screamed. "Stay down."

She either didn't hear me or ignored me. She sprinted toward the woman. The next shell landed just yards from her. She went down like a rag doll flung to the ground by an angry child. She didn't cry out. She didn't move.

I rushed to her. Several pieces of shrapnel had speared into her body. She lay motionless on the crusty mud, the crimson of her life pooling beneath her, her bright azure eyes staring lifelessly at the cloud-dotted Burma sky overhead. Doc Bonner, bad ankle and all, was at her side in an instant, frantically attempting to breathe life back into the woman I had grown to love.

The sounds of exploding mortar shells and the ripping fire of Blackie's Brens filled my ears, my head, my soul.

Bonner glanced at me, shook his head, went back to work. But Eve was no longer with us. I knew that, knew it for sure, because my soul had gone with her, carried away and crushed on her final flight. One she made without saying goodbye, without giving me—us—a chance.

I stood and howled like a wounded animal, an emotion so

atavistic it had no roots in my own existence. I tilted my head back, my face toward heaven, and cursed God with every foul word I could bring to bear. I cursed the Japs. I cursed life.

Bonner screeched something at me, but I could hear or feel nothing save for an excruciating pain where my soul had been ripped from my being. Bonner reached for me, attempting to drag me down.

Too late. I sensed a percussive explosion. An anvil block struck the back of my head. A broadsword sliced my legs from beneath me. I spiraled into a beckoning darkness of nihilism and nothingness. Of silence. Of death, oh so welcomed death.

The roof of the world and its rugged alabaster rafters lay far below me.

27

112th Station Hospital
Calcutta, India
Mid-November 1943

As much as I had wanted to, I didn't die. Or if I did, then heaven looked very much like an Army hospital. I lay in bed in a large open room with a couple of dozen other wounded men. Ceiling fans spun in lazy revolutions overhead, while nurses and Red Cross volunteers flowed silently among us doing whatever they do with great efficiency. Occasional moans and groans rode the gentle air currents, as did the smells of antiseptics and cleaning agents. No, it wasn't heaven.

A nurse stepped to my bedside and peered down at me.

"It's good to see you awake, Major Shepherd."

"Is it?" I wasn't so sure.

"How are you feeling? Much pain?"

She seemed sincere enough, and attractive in a matronly sort of way, so I didn't want to snap at her, but I hurt. All over.

"Yes. The pain is doing its job. My legs are throbbing like

hell and there's a little guy inside my head with a very large hammer."

I looked at my legs. The right one was encased in a cast, the left one heavily bandaged. And it felt as though my head was swathed in a cotton turban. I sensed I looked like a Sikh. A tube from an IV bottle snaked into my right arm.

"I'll get you some pain medication," the nurse said. "We need to get you started on orals."

"Thank you, Lieutenant . . . ?"

"Ressler. Betty Ressler."

"Well, Lieutenant Ressler—"

"Betty will do."

"Okay, Betty, a few questions."

She nodded.

"To start with, where am I?"

"Calcutta."

Her response stunned me. I had no recollection of being transported anywhere. The last thing I remembered was standing over Eve's inert body on a Burmese jungle mountaintop and cursing the universe.

"Really?"

"Really."

"I don't remember getting here. I have only vague memories of light and dark, sound and silence." I swallowed hard—at least that didn't hurt—because I couldn't believe I had to ask what I did next. "Betty, would you be so kind as to tell me what date it is?"

She smiled softly and laid her hand on my forearm. "It's Monday, November fifteenth."

"My God," I muttered.

"You've been floating in and out of consciousness ever since you got here."

"When was that?"

"Two weeks ago."

I expelled a long sigh, then a groan.

"I'll get your pain meds," Betty said, "and get you unhitched from that bottle."

She went to get the meds while I lay in bed staring at the ceiling. Not that I could do anything else. Visions of Eve in all her snarkiness, all her pain, all her beauty, and all her vulnerability filled my mind and sifted through my soul. Tears brimmed in my eyes and drained down my cheeks in streamlets of despair. So much loss. Trish. Zim. Colonel Willis. Eve. Why? But I knew there were no answers, only the pointlessness of existence.

Betty returned and without saying anything or questioning me, gently wiped the tears from my face. She unhooked me from the IV feed, helped me sit up, and gave me a cup of water and some pills.

I thanked her in a croaky voice. Then, hoping against foolish hope, I asked, "Did anybody else come in with me . . . male . . . or female?"

"No," she said. "All I know is that you arrived here on a medevac flight out of Chabua."

"Any idea how I got to Chabua?"

"I'm sorry, sir. There are dozens of patients arriving here every day—we've got eight hundred beds—so I really don't get a chance to learn much about anyone's personal history."

"I understand." I felt my eyes getting heavy. "I think I'll doze for a while."

When I awoke again, a tall, white-haired doctor stood over me. He wore a physician's smock with his name and rank embroidered on it: Colonel Daniel L. Peterson.

"Mind if I take a listen?" he said, an easy Southern drawl

coating his words. He didn't wait for me to answer, but placed the eartips of his stethoscope in his ears and moved the diaphragm over my chest and neck, stopping for short periods to concentrate on particular spots. He kept saying, "Mmmm" or "uh-huh," to himself, and I didn't know if that was bad or good.

Finished, he said, "Sounds good. You were lucky, son."

Bullshit, I thought, but kept my mouth shut.

"You got slammed pretty hard by shrapnel from a mortar shell. Several pieces sliced through your legs, and you got whupped pretty good by a big ol' chunk in the back of your head. But I think you'll be just fine."

Think? "Just fine meaning?"

"Well, you'll probably have a little hitch in your giddy-up when you walk, and perhaps some nasty headaches and blackouts every once in a while, but those should improve with time."

I let that wonderful piece of news sink in, then asked, "Will I be able to fly again?"

Colonel Peterson issued an avuncular chuckle. "Only if pigs sprout wings. But you should be able to live an ordinary life." He patted me on the shoulder. "Let's get you going on some physical therapy. We'll have you up hobbling around in no time."

Just what I wanted to hear: hobbling.

"Sir," I said, "do you happen to know how I got out of Burma?"

He tilted his head back and closed his eyes, seeming to summon his recall of events. "Yes. I heard the search and rescue bird that was helping you also turned out to be a sort of gun platform. A couple of the guys onboard had Brens and opened up on the Japs that were after you. Nailed about a dozen of them. End of problem.

"After that, you were carried on a makeshift stretcher by a squad that got you to a road where a truck was waiting. The truck got you to Chabua. Took about a week, I understand. The hospital there couldn't do much for you except get you stabilized. That's why you were airlifted down here where we could perform surgery and get you back into shipshape. Count your blessings, son, cuz I heard not everyone in your group made it out alive."

"I know, sir." I choked back a sob. "Thank you for what you did for me." The words came out broken and scratchy. Even though I knew the colonel was attempting to be upbeat with me, I could see in his eyes he sensed my emotional pain.

He gave me another pat on the shoulder and departed.

I lay in bed—like I had a choice?—and contemplated my nonexistent future. I would be discharged from the Army on disability and shipped back to the US where I could . . . what? I couldn't fly, and I certainly wouldn't be of much value to a corporation if I suffered from headaches and blackouts. Maybe a job as a janitor? Yeah, great. The returning war hero.

Later that day a small man who bore some resemblance to Santa Claus, without the red suit and snowy beard, strolled up to my bed.

He extended his hand. "Chaplain Dominic Rana. Just call me Padre Dom, if you'd like."

I grasped his hand and nodded.

"Thought we might chat for a bit, if that's okay?"

I nodded again—though I really didn't care one way or another—and he pulled up a chair and sat.

"I've heard you've been through a lot, lost some friends. If you'd like to talk about it, I'm here to listen. Otherwise, we can just gab about fishing, baseball, women, whatever you'd like."

He waited for me to speak. I didn't want to, but having nothing else to do . . .

"Women," I rasped.

"Okay," he said, holding his voice low.

"I've lost two I loved." Emotion overcame me. The follow-on words wouldn't come.

Padre Dom laid his hand on mine. "When you're ready."

Except for the clink of trays and glasses, and muted conversations, silence hovered over us. I finally choked back my despair and continued.

"My wife passed less than a year ago. We'd been married only three years." I drew a deep breath before pushing on. "Then there was a nurse. We, well, grew close. I guess I was falling in love with her. We had quite an adventure in Burma. That's where I got wounded, and she was . . . killed." A silent sob leaked out of me.

"I'm so sorry, Major."

"That wasn't all." I paused, struggling with my despondency. "My best friend was killed in an air crash. And I lost a medevac patient when the Japs shot me down over Burma."

"You've suffered a lot."

"God doesn't particularly care for me, does He?"

The chaplain seemed to consider his words before responding. "I don't think it's personal, my friend. I don't believe God arranges our lives in chessboard-like moves or engineers our fates. I suspect He's much more concerned with our eternal souls than events in our secular lives. Life can be —as we soldiers are wont to say—a SNAFU. And it sounds like yours has been more SNAFU-ie than most."

"Life is unfair, right?" I snapped. I didn't mean to aim venom at Padre Dom. He just got in the way of my overall disillusionment with the world.

"It is unfair, Major. Enhanced in wartime, of course."

"Maybe God should go back to the drawing board."

"Rewrite Genesis?"

"I don't know. Maybe. All I know is . . . well, why in the hell do we need Him?"

Nurse Betty appeared at the foot of my bed, apparently ready to do a quick check on me. The chaplain waved her off and asked if we couldn't have a couple more minutes. She agreed.

"Thank you," Dom said to her, then turned back to me. "I don't mean to get into a deep philosophical discussion of spirituality, but I believe that because things *are* in such a mess here on Earth, that's precisely why we need God. The hope He brings to us, the love, the strength, the direction. Let's give Him a chance. Would you like me to pray for you?"

"No. I know you mean well, Padre, but it's a little late for me. Let's skip the mumbo jumbo, shall we?"

He nodded. An immutable sadness appeared on his face. "Perhaps there is something else I could do for you, then?" He removed his hand from mine.

"Well . . ."

"Please, tell me."

"The nurse, a flight nurse. Her name was Captain Genevieve Johannsen. If you could find out where she's buried, I'd like to visit her before I depart India. You know, to say . . . goodbye."

Dom smiled. "I'll do my best. I'm going to New Delhi in a few days. I'll poke around in ATC headquarters when I get there and see what I can find out."

"Thank you, Padre. Sorry to be so negative about God and stuff, but, you know . . ."

"I do. You aren't alone." He stood, made the sign of the cross over me, and said he'd return after he got back from New Delhi.

I began my physical therapy the following day. It involved getting range of motion and strength back into my left leg so I'd be able to stand on it and use crutches. The right leg would take longer. Both the fibula and tibia had been shattered, and the breaks were ragged with missing pieces. They'd been glued back together—or whatever surgeons do to fix them— as best they could be, but that leg, I was told, would be a smidge shorter than the other. So I'd walk the rest of my life with a list and a limp.

The initial sessions were painful, and to make them even more fun, my head decided to join in the festivities. So I had pain shooting up and down my leg and back and forth through my head. The therapist, a burly nurse who I guessed had played rugby in college, didn't seem sympathetic. She said her name was Ruth. I referred to her as Ruth the Ruthless, but that didn't go over well. She said her efforts were for my own good, then doubled down on inflicting pain on me.

After about a week, I was able to be transferred into a wheelchair and periodically rolled out into a courtyard to get some fresh air. Although this was Calcutta. There was no damn fresh air. It still stank of garbage, traffic, death, and despair.

The first time out, a young orderly, a private, pushed me into the grassy enclosure.

"Sorry, sir, I know it stinks out here. But at least there's some sun, and the buildings cut out a bit of the noise from the city."

The structures looked like three-story apartment buildings. I mentioned that to the private.

"They were," he said. "That's how the hospital started out last April, in two apartment buildings. Since then, they've been building additional wards and facilities like crazy.

Rumor has it we'll be designated a general hospital within a few months."

My visits to the courtyard became routine, and I came to think of them as rewards after my sessions with Nurse Rugby.

At least by this time of year, the heat and humidity had abated in Calcutta, and the sunny afternoons proved relatively pleasant. Still, the stench and racket of the overcrowded, underfed, and death-ridden metropolis continued to weasel their way into the courtyard. I knew recollections of the stink and noise would always remain with me, as would the melancholy memories of Trish and Eve.

One afternoon, late in the month, I nodded off in the courtyard under the comforting embrace of the Indian sun. I thought of cabbages and kings, and why the sea is boiling hot —and whether pigs have wings. Thank you, Lewis Carroll and Army Air Forces Captain Pete Zimmerman.

I thought of crippled "war heroes" pushing brooms through empty buildings and being smothered in loss. I thought of them tripping over shattered dreams and falling face-first into the shit piles of their futures. Ah, the rich rewards of being a wounded Hump pilot.

A tap on my shoulder wrested me from my bleak brooding. Padre Dom.

"Didn't mean to wake you," he said.

"I needed to be. Good to see you, Padre."

"I come with news."

I nodded.

"First, I have a message from your boss, a Lieutenant Colonel Ellsworth."

"Yes?"

"He says, and I quote, 'Get your ass back here. I can't run this squadron by myself.'"

"He does know I'm through as an Army officer, doesn't he?"

Dom smiled. "He's already processed a waiver that will get you returned to duty in New Delhi and the Tenth Weather Squadron. He claims even if you're gimpy and dopey, you'll still be better than ninety percent of the men he knows."

Slack-jawed, I stared at the chaplain.

He extended a sheath of papers toward me. "Your orders."

I took them, glanced at them, and placed them in my lap. "Did you find out anything about Captain Johannsen?"

Dom squatted in front of my wheelchair. "I did. It turns out she was carried out of Burma, too. You and she, side by side. You made the journey together."

I could feel the tears welling in my eyes. "They got her body back to Chabua, then?" I managed to choke out.

Dom nodded, and cast his gaze at my feet. I'm sure he sensed the agony of my loss.

"She has a message for you," he muttered.

"What do you mean, '*has* a message?' She's dead." I could barely get the words out of my mouth.

The padre didn't respond.

A voice came from behind me, something out of the past. "Keep your hands in your pockets and your pecker in your pants, and we'll get along famously."

Dom burst out laughing. I burst into sobs and unmanly tears. And Eve Johannsen burst into my arms. We embraced and kissed so passionately I thought a surgeon might have to unfasten us.

"How, how, how?" I panted after we released each other.

With her flushed cheeks flooded in tears, too, she said, "I thought you knew. I thought somebody might have told you, gosh, that the flight surgeon, Doc Bonner, stanched my bleeding, breathed life back into me, and got me stabilized. My heart had actually stopped, you know. I was really badly shot up, but I made it.

"Lucky for me, Bonner knew there was a cardiothoracic surgeon at a small hospital unit in New Delhi, so he had me airlifted there. The surgeon patched me up and has been keeping an eye on my internal machinery since then. I guess everything is working okay, but I'll be on medical leave and in rehab for quite a while. I can't believe you didn't know."

"I guess by the time I'd rejoined the world, all the guys who'd had firsthand knowledge of what happened had disappeared. Had a war to fight, you know."

"And that's why I knew I had to get to Calcutta," Eve said. "That's why I knew I had to get to you. To let you know. In Burma, you came for me. So there was no question I was coming for you. Padre Dom and Colonel Ellsworth navigated a three-ring circus of bureaucracy to get me here. I'm so grateful." She nodded at Dom, her frail body still heaving with silent sobs.

We embraced and kissed again. My heart hammered so violently I thought *I* might need a cardiothoracic surgeon.

"Don't squeeze me too hard," Eve warned, "I could spring a leak."

I relaxed my hug. "You still wanna be my gal?" I whispered, struggling to force the words out as my emotions attempted to strangle them.

"If you want one with holes in her chest."

"It looks like the essential equipment was spared. You have to decide if you want a guy with a hole in his head . . . and a gimpy gait."

"I do." She delivered her declaration in a soft, firm voice.

The melodious chirping of a small bird in the branches of a nearby tree accompanied it. As did the distant, impatient tooting of vehicle horns in the chaotic streets of Calcutta. And from far overhead came the reverberating bellow of an American transport as it winged its way toward Assam, or maybe New Delhi, or perhaps even the Roof of the World.

By the old Moulmein Pagoda, lookin' lazy at the sea,
  There's a Burma girl a-settin', and I know she thinks o' me;

THE END

DOWN A DARK ROAD
Book 4 of When Heroes Flew

Down a Dark Road transports readers to the shadowy forests of WWII Austria, where a weary and battle-worn Army platoon is about to discover the war's darkest secret...

As the war in Europe draws to a close, young Army lieutenant Jim Thayer finds himself and his platoon on the point of the American advance into Austria. They are no strangers to the horror of war. But what they find hidden in the forests of Western Austria is beyond anything they have yet experienced.

Battling remnants of the legendary Waffen SS, Germany's elite fighting force, Jim and his men come face to face with the cruel brutality of the Nazi regime.

Determined to hunt down the architect of this atrocity, Jim dispatches an unofficial team of unlikely allies—an American bomber pilot, a German Luftwaffe fighter pilot, and a young Austrian woman.

The war may be ending. But for these strange comrades in arms, the final battle has only just begun...

In Down a Dark Road, former Air Force officer H.W. "Buzz" Bernard plunges readers into the final dark and bloody chapter of the war, as they follow Jim and others into the true heart of darkness.

Get your copy today at SevernRiverBooks.com

ALSO BY H.W. "BUZZ" BERNARD

The When Heroes Flew Series

When Heroes Flew

The Shangri-La Raiders

The Roof of the World

Down a Dark Road

Standalone Books

Eyewall

Plague

Supercell

Blizzard

Cascadia

Never miss a new release! Sign up to receive exclusive updates from author Buzz Bernard.

SevernRiverBooks.com

AUTHOR'S NOTE

Rod and Eve were fictional characters, of course, but a number of the people around them were not. With that in mind, I'd like to illuminate the real ones.

Dick Ellsworth was, indeed, the commander of the Tenth Weather Squadron. And he, along with his copilot, Tex Albaugh, really flew a C-47 named *Betsy*. Leading by example, Ellsworth flew four hundred combat missions and helped pioneer regular night flights over the Hump.

As a leader, he had few peers. A gentleman who worked with Ellsworth for over twenty-five years noted, "He's the best field commander I've ever run into anywhere."

Ellsworth was promoted to full colonel in December 1943 and to brigadier general in September 1952. He lost his life in a military airplane crash in Newfoundland in 1953. Ellsworth AFB near Rapid City, South Dakota, is named in his honor.

Tom Hardin was also a real character. His primary mission in the CBI Theater was to increase the tonnage ferried over the Hump. He did that. Deliveries rose from 4,624 tons in September 1943 to 23,675 tons in August 1944. But that accomplishment came at a high cost. For every thousand tons of supplies airlifted into China, three Americans gave their lives.

Hardin retired from the Air Force in 1955 as a major general, and passed away in 1968.

Another real person portrayed in the novel was Captain John "Blackie" Porter, who created Blackie's Gang.

Blackie developed search and rescue tactics that were later honed by a unit formed specifically to find and retrieve airmen who'd gone down on the Hump route. Blackie's Gang itself is credited with rescuing one hundred twenty-seven Army flyers, plus the men on Eric Severeid's ill-fated flight.

Blackie lost his life in December 1943 while flying a B-25 on a rescue mission. Japanese fighter aircraft jumped the bomber and shot out its engines. It crashed and exploded, killing all aboard except for the copilot whom Blackie managed to shove out an escape hatch just before the bird smashed into the Burmese rainforest.

Generals Joseph Stilwell and Claire Chenault, of course, were real figures. Much has been written about them.

The violent storm over the Hump depicted in Chapter Ten is based on one that hammered the Hump in early January 1945. That brutal tempest claimed nine ATC aircraft plus six from other commands. Thirty-one people, airmen and passengers, were killed or reported missing.

There is a wide range of figures cited for the total number of aircraft lost during Hump operations from 1942 to 1945, but the most commonly used is five hundred ninety. The tally for aircrew members killed stands at 1,314. Another 1,200 were rescued or hiked to safety.

All in all, the airlift ferried 650,000 tons of avgas, weaponry, food, medicine, and men from Assam, India, to China in support of the Chinese army and the US Fourteenth Air Force in their struggle against the Japanese. Some have argued that the cost of the airlift, in terms of lives and planes, wasn't worth it; that the tonnage delivered was quite small relative to the wartime requirements of the Chinese.

Maybe. On the other hand, in the game of baseball, a sacrifice bunt moving a runner into scoring position isn't going to make headlines. But if a base hit brings that runner home and wins the game, you could argue the uncelebrated bunt made all the difference.

For want of a nail . . .

There are a number of excellent books about flying the Hump and the key characters involved from which I was able to choose in support of my research. The ones I selected were: *Flying the Hump* (which included a plethora of wonderful color photographs) by Jeff Ethell and Don Downie; *Hell Is So Green* by Lt. William Diebold; *Hump Pilot* by Nedda R. Thomas; *In Search of History* by Theodore H. White; *Thor's Legions* by John F. Fuller; and *Other Veterans of World War II* by Rona Simmons.

Numerous well-written articles about flying the Hump— and about WWII hospitals and nurses— are available on the internet. One has to be careful, however, to make certain the information and data supplied in particular pieces are supported by other reliable sources. One of the more illuminating works I found on the internet was "The Hump, The Historic Airway to China was Created by U. S. Heroes," written by Theodore White for *Life* magazine in 1944.

Allow me to slip in a note here about the use of some of the slang terms in the novel, such as Japs and Chinks. These are offensive sobriquets these days. But during WWII they were common and accepted. It was a different era then with different sensibilities.

Finally, a book is not created by an author alone. Many others are involved. In my case that includes my cadre of trusted beta readers: my newly-minted wife, Barbara; my long-suffering brother, Rick; Gary Schwartz, who's supported me since my very first novel, *Eyewall*; G. R. "Lurch" Murchison, who did a superb job for me on *When Heroes Flew: The Shangri-La Raiders*; Tom Young, a wonderful friend, a first-rate novelist in his own right, and decorated Air Force veteran who crewed on transport aircraft in combat; and my rookie reader, Tom Rodgers, a highly decorated Vietnam War-era Air Force fighter pilot as well as a retired American Airlines first officer.

As always, there's the great team at Severn River Publishing led by Navy vet Andrew Watts, another marvelous novelist, by the way. Additional members of the SRP team include Publishing Director, Amber Hudock; Social Media Manager, Mo Metlen; and a superb editor and proofreader, Cara Quinlan.

Thanks to all for helping me bring to life the valor and determination of the men who challenged the ruggedest topography and worst weather on the planet in WWII as they flew twin-engine aircraft over the Roof of the World.

ABOUT THE AUTHOR

H. W. "Buzz" Bernard is a bestselling, award-winning novelist. A retired Air Force Colonel and Legion of Merit recipient, he also served as a senior meteorologist at The Weather Channel for thirteen years. He is a past president of the Southeastern Writers Association and member of International Thriller Writers, the Atlanta Writers Club, Military Writers Society of America, and Willamette Writers. Buzz and his special needs adult grandson live in Georgia with their fuzzy, strangely docile Shih-Tzu, Stormy... probably misnamed.

SevernRiverBooks.com